Chicks with Sticks

ALSO BY ELIZABETH LENHARD

Chicks with Sticks (It's a purl thing)

Chicks with Sticks

(Knit two together)

ELIZABETH LENHARD

DUTTON

DUTTON CHILDREN'S BOOKS
A division of Penguin Young Readers Group
Published by the Penguin Group
Penguin Group (USA) Inc., 375 Hudson Street, New York, New York 10014, U.S.A. · Penguin Group
(Canada), 90 Eglinton Avenue East, Suite 700, Toronto, Ontario, Canada M4P 2Y3 (a division of
Pearson Penguin Canada Inc.) · Penguin Books Ltd, 80 Strand, London WC2R 0RL, England · Penguin
Ireland, 25 St Stephen's Green, Dublin 2, Ireland (a division of Penguin Books Ltd) · Penguin Group
(Australia), 250 Camberwell Road, Camberwell, Victoria 3124, Australia (a division of Pearson Australia
Group Pty Ltd) · Penguin Books India Pvt Ltd, 11 Community Centre, Panchsheel Park, New Delhi–
110 017, India · Penguin Group (NZ), Cnr Airborne and Rosedale Roads, Albany, Auckland 1310,
New Zealand (a division of Pearson New Zealand Ltd) · Penguin Books (South Africa) (Pty) Ltd,
24 Sturdee Avenue, Rosebank, Johannesburg 2196, South Africa · Penguin Books Ltd,
Registered Offices: 80 Strand, London WC2R 0RL, England

Library of Congress Cataloging-in-Publication Data
Lenhard, Elizabeth.
Chicks with sticks: knit two together / by Elizabeth Lenhard.—1st ed.
p. cm.
Summary: Chicago high-school juniors Scottie, Amanda, Tay, and Bella, rely on their friendship and
their shared passion for knitting to help them as they navigate their relationships with boys.
ISBN 0-525-47764-0 (alk. paper)
[1. Knitting—Fiction. 2. Friendship—Fiction. 3. Interpersonal relations—Fiction.
4. Chicago (Ill.)—Fiction.] I. Title: Knit two together. II. Title.
PZ7.L5389Chk 2006
[Fic]—dc22 2006003872

Published in the United States by Dutton Books,
a member of Penguin Group (USA) Inc.
345 Hudson Street, New York, New York 10014
www.penguin.com/youngreaders

Designed by Irene Vandervoort

Printed in USA   First Edition
1 3 5 7 9 10 8 6 4 2

For Paul

Acknowledgments

I can't express enough thanks to . . .

Julie Strauss-Gabel, who does a brilliant job of looking out for me and the Chicks

Jodi Reamer, always there with wisdom and endless humor

Sarah Shumway, for her Xtreme organizational skills and knitting patterns

Sarah Pope Greene, for her super-cute patterns

Scottie Bookman, who let me borrow her name

My knitty mentors: Patti Ghezzi, Shirley "WWSD" Robb, and the Wednesday morning crew at Needle Nook

Tamara Derosia and Ben Brown, Web designer and Web master extraordinaire

Lynn Barfield, patron saint of postcards

Meg Cabot and her book club!

My far-reaching girls' club of confidantes, who've given me so much fodder for the Chicks' uncommon friendships

My growing family—particularly my parents, Bunny and Bob Lenhard—who are the Chicks' biggest cheerleaders, and mine, too

And Paul Donsky, who read each chapter the moment I finished it and fretted over Scottie and co. right alongside me; my boyfriend for life, my joy

Chicks with Sticks

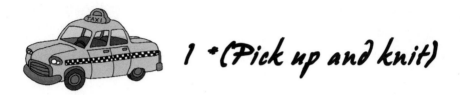

1 *(Pick up and knit)*

In the dust-motey haze of the near-empty Olivia Stark School hallway, Scottie finally found out what it was like to have a boyfriend.

Unfortunately, the boyfriend wasn't hers.

"I've *had* it, Charlie!"

The girl's voice, shrill and seething with anger, hit Scottie with an almost physical force as she walked past the cracked door of a history classroom. Instinctively, she froze.

"You're overreacting." This was a boy's voice. "As usual."

"No . . . I . . . am . . . not," the girl said. "And you *know* I hate it when you say stuff like that. Could you be any *more* condescending?"

"Could *you* be any more loud?" Charlie said. "Zoe, we're in school."

Charlie and Zoe, Charlie and Zoe, Scottie thought, going through a mental catalogue of her school's It couples. She had it narrowed down to either the girl with the purple lipstick and black bob who was always sucking face with some shaggy-haired senior, or the glossy blond couple who looked like their match had been arranged by the Daughters of the American Revolution.

"This isn't the country club, Charlie," Zoe spat. "I don't care if anybody hears us. In fact, I *want* someone to hear us. Because then the word will get around—Charlie Whitfield is a commitmentphobic *jerk*."

Definitely the blonds, Scottie thought smugly. In the next instant, though, her eyes went wide and she touched her fingertips to her lips. *Oh my God, what am I doing? I'm the creepy lurker that Charlie's afraid of.*

She darted past the doorway, fully intending to head to the front steps to meet her friends—

"I told you I loved you," Charlie said quietly. "How is *that* commitmentphobic?"

He loves her?!

Scottie's stomach swooped. She felt like she'd stumbled into a real live chick flick, the kind she, Bella, Amanda, and Tay watched on a regular basis between knits, purls, and handfuls of Garrett's caramel-cheese popcorn.

Maybe that's why she stayed, pressed against the sliver of nubbly, ochre plaster between the doorway and a bank of lockers. Because, suddenly, Zoe and Charlie were just fictional characters—the quintessential popular kids all broken and bruised beneath their shiny veneers.

"If you love me," Zoe said, a tiny catch in her voice, "why didn't you call me back last night?"

"Because it was too late," Charlie said defensively.

"I keep my cell phone in my room and you *know* it's on vibrate," Zoe lashed out. "Nobody would've heard. You're lying."

"Well maybe," Charlie yelled, "that's because—"

He stopped himself. Scottie felt sick. She sensed a big revelation coming on, and from Zoe's silence, Scottie could bet she felt it, too.

"You never said it back." Charlie said this so softly, so sadly. "Maybe *you're* the one who's commitmentphobic."

"What?" Zoe said. "Said what back?"

"You never said that you loved me, too," Charlie said. His voice was raw and raspy now, barely more than a whisper. Scottie had to crane her neck to hear it.

"I . . . but I . . ." Zoe stuttered. "I mean, Charlie! Come on."

"See! You still can't say it."

Zoe? What are you thinking? Shiny, blond Charlie loves *you. Do you even know how lucky you are?*

Stunned at the injustice of it all, Scottie's mouth had dropped open—which must have been why a scream left it so easily when she felt a rough tap on her shoulder.

She clamped her mouth shut and spun around. Of course, it was Tay who'd rapped her on the shoulder. Nobody else she knew thunked that hard. Amanda and Bella trailed behind Tay, looking perplexed.

"Scottie—" Tay began irritably.

"Shhhhh," Scottie whisper-screamed. She grabbed both of Tay's sharp shoulders and began to shuffle her away from the classroom.

"Ow!" Amanda cried as one of Tay's clompy boots came down on her frosty pink toes, which were completely exposed in a pair of turquoise-studded flip-flops.

"Ooh, are you okay?" Bella said in her high, squeaky voice. She curled her own toes in sympathy—though hers were polish free, and her flip-flops were made of more durable, ropy stuff.

"*Shhhhhh!*" Scottie repeated, waving her hands desperately at her buds.

But it was too late. Zoe had poked her head through the classroom door. Even in the throes of BF drama, she was gorgeous. Her hair was so thick and straight, it did that cascading thing that Scottie thought only happened on shampoo commercials. Her makeup was impeccable and her blue eyes were sparkly, even through her scowl.

"Mind your own business!" she screamed at the four girls. "And while you're at it, get a life."

She slammed the door so hard, Scottie felt the floor shudder beneath her feet.

"Holy crap," Tay sputtered. She scowled at the shut door. "What was that all about?"

While Scottie rolled her eyes, Amanda shot her a sly squint.

"You were totally eavesdropping," she accused with a grin. "Not that Zoe doesn't deserve it, the way she goes drama queening all over school. You'd think she was the first person in history to ever have a boyfriend."

"How do you know I was eavesdropping?" Scottie protested. "Maybe I forgot something. Maybe I was heading back to my locker to get it—"

"Scottie, I *know*," Amanda said with a laugh, "because I've known you for forever."

Which was true. Scottie and Amanda had been best friends since first grade, when Amanda had shown up on the first day of school wearing an outfit from Paris and carrying a leather lunchbox from Italy, but without a smock for art class. Since Scottie's mom was a painter, Scottie'd had a surplus of smocks and she'd loaned one to Amanda. It didn't matter that Amanda was a future debutante from the Gold Coast and Scottie was a shy, sorta scruffy Jewish kid who lived in an old bread factory—they'd been best friends ever since. Unless you counted the months last year when they'd barely been on speaking terms. Scottie called it their cartoon war.

"You were Jessica Rabbit," she'd said to Amanda one night during a shuddery flashback to those dark months, "And I was Flat Stanley."

"Oh, please," Amanda'd said, crossing one long, lean leg over the other. "You weren't *that* flat!"

"Amanda, my chest was *concave*," Scottie said. "Not a *hint* of sproutage. Meanwhile, you were loving life in your non-padded bra."

"It was an awkward period." Amanda shrugged.

"What awkward period?!" Scottie protested. "You went to Europe for the summer, and came back all perfect."

"Between us, I mean," Amanda had said, going a bit pink. "The awkward period."

So much had changed since then. Their awkward period? It was nothing but a bit of scar tissue in Scottie's memory bank, covered over with collective hours of dishing at their side-by-side lockers at Stark; with gallons of coffee and countless bags of candy; with sleepovers and long walks on the lakefront (when the blustery Chicago weather would allow it); and most of all, with knitting.

That was the most amazing thing to Scottie—that their friendship hadn't always been conducted to the *click-swish* music of their yarn and needles. Or that Tay and Bella hadn't *always* been there, making them a perfect quartet—the Chicks with Sticks.

"Amanda's right," Tay said, jolting Scottie back to the crisis at hand. "Shearer, you're *such* a snoop."

"No, it's just that she's a drama addict," Bella protested, enveloping Scottie in one of her quick, light-as-a-moth's-wing hugs. "She can't help it. It's like when Amanda gets around chocolate. She loses all perspective."

"Hey!" Amanda and Scottie said together.

But before they could protest any further, Zoe and Charlie's voices grew a shade louder behind the classroom door. Now it was Charlie who sounded shrill and angry, and Zoe who was pleading and placating.

"OhmiGod, they're gonna think I'm still snooping," Scottie squeaked. "Let's get outta here!"

She looped one arm around Tay's elbow, used the other to grab Bella's delicate hand, and began dragging them down the hall. Amanda trotted ahead of them, a hand slapped over her mouth to stifle her laughter. As soon as they'd all ducked into the nearest stairwell, Tay launched into full mockery mode.

"See?" she said to Scottie smugly. "You just admitted to snooping. End of discussion."

She balled up her fist and attempted to give Scottie a noogie, but Scottie dodged her. It hadn't been so long ago that such snark would have made Scottie cringe, but she knew Tay was only this jagged with those that she loved. And, in fact, Scottie was fully capable of defending herself.

"Dude," she said. "I'm not one of your guy friends from the skate park!" She aimed her own knuckles at Tay's head, but Scottie dissolved into a fit of giggles before she could even get close to making good on her threat.

"As if, Scottie," Amanda said. She shifted her Balenciaga bag from one shoulder to the other, grabbed the ancient wooden banister, and began to *flip-flop-flip* down the stairs.

"Anyway, Tay wouldn't care if you noogied her," Bella added. She pointed at Tay's supershort, spiky hair. Just like the rest of Tay—whose only jewelry was an eyebrow ring and who pretty much lived in cargo pants—her hair was strictly wash-and-wear.

"I don't want to talk about hair," Tay said, giving one of Bella's long dreadlocks a tweak. "I want to talk dirt. So, Scottie? What was so fascinating between Mr. and Mrs. Perfect up there?"

"Didn't sound so perfect to me," Amanda muttered.

"No," Scottie sighed. "What I got was that Charlie used the L word and Zoe *didn't*. Can you *imagine?*"

"Yeah." Tay shrugged.

"Sure." Amanda nodded.

"She must not be in love with him," Bella said nonchalantly.

Scottie heaved a deep sigh as she trudged down the stairs. Amanda, already on the landing below her, planted a fist on each of her impossibly curvy hips and gaped up at Scottie.

"You're jealous!" she said. "Even though Charlie and Zoe's relationship is a disaster!"

Okay, not that I'm not grateful for this BFF/mind-reader thing? Scottie grumbled inwardly. *But sometimes it can be completely annoying.*

Still, she knew it was futile to deny Amanda's accusation.

"I don't get why Zoe's just chucking it all!" Scottie cried. "I'd give *anything* to have a boyfriend."

"So you'd be happy with just anyone, as long as he was your boyfriend?" Tay scoffed. "You don't even care if the guy's right for you?"

"If he was my boyfriend," Scottie said with a little pout, "he *would* be right for me."

"Well, sometimes it's not that simple," Amanda said, glancing at Tay shiftily. Tay nodded almost imperceptibly.

•• Chicks with Sticks

"See!" Scottie cried. "The fact that you guys have boyfriends means you speak this secret language to each other. And every day when you wake up, you know that you're the first thing your boyfriends think about when *they* wake up. I don't even remotely know what that's like."

"I'm pretty sure when John wakes up," Tay said casually, "the first thing on his mind is frozen waffles."

"The first thing on *my* mind every morning isn't Toby, it's the weather," Amanda said. "I mean, I've gotta know from the get-go. Is this gonna be a straightening iron kind of day? Or a curling mousse kind of day?"

"Har, har," Scottie said. "Thanks for the empathy, you guys."

"Sweetie, you just have to be patient," Bella said as they thunked down the last of the stairs and emerged onto Clark Street. "Like meeeee!"

Bella capped off her advice by launching herself into an impromptu pirouette on the sidewalk. This was just the kind of thing Bella did. If she loved the way something tasted, she exclaimed with pleasure. Reveling in her freedom, and happy to be outside on a beautiful day, she twirled.

"You can take the girl out of home school . . ." Tay said, shaking her head.

". . . but you can't take home school out of the girl," Amanda and Scottie said together.

"Why do you guys always say that?" Bella wondered aloud as she spun again, her dreads fanning around her like a headdress of golden feathers. Her blowsy linen top fluttered prettily, too. All to the music of the stack of copper bangles on her wrist. Even if Bella had added the odd pair of denims or non-clog shoes to her wardrobe in the past year, she still pretty much preferred her standard look—gawky/gorgeous biracial yoga goddess, circa 1968.

"We say it because we love you," Amanda said briskly. "Now can we get back on message? Scottie, did you forget?"

"Forget?" Scottie blinked. She'd just lapsed into a mini daydream in which she was at her favorite diner, eating waffles with her cute, shiny boyfriend.

"Shearer!" Tay said. "You told us to meet you on the steps after school for a 'mystery trip.' Why do you think we all came looking for you?"

"Oh, my God!" Scottie said. "I did forget. But only for a second, I swear."

"You are *so* boy crazy," Amanda said.

"Can that be possible when I have basically *no* boy experience?" Scottie sighed. "I mean, other than Tom Castellucci snapping my bra strap every time he lands behind me in the lunch line?"

"Here we go," Tay muttered.

"I swear, you guys," Scottie whispered, wary of the other Starkers straggling out of the school. "It's humiliating. I'm a junior now. I'm reasonably normal. And I've never even been asked out! I can't take it anymore. Where *is* he? Where is my boyfriend?"

"Maybe he's waiting for us at the mystery destination?" Amanda offered wearily. "And he's got shaggy, dark hair, just like you like."

"And light eyes," Bella crooned, closing her own stunning celery eyes. "Blue or green or hazel."

"And he'll be skinny, not stocky," Tay droned with a grin. "Or so you've told us a zillion times. And he'll hate football and he'll always share his popcorn with you at the movies."

"Okay, okay," Scottie muttered. She stalked up to the curb and threw out her arm to hail a cab. Over her shoulder, she said, "You've made your point. I promise not to obsess about Boyfriendus Absentius for the rest of the day."

Amanda raised her eyebrows. She seemed impressed.

"Okay, for the rest of the hour, at least," Scottie revised.

"Whatever!" Tay cried. "Just tell us where we're going!"

"Wait!" Scottie yelled. "Here's a cab!"

An orange taxi screeched to a halt before them. Bella folded her lanky self into the front seat. Tay, Scottie, and Amanda clambered into the back.

"Head up Damen to Wicker Park, please," Scottie called through the Plexiglas partition. The cabbie, muttering into his cell phone, grunted, nodded, and peeled out into traffic.

Once they were settled, Scottie made her announcement.

"We're checking out a brand-new LYS," she exclaimed. "I found it on chicknits.com. It's having a soft opening this week."

"No way!" Amanda screeched. The cabbie jumped, then shook his head in annoyance. "How did I miss that?"

Of course, all the Chicks read chicknits, Chicago's coolest knitting blog. But clearly, none of them read it as slavishly as Scottie did.

"What's this place called?" Tay said.

"Stockinette," Scottie announced, as proudly as if she'd named it herself.

"*Pfuh,*" Tay said, scrunching as far down in the taxi's backseat as her long legs would allow (which was pretty far, since she was shamelessly scooching Scottie into Amanda's side of the cab). "Stockinette. It's too cute."

"You say that about everything," Scottie complained. She flopped her legs on top of Tay's outstretched ones. "Dude, it's a *yarn store*. What do want them to call it? Belly Button Lint?"

"*That's* uncute. Or how about . . . Pilled?" Amanda offered, lips twisted into a wry pucker. "Or Knot!"

"A Frayed Knot," Tay shot back. After a long moment, Amanda finally got it and unleashed a string of snorty giggles.

"How about just Local Yarn Store?" Bella squeaked, twisting to peek through the cab's Plexiglas partition. "That would be very postmodern."

"English teacher's pet," Amanda sing-songed.

"Dag," Scottie said, slumping down in *her* seat (or more precisely, slumping into Amanda's rib cage). "You guys are so neg. How long have we been waiting for a new LYS to come along?"

"Do you have to say LYS?" Tay sniffed. "It reminds me of LOL."

"Tacky," all four girls said at once.

"Address!"

Scottie jumped. The cabbie had put his cell buddy on hold to bark at her.

"Um, Division and Wolcott," Scottie squeaked.

The cabbie shook his head. Apparently, this wasn't good enough.

"Address!" he ordered again.

"Ummmmm." Scottie pulled open her stripey, felted Suki bag—which she'd knitted after discovering the pattern online—and pawed desperately through it. "It's uh . . . it's called Stockinette. Do you see a sign anywhere?"

"No! I need address!" The cabbie's thick eyebrows furrowed until they almost landed on the bridge of his squashy nose.

Okay, Scottie gulped. *Compared to this guy, my friends are just* radiating *positivity.*

She sifted frantically through a couple school notebooks, the latest *Interweave Knits* magazine, errant pens and knitting needles, but the little pink Post-it where she'd written the address that morning was gone. It was probably at home, stuck to her hairbrush or something.

When Scottie gouged a finger on an embroidery needle, she gave up.

"This always happens to me," she told the driver, whose nose looked both red *and* squashy now. "I lost it. All I can tell you is Division and Wolcott."

The cabbie sniffed violently, swung the cab across two lanes, and came to an abrupt halt at the corner. He sniffed again, and louder, as the girls all dove for their wallets to dig up the eight-dollar fare. Before Tay, Bella, and Scottie could pool their wadded singles, Amanda, as usual, extracted a crisp ten-dollar bill from her patent leather wallet. She slid it into the little dish in the Plexiglas partition, grabbed Scottie's arm, and yanked her out onto the sidewalk.

"Oh, okay, bye!" Bella chirped to the cabbie as she slithered out of her seat up front. Tay didn't say a word. She just heaved herself out the street-side door. An oncoming car promptly whizzed by her, scarily close.

"Chicago drivers *suck!*" Tay yelled at no one in particular.

The cabbie, clearly thinking she was talking about *him*, peeled away with screeching tires.

"Hello?" Tay called after him. "This is Wicker Park. Yuppie central. The whole butch act won't fly."

"Then why are *you* doing it?" Scottie yelled. "Have you noticed you're still standing in the street?"

Tay shrugged as she walked—slowly—to join her friends on the sidewalk.

Okay, could the energy on this little field trip be any worse?

Scottie vaguely noticed that she was thinking in Bella-speak. Bella was the one in their group who riffed about karma and energy and fate and stuff. Mostly Scottie didn't believe in that kind of thing. At least she hadn't—until she'd discovered KnitWit.

The LYS to end all LYSes, Scottie thought before she cringed and shot Tay a sheepish look. *LYS. She's right—that* is *the goofiest term....*

There was nothing goofy about KnitWit, though. The shabby little shop—and its sproingy-haired owner, Alice—had brought the Chicks together.

Sometimes it still felt freaky to Scottie, that all of them had landed in the same random yarn store on the same random Tuesday night the previous fall.

Freaky in a good way. Scottie smiled—just as she spotted Stockinette's shingle about halfway down the block. The sign was slickly sweet, a porous afghan "knitted" of copper wire, with the shop's name laced in with bright pink twine.

And now, here we are again. Another autumn, another yarn shop.

Since Alice had closed KnitWit last winter, the Chicks had found their fiber wherever convenient. They'd bought it online, scrounged around the occasional craft fair, and picked up skeins in Chicago's various yarn stores. None of those places, though, had even approached KnitWit's perfect balance between shabby and chic, quirky and cool.

But maybe we've been looking for a new KnitWit, Scottie realized, *without even realizing it. Maybe that's why we're all so tense right now.*

Scottie had thought the jaunt to Stockinette would be just another knitty afternoon; some sticks, snacks, and gossip. The usual.

Now, I'm starting to think this little field trip is more important than I knew.

2 *(Place marker)

As she began walking toward the shingle, Scottie's stomach twisted. Hope and the certainty of disappointment were mixing it up in there, making her a little nauseous. For an instant, she pictured KnitWit—its sunset-colored foyer that made you feel like James walking into the giant peach; the yarn tucked into old soda crates, bookshelves, and cracked ceramic bowls; the pregnant, blue-gray cat named Monkey, meowing irritably at everybody who approached her; Alice whispering knitty wisdom into her students' ears. . . .

Stop it, Scottie interrupted herself. *KnitWit's gone. Give this place a chance.*

She stopped in front of the little store and squinted at Stockinette's glass door. At first, all she could see was her own wavery reflection. Her long, light-brown hair was flattened on one side after a long day of propping her head on her hand at school. Her recently glossed lips made her heart-shaped face look a little less pale than usual. The scoopy neck of her cotton sweater sat just right on her collarbones (due to relentless sizing and blocking).

With an extra squint, Scottie's see-through self disappeared and the shop came dimly into view. Now she saw sherberty walls, a white leather sofa, track lighting, and a strip of burlap stuck through with knitting needles. The skewered fabric hung from the ceiling, fluttering in the breeze of the air conditioning. . . .

(Knit two together)

Scottie felt another rush of queasy hope. Willing herself again to forget her KnitWit rewind, she gave her buds a quick glance, then plunged through the shop door. She stopped the moment she crossed the threshold. *Was* stopped, was more like it—by a series of aromas that thudded her gently in the gut. She smelled dry wool; sunshine trapped in the grooves of the wooden floor; warm sugar. They weren't exactly on the standard aromatherapy roster, but they were just about Scottie's favorite scents on the planet.

The long, narrow shop was lined with galvanized tin buckets, mounted horizontally and stuffed with yarn. The poofs and puffs were candy-colored; unnatural in the best way. The bucket-free parts of the walls were splashed with a mellow shade of raspberry and the iMac on the front desk was a retro orange. A woman wearing mega-low jeans was perched behind the iMac, weaving I-cord out of some glinty thread.

"Oh my God," Scottie breathed as the vibe hit her full-on. Her girlfriends crowded up behind her. They spent a good minute soaking it all in before Tay spoke up.

"I don't get it," she said. "This *is* a knitting store, right? Where's the dowdy?"

"Tay!" Scottie blurted, glancing shyly at the young woman at the iMac. Luckily, she wasn't a hoverer or worse, a knitevangelist. She simply giggled at Tay, then returned to her I-cord. Scottie turned her back on the woman and spoke through gritted teeth.

"How can I put this so you'll *get* it?" she whispered. "Okay, here's you: fifteen years old; tattooed and pierced; badass extraordinaire; in no way dowdy. You also happen to be a genius with yarn and sticks. So how can knitting be dowdy if *you're* a knitter?!"

"A equals b, and b equals c, so a equals c," Bella piped up.

"Bella," Amanda sighed, pointing at Stockinette's fibrous bounty. "We're in the presence of beauty. *Must* you bring algebra into it?"

"Sorry, sweetie," Bella said, giving Amanda's shoulders a squeeze.

"Oh, you *would* love this place," Tay scowled at Amanda. "It's like they polled a thousand Amandas before they built it. It's your Malibu Dream House."

Amanda didn't bother to drag her eyes off the yarn as she popped out an instant retort: "I can't even care that you're totally stereotyping me, *as usual*. This time, you're right. This place is perrrrfect."

"That's exactly what it is. Perfect," Scottie breathed. "Perfect, knitty goodness with frosting on top."

Tay stomped to the front of their little cluster and stared her friends down.

"You *guys*," she protested. "It's completely pink! And it's making Scottie channel *CosmoGirl*. 'Knitty goodness with frosting on top'?"

"I'm *serious*," Scottie protested. She pointed at the shop's requisite Stitch 'n Bitch region in the center of the store. Within a quad of mod white loveseats and squishy chairs was a coffee table on which rested— in addition to a stack of Debbie Stoller tomes—a triple-tiered tray of mini-cupcakes.

With pretty lavender icing.

Tay gasped in horror.

"Cupcakes?!" she squeaked. "Wasn't the pink enough?"

Scottie didn't even try to stifle her snort of laughter.

"Just ignore the cupcakes," she sighed. She gave Tay a push toward a little cluster of buckets stacked with just the kind of serviceable cotton Tay loved. "Go over there. Find your yarn fizz."

While Amanda and Bella went to hover over some fuzzy yarn, arrayed like so many scoops of ice cream in an antique baby bath, and Tay cruised the store with a purposeful scowl, Scottie plucked a cupcake from the tray. When she bit into it, the cake and frosting melted instantly in her mouth. It was little more than sweetened air.

Oh. Wow.

Scottie groaned with fresh-baked happiness, just as Tay tapped her on the shoulder with a springy skein of Risdie Suede.

"Want some trendy with your trendy?" she asked.

Scottie almost dropped her cupcake as her eyes fell on the amber yarn.

"Risdie isn't trendy, it's gold!" she cried, grabbing the skein from Tay. "I read on that blog that they had it here, but I didn't believe it. Yes!"

With one hand, Scottie buried her fingers into the unspeakable, completely unnatural softness of the suede yarn. With the other hand, she gingerly maintained her grip on the Best. Cupcake. Ever. Tay raised one eyebrow at it.

"Whatever," Scottie said. "So cupcakes *are* trendy. But I so don't care and neither will you when you get a taste of this."

She thrust her airy treat toward Tay's mouth. "Try it!"

"No way am I eating a *cup*cake!" Tay scoffed. "Miniature food skeeves me out. It's like playing with a dollhouse where everything's shrunken."

"And?" Scottie said.

"What do you mean?" Tay sputtered. "Am I the only one who thinks dollhouses are creepy? They're worse than clowns."

Tay tried to flick the cupcake away from her—and ended up with a big dab of purple frosting on her fingertip.

Scottie giggled.

Tay rolled her eyes. She had no choice. She popped the stuff into her mouth. Her eyes went big and her lips twisted into a pucker that could only signify supreme pleasure.

"Oh, my God," she swooned.

"Ha!" Scottie yelled triumphantly.

"You guys, c'mere!" she called to Amanda and Bella, who were still ogling their yarn. "The cupcakes have defeated even Tay. You've gotta have some. Oh, wait, Bella, you're not vegan this week, are you?"

"No," Bella sighed, looking guilty. "Ovo-lacto. *Majorly* ovo-lacto. This morning, I had an *omelet*. It was the best thing I've tasted since—"

"Since we went for ice cream two nights ago?" Scottie said.

"Oh, I forgot about that!" Bella's eyes opened wide with guilt.

•• *Chicks with Sticks*

"Whatever," Amanda said, scooping up a puff of melon-colored yarn. "Bella, this is Manos del Uruguay. It's made by this co-op of South American women. It's PC *and* pretty. I'm sure it cancels out a few dairy products."

"Yeah, don't sweat it, B," Tay said. Managing to curl her lip only a little bit, she picked up a cupcake and delivered it to Bella.

Amanda looked at Scottie, her eyes wide and questioning.

I know, Scottie thought, grinning at Amanda. *It's like every day, Tay becomes a little less cactus-like. Who knows, maybe she'll even consent to getting The Tattoo!*

Scottie had hatched an idea a while back that the Chicks should get matching tattoos—a cute little ball of yarn and some sticks, etched onto each of their ankles.

So far all three of her friends had shot the idea down. Bella was terrified of needles and Amanda was terrified of the prolonged meltdown her parents would have if she ever came home with inked skin.

Tay had simply scoffed.

"A cute ball of yarn? That's not a tattoo. *This* is a tattoo."

She'd pointed at the black barbs that encircled her bicep and added, "And guess what, Shearer? This tattoo thing may be your idea, but I don't think you're ready for it. Beginning major rebellion at sixteen could give you the bends or something. Maybe you should start small. You could try, I don't know, refusing to wear your safety goggles in chem class. Or being late to school more than once a year. Work up to the tattoo."

"Hey," Scottie had protested. "I rebel!"

"Dude," Tay had said, "breaking curfew to buy yarn doesn't count."

Okay, so she was totally right, Scottie told herself now, glancing down at her still-bare ankle. *I have a little issue with being bad. I even call my parents when I'm not gonna make curfew, because hello? Tay was right. I only break curfew for yarn or because I'm hanging with my girlfriends. It's not like I have anything worth hiding, like Tay and Amanda do. I'll never stay out 'til two doing . . .*

stuff with my boyfriend because my boyfriend *exists only in my pathetic fantasies.*

Scottie drifted to the Risdie table. It was a small, round pedestal stacked with a wedding cake of yarn and stationed just next to the front desk, probably to prevent shoplifting.

Smart, Scottie thought. *The stuff isn't just expensive, it's also impossible to find in Chicago.*

She'd heard that the company purposely made tiny lots of its stock to feed yarnheads' hunger. Knitting blogs murmured about a beanie baby–style conspiracy.

Yet here it was at Stockinette. Along with Manos del Uruguay, Lorna's Laces, ArtYarns, and tons of homegrown handspun.

It really is perfect, Scottie thought. But even as she set out to choose a few precious skeins of Risdie, she sighed. *It's not KnitWit, though.*

Just like the Chicks with Sticks, while perfectly devoted to Scottie, were not Scottie's shaggy-haired, light-eyed dream boy.

The thing about perfect? Scottie thought. *I keep thinking I've found it, but then it turns out I was wrong.*

Just a couple weeks ago, for instance, Scottie thought she'd found the perfect shirt at H&M. It was cheap, but adorable, an eggplant, empire-waisted, wear-it-once-a-week revelation. It created the illusion of cleavage. It was made of whisper-soft cotton jersey. Scottie was in love.

And then I got it home and turns out, it's got an unsnippable tag, Scottie thought. *That thing scratched at me and rubbed at me until I wished I'd never found my perfect eggplant shirt in the first place.*

Perfect was bad, Scottie knew. Because perfection—or the perception of it, anyway—never lasted.

3 ✳ (Work in the round, being careful not to twist)

"You know, Scottie," Amanda said, popping a grape into her mouth, "your boy problem is that you don't actually *like* boys."

They were sitting with Bella on the front steps of Stark the day after their Stockinette run. Since Tay was running late, they'd already broken out their after-school snacks.

"Okay, *where* would you get an idea like that?" Scottie said, heaving a long-suffering sigh.

"Yeah," Bella added. "Scottie likes half the boys she lays eyes on."

"Thanks," Scottie said. "I think."

"She doesn't *like* those boys," Amanda corrected. "She *crushes* on them."

"Yeah, I guess that's not the same thing," Bella agreed, fishing a Tupperware container out of her woven backpack. "Just like this lime soy mousse is *so* not the same thing as ice cream."

"Man, when you go ovo-lacto, you *really* go ovo-lacto," Scottie said dryly. She pulled a packet of M&M's out of her Suki and held it out to Bella. "Want some?"

"Don't try to change the subject," Amanda giggled, nudging Scottie with her foot. Today's flip-flops had pink Gerber daisies nesting between her toes.

"The subject being liking versus crushing?" Scottie shrugged.

"The subject being the one-note song you've been singing," Amanda said. She made her face go wan and mimicked Scottie: "'Will I *ever* get a boyfriend? Am I *totally* invisible? Oh, Amanda, you're so lucky to have Toby. I'll *neeeeever* find *looooove*.'"

"I do not sound like that," Scottie gasped. She glanced at Bella. "Do I?"

"Well . . ." Bella shifted uncomfortably and fussed with one of the billowy cuffs of her bell-bottom jeans. "You *were* kind of obsessing at lunch. And yesterday after the eavesdropping."

"And the day before that in psych class," Amanda droned.

"Oh my God, you guys!" Scottie said, feeling her face go warm. "Gang up on me, why don't you?"

"Wait!" Amanda cried. "Don't get all splotchy. I'm telling you, I think I've figured out what you can do to solve your problem!"

"Does this involve a fashion makeover?" Scottie sighed. "Because I *still* haven't worn that tube top you forced me to buy this summer."

"No!" Amanda sputtered. "Although it wouldn't hurt you to wear a *few* more bright colors. . . ."

"*Wah!*" Scottie cried, throwing her arms over her head.

"Okay, okay, here's my point," Amanda said. "You have *no* guy friends. They're like this foreign species to you."

"Duh," Scottie said. "That's why they're so intriguing!"

"But that's not good," Amanda said. "I mean, you have to figure out how to relate to guys as, like, normal creatures. To you, they're either absolutely gross or they're Jake Gyllenhaal."

"Jaaaake," Scottie swooned.

"Scottie!" Amanda said. "I'm serious. I think guys sense that you think of them that way."

"*I* think you've been taking our psychology class for only a few weeks, which isn't nearly long enough to have this much insight into my brain," Scottie pouted. "That's a totally weird theory. I mean, I'm friends with Toby, aren't I? He's a guy."

· · *Chicks with Sticks*

"Friends' boyfriends don't count," Bella said. "They're like your brother."

"Same goes for underclassmen," Amanda said, "and male teachers."

"Okay, then," Scottie shot back. "What about Darius, that guy who's always at the coffeehouse? I chat with him sometimes."

"The caffeinedicted poet who always shows up first for open mike night?" Amanda shook her head. "He talks to *everyone*. He's totally hyper and strange. Pity chatting doesn't count."

"Well . . ." Scottie bit her lip. "Oh! There was that guy Regan brought to the Stitch 'n Bitch that time. We had a friendly thing going on."

"Nuh-uh, Scottie. You totally fell for him," Amanda said. "It was only after he started talking about his boyfriend that you became 'friendly.'"

"Gay boys don't count, either," Bella said, "because the romance potential isn't there."

"Okay!" Scottie half-shouted. "Okay, so you're right. I don't like boys. I only like-like them. But what am I supposed to do about it?"

"Just change the way you think of them." Amanda shrugged. "Get to know someone before you fall for him. Or better yet, don't fall for him at all. Just *be friends*. Before you know it, he'll have fallen for you!"

"Oh, like it's so easy," Scottie spat. She was too irked to eat her M&M's so she pulled out the WIP she'd been nursing for a while—a pale yellow tank called Buttered Toast—and started ribbing madly. "And besides, that's not how it happened with Toby. Don't you remember? You were all, 'From the moment I laid eyes on him, I felt like I'd known him forever!' It was like insta-soulmate. Just add water."

"I did not!" Amanda cried. She tossed a grape at Scottie. "I would never have said anything that cheesy."

"I'm just saying," Scottie said. Her fingers started grooving to the riff that always cycled through her head when she ribbed: *purl, purl it again, knit, knit it on, purl, purl it again*. "You found the perfect boy purely by accident. So I don't see why *I* have to follow some formula to find mine. And how do we know it'll even work?! Boys aren't *that* predictable, are they?"

"Definitely not," Bella said casually. "Did I tell you that I've totally given up on boys?"

"What?!" Scottie and Amanda blurted together.

They shot each other a quick look that communicated half a dozen things at once. *There was a boy to give up on? What happened? Wait, does this mean that Bella's into girls? Um, okay, how do we feel about that? And hello? Why didn't we know about any of this? Guilt, guilt, guilt. . . .*

Arranging her face into the picture of calm acceptance, Amanda turned to Bella and said, "Um, no, sweetie. You sort of didn't mention that to us. Even though it's kind of major, don't ya think?"

"It's my fault," Scottie wailed. "I've been angsting about my boy stuff and Bella couldn't get a word in edgewise."

"Oh no, that's not true," Bella said quickly. "I mean, you *have* been pretty angsty. *That's* true. But that's nothing new."

Amanda snorted. Scottie wanted to shoot her a quick pout, but she was too focused on Bella.

And besides, when Bella's right, she's right, Scottie thought with a cringe.

"But that's not why I didn't say anything," Bella went on, licking another dollop of mousse off her spoon. "I'd actually sort of forgotten about my whole no-boys thing."

"How?!" Scottie screeched.

Bella shrugged.

"I decided at Camp Hippie and you know, that was more than a month ago."

"Camp Hippie!" Amanda said. She leaned forward to look at Bella intensely. "We saw you the day after you got back from Camp Hippie and you were all, 'Oh, it was the usual. Weeding the organic garden and milking goats and kayaking and toasting up vegan s'mores.' You might have mentioned that you also made a major lifestyle choice. I mean, I told *you* guys all about my beach trip with my folks and Toby."

"Yeah," Scottie said with rolling eyes. "*All* about it. I'm still wishing I didn't know that Toby chewed on your earlobes. TMI, Amanda!"

"He didn't *chew* on them," Amanda said, sitting up haughtily. "He, er, nibbled them."

"*Uch*, yeah, one of my guys tried that," Bella said with a shudder.

Again, Scottie and Amanda gaped at each other before pouncing on Bella.

"Okay, *backtrack!*" Scottie cried. "You've got to start at the beginning."

Bella blinked at her friends. For about the zillionth time, Scottie marveled at Bella's eyelashes, which were so long and curly they brushed up against her eyebrows when she was surprised.

"You know, Scottie," Bella said, "*you* might want to think about easing off the caffeine a bit."

"Who's changing the subject, now?" Scottie teased. "Start spilling, Bellissima."

"Okay," Bella said. She took a deep breath. "Um, well, when I was five, my parents decided they didn't want me to grow up in a totally urban environment and that we should spend our summers in the country. And it just so happened, one of my dad's old college friends had just bought a big farm in Ohio. So we and nine other families started spending every summer there—"

"Bella—we know this part," Amanda said impatiently. "Everybody slept in tents in a meadow and spent their days working the land while you little kids ran around all dirty and barefoot, singing Carole King songs and making macramé bracelets."

"And when you were eight and your friends started going to sleepaway camp," Scottie said, "you told them you'd been going to sleepaway camp forever. When they wanted to know the name of your camp . . ."

". . . the only name I could think of was Camp Hippie," Bella grinned. "My parents thought that was the cutest thing ever."

"Reason number three hundred twenty two that I can't believe your parents and my parents are the same species," Amanda giggled. "My mom doesn't even take care of her own potted plants. She might ruin her mani."

"Back to Camp Hippie," Scottie said. "So, what happened? With the *boys?*"

"I don't know, it was weird," Bella said. "Last summer, it was like, we were all little kids. We rode our bikes all day and swung from the super-long tire swings that hung from the black walnut trees. We were always making stuff. We'd hand-crank ice cream or make soap or dry flowers."

"Sounds very Laura Ingalls," Scottie said.

"Yeah!" Bella grinned. As usual, she didn't hear the affectionate tweak in Scottie's voice. "Of course, this year, I was all set to teach everybody how to knit. I was even going to shear our goat and try to spin some yarn of my own. But nobody else was into it. Suddenly, everyone—well, at least, us older kids—decided they were bored and that the farm was lame. Nobody talked about it, it was just kind of . . . known."

"Wait, remind me of the Hippie kids again," Scottie said.

"Well, of the older kids, it was me, Liesel, the twins Tobias and Teddy, Tamara, Aidan, and Maya," Bella listed. "We were all fifteen and sixteen. And then there were the seventeen-year-olds—River, Huckleberry, and Peter."

"Why am I not surprised that there was a River?" Amanda drawled, biting into another grape.

"And a Huckleberry!" Scottie said. "Who names their kid Huckleberry?"

"Scottie, don't make fun of him," Bella said. "Huckleberry is a hottie!"

"Oh my God!" Amanda cackled.

"Are you saying," Scottie choked out, "you and Huckleberry . . ."

"We kissed," Bella said bluntly. Scottie's stomach did a sickening flip-flop. She had to admit—she'd always taken comfort in the fact that she wasn't the *only* Chick without a speck of experience. But suddenly, with Bella's casual revelation, that had all changed.

"It was so weird," Bella went on, oblivious to Scottie's trauma. "Suddenly, nobody was churning ice cream and everybody was just, you know, sneaking off with each other to make out. Isn't that bizarre?"

While Scottie nodded, Amanda blurted, "No! Believe me, Bella, kissing is much better than ice cream. Toby and I—"

"You were *saying*, Bella?" Scottie cut in with a quick glare at Amanda. One spit-swapping story at a time was all she could handle.

"Well, anyway," Bella said, "I thought it was weird until Huckleberry and I were walking some eggs from the henhouse to the communal kitchen . . ."

"Now *that's* weird," Amanda giggled.

"No it's not," Bella explained. "Hardly anybody on the farm was vegan so it was okay."

"I meant—" Before Amanda could get any further, she shook her head. "Just . . . go on."

"So we're walking and suddenly Huckleberry reaches out and grabs my hand!" Bella said, her eyelashes reaching for her brows again. "And it was all sweaty and hot, his hand, I mean. But it was also really nice."

"Kinda zingy?" Amanda said with a knowing look in her eyes.

"Totally zingy!" Bella agreed.

Okay, I don't know from this zing, Scottie thought wistfully. *As usual.*

"So then Huckleberry said, 'Bella, my beauty, may I kiss you?'"

"Shut! Up!" Amanda cried. "No guy says that."

"Huckleberry did." Bella shrugged. "I mean, if you knew Huckleberry . . . that's just the way he talks. He writes poetry, too."

"Okay, so then you kissed," Scottie blurted, cutting to the chase. "So how was it?"

"Gross!" Bella wailed. "I mean, I didn't know there were *tongues* involved! Which is crazy. My parents gave me The Talk practically before I could talk. I've known about bodies and hormones and stuff for forever. But there was nothing about tongues in The Talk."

"Cuz *that* would have been weird," Scottie said through her laughter. "So then what? Did you have to break up with Huckleberry?"

"No need," Bella said. "A couple days later, Huckleberry kissed Liesel and I kissed Todd."

"Whoa, you farm kids are fast," Amanda choked out. She was laughing so hard, she was doubled over.

"All I have to say is Todd was even worse," Bella said glumly. "He was the ear chewer. Yuck. But then . . ."

"There's more?" Scottie cried.

"There's Peter," Bella said. She clasped her spidery fingers in a knot beneath her chin and smiled beatifically.

"Peter wasn't gross," Scottie stated.

"Peter was wonderful," Bella cooed. "He was the only reason I decided to give boys one more chance. He had the cutest farmer's tan and he smelled like pollen and . . . I don't know, he was just kind of yummy! I kissed him twice."

"And then what?" Scottie said, feeling a little out of breath. "You had to come home?"

"No." Bella's pretty face suddenly took on an unfamiliar glower. "He got a call *from* home. Specifically from his *girlfriend*."

"No!" Amanda and Scottie cried together.

"Oh, thanks. I can see you're really happy to see me."

Scottie jumped. Standing a few steps above them was Tay. John—even lankier and skinnier than Tay—was standing next to her. Two of his fingers were hooked through one of her cargo pants belt loops. That was about as much PDA as Tay would allow him.

"Hey!" Scottie said. "What took you so long?"

"Mr. A," Tay said with an eye roll—one that Scottie knew was just for show. Tay actually liked her bimonthly meetings with her woolly-eyebrowed guidance counselor, even if she did object to the fact that she was *required* to go to them.

The Starkers That Be (as Tay referred to their school's head honchos) had first sent her to the counselors' offices a few years ago after deciding that Tay's "broken home" had left her with some "anger issues."

The order, of course, had brought on fresh, new waves of anger the likes of which the elder-Starkers had never seen before. The first wave came after they made the mistake of sending Tay to Mrs. Sczielwiak, a nervous, twitchy woman whom Tay had calmly and efficiently stonewalled from day one. Mrs. Sczielwiak broke down in tears at the end of their third meeting, whereupon Tay was transferred to Mr. Smith (privately nicknamed by Tay: Mr. Smellth), quickly followed by Ms. Klein-Rosenzweig. ("A prime example," Tay said dismissively, "of someone who became a social worker to deal with her own junk.")

Mr. Adrian, as Stark's only other counselor, had been Tay's last chance. Maybe that was why they'd hit it off.

"Or maybe," Tay said when Scottie asked her about it once, "it's because he doesn't treat me like some Case. Because, hello? There are plenty of bulimics and meth-heads to go around in this school. My little divorce is nothing compared to that."

It seemed to be true. Sure, Tay still hated the constant hamster wheel of shuttling from her dad's place in the Ukrainian Village to her mom's in Andersonville. And yeah, she studiously avoided talking about the years when her parents had still been together, fighting like caged cats. But from what Scottie could see, Tay's "anger issues" didn't seem like issues at all.

Tay's got quills, that's all there is to it. In more ways than one, Scottie thought, smiling at the knitting needles poking out of Tay's pants pocket. *I wouldn't recognize her without 'em. Seems like the only people who can't handle it are the people who are supposed to have a clue—the adults.*

"So what's today's big drama, Scottie?" Tay said, kneeling gracefully next to Scottie.

"Me?!" Scottie squeaked. "Don't look at me. It's Bella's turn!"

"She's got an announcement," Amanda said.

Tay raised her eyebrows at Bella, who flushed and fluttered her fingers nervously.

"Well, I was just saying . . ."

Bella cast a careful glance at John, who'd sunk into an easy slouch on the steps behind Tay. He was pulling out his own snack—a Big Grab bag of chips—and his math homework.

"Um, well, it's nothing," Bella said, taking a quick bite of lime mousse and gazing at the sky as she puckered through it.

"Liar," Tay accused. "What's the deal?"

"Bella's ditched boys," Amanda stage-whispered to Tay.

"Amanda!" Bella squeaked. She pointed exaggeratedly at John. *"He's a boy, you know!"*

"Well, he's taken," Scottie provided. "So he doesn't really count."

"Of course he counts," Bella whispered, patting Tay's knee. "And I don't want to hurt his feelings."

All the girls peeked at John, who seemed much more interested in his junk food and geometry than their conversation.

"The dude is oblivious," Scottie whispered.

"Unless, of course, Tay snaps her fingers and asks him to peel her a grape," Amanda joked.

Tay rolled her eyes, but even as she did, John's hand drifted to the back of her neck, giving it a quick, absent-minded squeeze.

Where any other guy might see Tay as dangerously thorny, John found her to be irresistibly touchable. He grabbed for her hand at every opportunity. Whenever they sat next to each other, his knee crept sideways until it was just tapping hers. Sitting around, just reading or watching TV, John massaged Tay's shoulders, fluttered his fingertips over her hair, or traced the veins on the inside of her wrist. And that was when they were around other people!

• • Chicks with Sticks

Scottie forced herself to look away from John's easy, loving gesture. She turned back to Bella.

"Just finish the story," she whispered. "What happened after you found out about kisser number three's girlfriend?"

"Whoa!" Tay said. "I *did* miss a story."

With one more shifty glance at John, Bella said, "Well, I decided that I'd given boys a fair shot and—I don't like them! I'll wait for them to grow up before I get near one of them again. I'm thinking maybe senior year."

"But that's only next year," Scottie said.

"Of college," Bella said with a decisive nod.

"Oh," Scottie whispered. "So that's the end of the story?"

"Well . . . I might have also dumped a pail of goat's milk on Peter's head," Bella said, covering her mouth with her hand.

"No way!" Tay cackled. "B, way to come over to the dark side!"

At the sound of Tay's triumphant voice, John roused himself, brushing sour-cream-and-onion dust off his hands.

"Hey," he yawned. "Why are we just sitting here when we could be at Joe? It's Tuesday, isn't it? Stitch 'n Bitch day? So are we gonna knit or what?"

Scottie blinked.

John's knitting? *Basketball forward, cheese-fry-chugging, chiseled-chin* John? *Well . . . that's new.*

She looked from John's grinning, sheepish face to Tay's pale, simmering one.

"Surprise, Tay-Tay!" John said.

And not just to me!

A few minutes later, the Chicks with Sticks were digging into their knitting bags in the shabby lounge in the back of Joe. Bella was in her usual spot, plopped into the almost-beanless beanbag chair. Amanda, Scottie, and Tay were wedged into a very hard old church pew along the wall, which was *not* their usual spot.

"This is just weird," Tay grumbled.

"I know," Scottie said, already feeling the butt-numbing effects of the pew. "I mean, *we* created the Tuesday Stitch 'n Bitch. Yet here we are, only ten minutes late, and *nobody* saved us any seats."

Scottie peered around the dusky place. The pub-turned-coffeehouse was always crowded with Starkers, being right across the street from school. But crowded with *knitters?*

Scottie wasn't surprised to see the regulars, like Amanda's friends from the University of Chicago, Polly and Regan. Polly was sitting cross-legged in front of the beat-up coffee table, freeforming her way through a long, pointy hat and Regan was curled up in a saggy chair, sketching her latest yarny brainstorm. Either that or writing code for one of her computer engineering classes.

Maryn, who held an immutable spot on Stark's A-list, had today snagged a spot on Scottie's favorite loveseat. She was showing her BFF, Tiff, several balls of yarn, all variations of the same corally pink.

"I'm trying to find the perfect match for that OPI nail polish I love," she was saying.

"Melon of Troy?" Tiff said automatically. "Fab idea! Pick that one!"

She pointed one of her perfectly manicured fingers at one of the pink-orange poufs. Scottie laughed.

Only Maryn would spend months knitting a sweater to match her mani.

A couple other regulars were camped around Joe's knitarena, too, but there were also about a dozen people Scottie barely recognized, many of them clutching pink Stockinette bags and wielding shiny new needles. They had no idea they were crowding out the very founders of the Never-Mind-the-Frogs Stitch 'n Bitch.

"Tay's right. Like, who are they?" Scottie whispered, furtively jabbing her needle in their direction. "Refugees from a paint-your-own-pottery class?"

"Whoa, snark much?!" Amanda said.

"And besides, the trendheads aren't the ones weirding me out," Tay muttered. "It's the boy in our midst."

"John?" Bella said. She peeked over at John, who was perched on the coffee table. He was peering at a page in a book called *Knitting for Total Fools* and struggling to cast some French blue worsted onto a bamboo needle.

"Wait, you're saying John shouldn't be knitting because he's a *boy?*" Scottie whispered. "You of all people, Tay, aren't hung up on gender roles, are you?"

"Of course not," Tay scowled. She looked down and skimmed through a series of stitches. "I don't know, it's just weird, that's all. I mean, knitting? Knitting's . . ."

"Your thing?" Scottie said sympathetically.

"No," Tay said, shaking her head, frustrated to be so confused. "Well, yeah, maybe. Oh, I don't know. It's just weird, that's all."

"Um, guys?" John piped up. The Chicks jumped and looked over at him guiltily. "I've kind of already screwed up. Like, majorly."

He held up his needle, strung with a tangle of knots upon knots— nothing like the neat little swerves that Scottie knew as casting on.

Amanda laughed and glanced at Tay. But Tay made no move to get up and go to her boyfriend's yarn-aid. Instead, she looked more freaked than ever.

"I'll show you," Amanda offered quickly. "Tay's kind of at a sticky point in her hat herself."

"Glove," Tay muttered, but she didn't try to interfere. Amanda unwedged herself from the church pew and knelt beside John at the coffee table, its wood surface pitted and gouged with the graffiti of hundreds of Starkers. Sliding *Knitting for Total Fools* out of the way, Amanda began to pull John's hopeless knots off his needle.

As Scottie absently stitched a round into Buttered Toast, she gazed at a particular corner of the coffee table. A long time ago, *she'd* been the

(Knit two together)

one carving into it. Somewhere beneath a new layer of scrawlings was a quartet of letters: *S, A, T,* and *B,* knifed in by each Chick with a knitting needle. In the center of those initials, like the hub of a wheel, were the letters *C w/ S.*

Scottie glanced again at John, who was now stuttering through his first knit stitches under Amanda's watchful eye. She eyed a cluster of popular seniors as they pulled skein after skein of Risdie yarn out of their pink bags. She took in this chaos of coffee, yarn, and chatter that she and her friends had wrought without even meaning to. And she felt desperately grateful for that imprint on the coffee table. It was permanent. Grounding. Even if it was no longer visible.

Even if it was no longer enough.

4 *(Use contrasting color)

That night in her bedroom, Scottie frowned at Buttered Toast. She'd spent the afternoon at Joe stitching a series of sweet scallops into its hem, but now they didn't look right to her (even if they did look exactly like the illustration in her pattern).

Jagged little points, she realized. *That's what I want.*

Without stopping to reconsider, she plopped onto her bed and frogged a good half of the stitches she'd worked into the tank at Joe. She wasn't even upset about destroying the hour's worth of work. Pulling stitches out had become as much a part of knitting for her as weaving them in. She'd discover that the decrease that was supposed to create a nipped-in waist landed somewhere around her rib cage. Or a hat was knit up too tightly to make gauge. Or suddenly, that lavender sportweight wool seemed much better suited to a pair of slouchy socks than the fingerless gloves she'd originally imagined.

Besides, in a perverse way, Scottie liked how it felt, pulling out stitches. The interconnected loops burst apart, like a silent version of the plastic pop-beads she'd had as a little kid. She used to *pop* all those shapes and colors together and apart, together and apart for hours. It got to be such a habit that sometimes she'd do it while she watched after-school TV or read a book, absently *pop-pop-popping* away.

Added bonus—the noise had always driven her older sister crazy.

With her frogging finished, Scottie rolled onto her stomach and grabbed her pattern off her nightstand. But every time she tried to find her place in it so she could scribble in her alterations, her eyes glazed over.

Sighing, Scottie glanced at her bedroom door. Music was floating over it. (Because of course, the fact that Scottie actually possessed a bedroom door didn't mean she had total privacy. Not in a loft with twenty-foot ceilings, where all the rooms were made of partitions as opposed to actual walls.)

Music pumping into the loft meant that her mom was painting in the canvased-off corner that was her studio.

With a start, Scottie realized that this was the first time she'd heard painting tunes in weeks. Her mom had been a bit fallow lately. For days, she'd been stomping grumpily around the loft (as much as you can stomp when the floors are made of cement). She'd grab at pieces of junk mail or paper napkins when an idea struck and begin sketching wildly, a mad grin growing ever larger on her face. But almost the instant she finished her brainstorm, she'd glance at the result and her face would fall. She'd crumple it up, chuck it, and trudge away, muttering anew.

Finally, Scottie had pounced on her that morning, just after her mom had penciled an idea on a corner of the *Chicago Tribune,* then viciously crossed it out until it was a just shiny, black slash.

"Mom," Scottie complained as she scraped butter onto her toast, "I feel like I'm watching a bad movie montage: angsty artist, deep in thought."

Her mom slurped at her black coffee and pulled at her bright red hair until it stood up on her head, spikier than ever.

"I know," she sighed apologetically. "I'm feeling a whole new wave coming on, and it ain't pretty."

"What do you mean?" Scottie asked.

"I mean, I think I need to get back into representational paintings," Mom replied, doodling a sleepy eye into the *Trib*'s margin.

"Representing . . . what?" Scottie said.

"People. Stuff. Life!" her mom said.

"I thought you did abstracts to *reject* all that," Scottie said. She tried to remember some of the arty banter her parents flung about at the monthly openings in their gallery space next door. Their party chat had never made much sense to her, but she'd retained just enough to regurgitate now. "Isn't your stuff about going deeper than representation? I thought you painted the, um, feelings that drive life? Or, y'know, something like that?"

"That's not working for me anymore." Her mom sighed. Now she penciled a tiny pig underneath the eye, its mouth open and squawling. "I'm not seeing in abstracts at the moment. You know what I mean? Is it ever like that for you?"

"In my knitting, you mean?" Scottie swallowed hard, forcing down the bite of toast she'd been chewing. She tried to hide the syrupy smile that'd just erupted on her face. She made every attempt to be blasé about the whole artist-to-artist commiserating thing.

But she couldn't. She just couldn't hide her goofy grin as she nodded and said, "Yeah, it is. It is right now, as a matter of fact. It's like nothing I knit is quite right. I keep ripping and ripping, reknitting and reknitting."

"Join the club," her mom said. "But it's all part of the creative process, right?"

"Right!" Scottie blurted. Not that she *really* knew what her mom was talking about. But she was enjoying the conspiratorial vibe too much to point that out. For a long time, Scottie's sister had been the only one on Mom's artistic wavelength. Jordan, who was at NYU film school making "experimental shorts," was always riffing about compositional theory and concept versus aesthetic. Just as their painting-obsessed parents were always throwing around names of artists that Scottie never recognized.

It used to bother Scottie, this thing with her family. When her parents and Jordan would go on one of their artsy-fartsy tears, an old *Sesame Street* ditty would hum through Scottie's head: "One of these things is not like the other, one of these things does not belong. . . ."

But these days, that hardly ever happened. Because Scottie's mom had pulled her into the artist trenches with her. Not as some pretentious "fiber artist" or yarn sculptress or whatever. But as a knitter. As herself.

Who knows, Scottie thought now, swiping her laptop off her desk and padding out of her bedroom. *Maybe our little chat helped Mom unblock and I'm responsible for some fabulous new art breaking into the world. I wonder if that makes up for the fact that my needles have been totally stalled lately.*

Scottie pushed the thought aside as a distraction trotted out of the kitchen—her wobbly little kitten.

"CC," Scottie cooed, kneeling to give the kitty a quick stroke. Just like her mother, Monkey, CC was bluish gray. Except for her tail, which was black. Hence her name, CC (as in Contrasting Color).

Frankly, CC was much sweeter than Monkey, who'd pretty much terrorized everyone at KnitWit except Alice. Unfortunately, CC's brother—whom Bella had adopted and named Eden—was even worse than Monkey. Bella adored him, even as she was constantly fighting off his random attacks on everything she owned, from her favorite rosewood knitting needles to the delicate, blowsy skirts hanging in her closet. Eden had even been known to shred Bella's socks while she was still wearing them.

CC on the other hand, was utterly harmless. She was tiny and delicate—having been the runt of Monkey's litter—and walked with a wobbly, side-swaying gait. Though she was no longer *really* a kitten, her fur still looked like baby fluff—all tangly and disheveled. Objectively, Scottie knew that she was a little odd. The veterinarian had told her

•• Chicks with Sticks

that it was possible that CC had sustained some nerve damage in her difficult birth. But this only made Scottie love her more.

Still cradling her laptop, Scottie scooped CC into her other arm and headed over to the assemblage of angular couches floating on the giant rug just outside her mom's studio.

Humming along to her mom's Andrew Bird CD, Scottie flopped onto the red couch, swung her legs up over the back, and nested her computer on her stomach to surf some blogs. CC curled up under the bridge Scottie had made with her legs.

Scottie had barely begun wending her way through her long roster of favorite knitting sites when her IM window popped up in the corner of her screen with a bubbly chime. It was her sister.

CINEWOMAN: Hey S. Thank gawd ur there. I totally don't get this SSK thing.

Scottie froze.
SSK?

KNITCHICK16: ??? What're you talking about?
CINEWOMAN: You know, slip slip knit. The decrease thing? I'm at Tea Spot with my S 'n B and we're stuck. Probably cuz we've only been doing this yarn thing for abt a minute.

"No you're *not*," Scottie whispered. Her fingers were paralyzed for a moment, hovering over her keyboard. A second later, she exhaled loudly and typed a curt reply.

KNITCHICK16: Clearly. SSK is way basic. Are you even purling yet?
CINEWOMAN: Duh. Why so harsh?
KNITCHICK16: Not. Just not really interested in tutoring long distance. Why don't ask your S 'n B organizer?

(Knit two together)

CINEWOMAN: Cuz I'M the organizer. I'm thinking of making a film about the whole NY knitting scene. With, like, nothing but close-ups of different hands knitting. Maybe . . . I'm still concepting.
CINEWOMAN: Anyway, the knit's totally HUGE here.
KNITCHICK16: It's huge here, too.

Scottie paused for a fluttery instant before she capped off her lame retort with a snarky addendum.

KNITCHICK16: Course, now the trendheads are taking over, which sux.

Scottie waited with a sour smile for Jordan's response. She predicted self-righteousness with a hint of shame between the lines.

Scottie's computer emitted an electronic chortle as Jordan's reply came in.

CINEWOMAN: I know, it *totally* sux. Hey, guess who I saw in Soho the other day? Debbie Stoller! Wearing the cutest little ribby tank. I stopped her and told her about my film idea. She was really into it.

Scottie gaped at her computer screen. She could barely breathe as she slammed out her reply. Conjuring up another famous knitster, she typed . . .

KNITCHICK16: Sorry, gotta go. Suss Cousins is on her way over. We're having a slumber party.
CINEWOMAN: Who? What about my SSK?
KNITCHICK16: You should get this xcellent book. *Knitting for Total Fools.* You'll find all your answers there. Buh-bye.

Scottie logged off in the middle of Jordan's reply-chime. Clicking her laptop shut, Scottie shoved it onto the coffee table, pulled CC onto her chest, and scowled.

That's so Jordan, she railed silently. *She just gloms onto knitting, then doesn't even realize that* she's *one of the trendheads.*

Deeper down was another complaint, one she didn't want to admit to, but couldn't help thinking: *And why knitting? My knitting. Being Miss Film Prodigy wasn't enough?*

"Hey, sweetheart."

Scottie looked up and saw her dad coming through the wide, frosty-glass door that led to Shearer Space, her parents' art gallery. As usual, his hands-free phone was bobbling in his left ear beneath his latest pair of arty glasses. Scottie's parents collected eyeglass frames the way some people collected T-shirts.

Of course, given that a lot of people in their paint-spattered social circle were all about leather pants and mock turtlenecks, Scottie thought she was getting off easy. Other than their eyewear, her parents were pretty presentable.

"Since your mom's on a roll," Dad said, "why don't we get some take-out. Indian?"

Scottie glanced at her computer. Indian was one of Jordan's favorites, which made Scottie want to vote for pizza.

But annoyingly, Indian was one of Scottie's favorites, too.

"Let's do it," she declared, letting CC scramble away and heaving herself off the couch. "I vote for saag paneer and tandoori chicken. And that nan with the caramelized onions?"

"Oh, wait," Dad remembered. "I think I saw a menu for Raja India down by the mailboxes. They always have coupons on those. Can you go grab one? I'm sure by the time you get back, you'll have added to your list."

"Already have," Scottie smiled as she headed for the door. She was pleasantly aware of CC trotting along behind her. "Mango lassi. Ooh, and that eggplant-chickpea thing!"

"I knew it," her dad said. "Oh, to have your teenage metabolism."

"Hey, a girl needs comfort food after getting IM'ed by her sister," Scottie blurted.

"What?" Dad said. He walked across the loft and crossed his arms over his soft midsection. "What's going on with Jordan? Anything wrong?"

Scottie contemplated indulging in some whining. Ever since Jordan had gone to college, her dad had become her confidante of sorts—maybe because *he* didn't get Jordan's movies any more than Scottie did. Dad's idea of heaven was a John Woo movie with stadium seating and a king-sized box of Good & Plenty.

Scottie—who happened to have inherited her dad's weird Good & Plenty gene—had a feeling he'd understand the injustice of a sister gone knitty.

But what do I say? That the whole world seems to be knitting, but my sister isn't allowed to? That'll make sense.

So Scottie just shook her head and attempted a grim smile.

"Jordan's fine," she said. "She was just telling me about some new avant garde movie in the works. Tell me, would *you* want to watch a movie with nothing but hands in them?"

"Like . . . sock puppets?" Dad said.

"With Jordan, who knows?" Scottie said.

"Maybe she'll ask you to knit the socks," Dad suggested as he headed over to the couch.

"Wouldn't be surprised," Scottie mumbled, knowing her dad couldn't hear her all the way across the loft. Louder, she called, "Be back in a sec."

"With your appetite, you might want to grab two of those menus," her dad called back to her.

"Har, har," Scottie said dryly.

Since the building's mailboxes were in the foyer, she didn't bother to put on shoes. She hauled open the heavy door—a pastiche of rusty panels stenciled with SUNFLOUR BREAD COMPANY that were relics of her building's former life as an industrial bakery. Just before she slipped into the long, echoey hallway over CC's squeaky protests, she caught a glimpse of herself in the little lipstick-check mirror hung next to the door. Her makeup was long gone and her nose had an oily sheen on it. Her hair was a bit sticky-uppy after being wedged into the couch arm.

Lovely, Scottie thought, slipping into the hallway. She skimmed her hand over her head to tamp down her tangles but didn't attempt any other prettying up. The bread factory was mostly home to artists, dot.com types, and a few caterers who took advantage of the giant old ovens still left in some of the lofts. When it came to dog-walking and mail-fetching wardrobe, Scottie had seen everything from magnifying goggles (on the jeweler who lived on the first floor) to pastry-caked clogs to the clay-mucked graying chest hair on that sculptor who always walked around with no shirt on. *Yich.* Compared to *those* ensembles, the pilly old lavender stretch pants Scottie had changed into after school, her bare feet, and her less-than-fresh face were completely tame.

Downstairs, she shoved her way through another high-concept metal door and shuffled over to the row of mailboxes embedded in the foyer's chinked brick wall. She bent over to sift through the long trough underneath the boxes where the mail carrier always stashed the daily sheaf of take-out menus, dry cleaner ads, and supermarket circulars. As she searched for a Raja India menu, she felt her stretch pants slip dangerously low on her hips.

Grrr—low-rise pants, Scottie thought, reaching back to yank up her waistband.

Oh, great, now *I have a wedgie.*

She straightened up and reached around to correct the situation.

Which was, naturally, when the clanky door swung open again. Loping into the foyer was . . . a boy.

A tragically cute boy—whose greenish eyes instantly fell upon Scottie. Scottie snatched her hand away from her butt in horror. At the

(Knit two together)

same time, the guy glanced at the floor. Basically, they were both doing that thing where they pretended that he hadn't actually seen Scottie yanking at her underwear in public.

The only problem was, the guy couldn't maintain the illusion. When he looked up, his eyes—maybe more of a hazel, actually—were crinkled into a smile. An I'm-trying-really-hard-not-to-laugh smile.

Feeling her cheeks flush, Scottie took one last look at the guy's face, cataloguing all its beauties before she returned her gaze, intently, to the trough under the mailboxes.

As she shuffled blindly through the box, she felt utter agony.

His eyes are definitely hazel. And they're shaped like teardrops and they're sort of crinkly at the corners. And his nose is kind of big, but in a really cute way. It totally goes with that shaggy, black hair of his. His chin is square and not slopey in the slightest. AND HE SAW ME PULLING A WEDGIE OUT OF MY BUTT!

Scottie stared into the mail trough so hard, her eyes almost began to water. She yanked out a wad of junk mail and began sifting through it quickly. Meanwhile, she could feel the guy standing behind her as if he was giving off heat.

Why isn't he leaving? Scottie angsted. *Hello, the foyer's like eight feet long. It shouldn't be taking him this long to find the front door.*

The Raja India menus were maddeningly elusive. Scottie shoved her wad of papers back into the trough. And that's when the boy alighted at a mailbox a few feet away. He unlocked the box and peered inside. Then he sighed heavily.

Wait a minute. He lives here?!?

She'd been sure that the guy was just passing through the foyer after visiting someone in the bread factory. Probably his girlfriend. Probably that gorgeous girl in 4-H with the long red curls and the Japanese letters tattooed onto the small of her back.

"Nobody loves me."

That was him. Him talking. And since nobody else was in the foyer, that must have meant he was talking to Scottie!

• • Chicks with Sticks

With a really bizarre opening line.

Scottie, hand frozen halfway through one last, desperate dig for the Raja India menu, took a quick peek over at him.

He was looking right at her. And from the crinkly-eyed smile he was flashing, it appeared that he was joking.

So, now, Scottie had to quip back. She had to issue some breezy, clever, flirty retort. Which would have been easy—if this boy were a girl.

Amanda's right, Scottie groaned inwardly. *I'm completely freaked by boys.*

The guy's smile was starting to fade, replaced by confusion. If Scottie hesitated a second more, the awkwardness would grow so loud, it'd be deafening.

Quip! She ordered herself desperately. *QUIP!*

"Aw, that can't be true," Scottie squeaked out, trying to sound flirty (but detecting a quaver in her voice). "Jesus loves you. Haven't you seen that billboard at Montrose and Ashland?"

The guy's smile? It was back. But the confusion? Still lingering.

"I mean . . ." Scottie faltered, "uh, that was a joke. I mean, there really is a 'Jesus Loves You' billboard at Montrose and Ashland. The Jesus is all rain-streaked and his eyes are kind of crossed and it always strikes me as funny, this battered old Jesus staring down on the people coming out of the Dunkin' Donuts on the corner."

The guy's expression was hard to decipher now. He blinked at Scottie a few times.

"I mean, not that Jesus is inherently funny or anything," Scottie babbled on.

Just dig that hole deeper, she told herself, feeling a quick burst of sweat bloom beneath her arms. *Go on.*

"What do I know?" she said with a nervous shrug. "I'm Jewish!"

The guy's smile was returning.

"Not that I'm all religious or anything," Scottie said, knowing she was prattling but powerless to stop herself. "I mean, I think the only reason my parents have a mezuzah on the door is because it looks cool."

(Knit two together)

That's it. Talk about your parents. *Because that's* so *attractive.*

"I'm Jewish, too," the guy said. "Well, half-Jewish, half-some nebulous, nonreligious form of Gentileness."

He was grinning. Maybe, by some miracle, he'd found Scottie's geeky gush charming?

"Actually, you could say my mom worships the gods of fashion," The Guy went on. "But we're from New York, which pretty much means the Jewish cancels everything else out. You know, every New Yorker's Jewish, even the non-Jews."

"It's all the corned beef and bagels," Scottie said—one could even say *quipped*—with a sage nod. "You know, you have to look long and hard to get a good bagel in Chicago."

"I've heard that," the guy said. "That's one of the countless reasons I begged my mom not to move out here. But it didn't work. 'They have good pizza,' she told me. 'You'll get over it.'"

Scottie laughed and leaned against the row of mailboxes.

"So when did you move to our bagel-forsaken burg?" she said.

"Like, a minute ago," the guy said. "It looks like our mail hasn't even been forwarded yet."

He pointed at the empty box and sighed again.

Which made Scottie finally understand what was behind his mock-udrama.

"Nobody loves you," she said, pointing at the mailbox. Then she clasped her hands beneath her chin and simpered, "*Awwwww.* That's *sooooo* sad!"

"Shut up," the guy said, waving her off with a grin. "You don't know what it's like."

"You're right," Scottie said, suddenly going serious. "I don't. I've lived here all my life. It's gotta be really tough. For you, I mean."

"It's okay," the guy said. He looked down at his hands suddenly.

His hands! Scottie couldn't believe she'd overlooked them before. They were substantial and on the knuckly side, with a prominent writer's callous and nice, square, unbitten nails. Scottie suddenly wanted to reach out and touch one of them. Instead, she clutched the edge of the junk mail trough.

"Hell," the guy continued, "I only have a year of high school left, so even if it's awful, it's only a year."

"Oh, it won't be awful," Scottie said immediately.

The guy actually seemed to derive some hope from Scottie's silly platitude. He looked up at her.

"Maybe you know something about the school I'm heading to," he wondered. "It's private, of course. My mom wouldn't even consider anything else. It's called the Olivia Stark School?"

"Shut up!" Scottie shouted. "That's my school!"

"You're kidding."

"It's true," Scottie said. "I've been going there since I was in first grade. I'm a junior now."

"This is amazing," the guy said eagerly. "I'm starting there at the end of the week. So, can you give me the dirt?"

"Well . . ." Scottie laughed and shifted her weight from one bare foot to the other. As she did, she realized that she felt halfway comfortable with this guy! Other than the whole wedgie fiasco. And, well, the Jesus thing. For the past few minutes, she hadn't given a thought to the chipped mahogany polish on her toenails, or to her shiny nose or flattened hair.

A growly noise emanating softly from her stomach also reminded her that she was into minute ten or so of a two-minute errand. It was entirely possible that her dad could get worried and come downstairs looking for her in a minute. He could mortify Scottie in a dozen different ways, even if he wasn't wearing a mock turtleneck.

Scottie closed her eyes for a split second. She knew what she had to do. She had to channel Amanda. She had to imagine what it was like to operate out of utter, effortless confidence, girded by a chest that was substantially larger than Scottie's own 32A.

"I've got to get back," Scottie said. Much as she tried, she couldn't inject even a hint of flirtiness into her voice. She was too nervous. She settled for angling her head and trying for a breezy effect. "But tell you what—why don't we head to school together on your first day and I can catch you up then."

The guy's smile was too quick and bright to be fake. Scottie felt her eyes widen. Was she detecting sparkage? Other than her own, that was?

"That'd be awesome," he said.

"Meet you right here at 7:45?" Scottie proposed. "You start on Friday, right?"

"You're a good listener," the guy said, his smile getting even beamier. "I wanted to just start Monday, but the guidance counselor I talked to said Friday would be better. Not only is it the mellowest day of the week, but in her words, I could then take the weekend to 'process' my first day."

"That's a Stark guidance counselor all right," Scottie laughed. "They don't come any more touchy-feely."

"So," he grinned, "I'll see ya Friday, then."

With a few more smiles and a little wave good-bye, Scottie glided out of the foyer, hoping to God that the guy couldn't see that she *still* had a major wedgie going on beneath her traitorous lavender pants.

She was almost at her loft before she realized that not only had she failed to snag a Raja India menu, she hadn't even gotten her new crush's name.

5 *(Knit through the back loop)

Scottie vowed not to tell anybody about The Guy until after their Friday Morning Walk. Not even the Chicks. It was too big to talk about—and too ripe for jinxing.

Trying not to *think* about it, on the other hand, was futile. On Wednesday at school, Scottie vacillated between wondering what his name was—*Jake? Robert? Alexander?*—and panicking at the thought of filling the half-hour trip from the bread factory to school with scintillating Stark-bits.

Remember the Jesus billboard, Scottie warned herself as she lolled her way through homeroom, doodling in her notebook. Scottie knew herself. When she got into nervous chatter mode, she was unstoppable.

Let's say he asks me about the cafeteria food, she imagined, shifting nervously in her desk chair. *The next thing ya know, I'll be waxing poetic about that time in fourth grade when Jonny Anton ate ten peanut butter-cornflake bars and puked all over Amanda's mary janes.*

Scottie shuddered.

Just don't think about it, she ordered herself sternly. *Overanalysis is death.*

She also wouldn't allow herself to write a script for the Friday Morning Walk—much as she was tempted. Instead, she went back to imagining her crush's name, writing each possibility in her notebook.

Ethan? Leo? Ulysses? Tito????? I know. Arthur. Definitely Arthur.

Scottie was almost grateful when the bell rang to take her to Chem 2, where she had a quiz. If not for that distraction, she might have filled up the whole notebook.

Isaac? Max? Jesus?

"What a morning," Amanda sighed at lunch time. She flopped into the cafeteria chair and fished an Izze soda out of her bag. "We had in-class essays in English."

"Oh . . ." Scottie said carefully, peering at Amanda's face for signs of distress. Amanda's learning disability meant writing—especially under the time gun—could be torturous.

But Amanda actually looked . . . happy! Nothing like someone who'd just endured fifty-five minutes of hell.

"So, was it okay?" Scottie asked her.

"It was, actually!" Amanda announced, taking a big swig of gourmet, grapefruit fizz. She plucked an olive out of her cafeteria-issue salad and popped it into her mouth before digging into her bag for her lunchtime knitting—a beret she was making out of some fuzzy pink novelty yarn.

"The thing is, I *did* the reading," Amanda went on. "It was this pretty awesome Eudora Welty short story. And I knew just what I wanted to say about it. So I just spent about five minutes doing some of the relaxation exercises I've been working on with Dr. Anderson at U of C and then . . . I did it! I wrote. I wrote really slow and the essay was really short, but whatever. Ms. McElroy knows all about my L.D. so I think she'll understand."

Scottie shook her head in wonder at Amanda. At this point last year, Amanda could barely stand to admit to *herself* that she had a learning disability, much less to her teachers and other people in her life. Now she was writing essays about Eudora Welty?!?

"Amanda, that's so fab!" Scottie squealed, unwrapping some tandoori chicken left over from the previous night's take-out. "Did you call Toby yet?"

"No!" Amanda declared. She looked intently at her salad, poking at a cherry tomato with her fork. "Okay *yes*. But he wasn't there. I left a message."

Scottie was about to make a crack about the vast amounts of cell chat that traveled between Amanda and her BF—but then she stopped herself. What if *she* were the one with the boyfriend? Not a college guy like Amanda's, but a Starker with hazel eyes and shaggy dark hair, loping across the cafeteria toward her with a big, cute smile on his poochy lips.

The vision made Scottie close her eyes and clasp her hands together, white-knuckled with hope. The last thing she wanted to do was ding her boyfriend karma by making fun of Amanda's relationship, so she kept her mouth shut.

Which left a window open for Bella, who'd just arrived at their table, toting her usual canvas lunch bag and a very *un*usual perturbed expression on her face.

"Hi," she blurted before flopping into a folding chair. Her long peasant skirt poofed up with air for a moment before settling into a silky pool around her.

"Ciao, Bella," Scottie greeted her. "What's wrong?"

"This . . . this *boy* just asked me out!" Bella said, sounding totally confused and outraged. "And he's the *second* one since school started."

"Bella, that's great!" Amanda said. She'd been frowning at her silent cell phone but emerged to shoot Bella a triumphant smile. It was no secret among any of them that Bella, for all her beauty, used to be con-sidered *girla non grata* at Stark.

Even by me, Amanda, and Tay, Scottie remembered with a guilty cringe. *I mean, we had no way of knowing what kind of cool lurked inside of Bella. All we saw was this geeky girl, fresh out of home school, who passed out groat muffins in the hallway and spent her lunch hours doing yoga in the court-yard.*

"It's *not* great," Bella said. "I told you, I'm not doing the boy thing. Not until college, at least. They're like walking hormones. Like this boy—um, what was his name . . ."

The question of the day, it seems, Scottie thought with a pang.

"Zach. That's it," Bella suddenly remembered.

"Zach . . . Isaacson?" Scottie said with wide eyes.

"That's the one," Bella said, pointing as if she were a crime victim choosing from a line-up of baddies. "You guys, I've never seen anyone *look* at me that way. Like I was a . . . a cheeseburger or something."

"That's how they all look at girls." Amanda shrugged. "You're just noticing this now, B?"

"Zach Isaacson!" Scottie repeated. "Bella, you do realize he is the closest thing to Orlando Bloom we have at this school. And he asked you out?"

"He's not my type," Bella said simply. "For one, he's a *boy*, and I've already told you how I feel about *them*. And then, there's the rest of him. He's all clean-shaven and short-haired and stuff."

"So you said no?!?" Scottie gaped. "Not to get too *She's All That* on you, but you do know that dating Zach Isaacson makes you an instant It girl, don't you?"

Bella blinked at Scottie blankly.

I forgot, Scottie thought morosely. *Even with the new and updated Bella—the one who actually owns a pair of jeans and can be spotted at the occasional party—the issue of popularity just doesn't compute. What's it like to be that way?*

Not that Scottie lived to be popular, or anything.

I mean, suddenly I am kind of popular, Scottie realized. *At least on Tuesday afternoons at Joe, where the Chicks seem to be the trendsetters du jour.*

Even now, as Scottie stole a quick glance around the cafeteria, she could see half a dozen bright pink Stockinette bags propped against cafeteria trays, trailing a Crayola box worth of colors. And at least one freshman weaving her way through a starter scarf was shooting admiring glances at their table, where Bella had begun whizzing her way through a row of stitches while she continued to brood about the boy sitch.

But instead of making Scottie feel anointed? Instead of giving her the glossy sense of belonging that she assumed every It girl carried in the core of her being? She could only squirm in irritation—just the way she had yesterday as she'd squeezed into the overcrowded Stitch 'n Bitch at Joe.

"What I want to know is why Zach even asked," Bella announced, cutting Scottie off before she could get any more broody. "Yes, I've seen him giving me that cheeseburgery look every day in our ethics class—which, if you ask me, is pretty ironic, objectifying me in *ethics* class."

Amanda snorted out a laugh.

"But I've sent Zach *no* signals whatsoever," Bella went on. "So why on earth would he be interested in me?"

"*That's* why," Amanda declared. "Duh, Bella. Not only do all boys objectify us, even the crunchy, PC boys. But they also *love* it when you're not interested. It's like an aphrodisiac to them."

Scottie started. Her popularity conundrum popped out of her head and The Guy popped back in.

"Oh, my God," she blurted, feeling a chill course through her. "Amanda, you're right. I've already ruined it!"

Feeling a sudden, surprising urge to cry, she flopped her head into her hands. Instantly, she felt pathetic.

You don't even know his name, she berated herself, swallowing hard to dissolve the lump in her throat. She glanced up at her friends, who were staring at her, totally bewildered.

Oh yeah, Scottie remembered. *He was also supposed to be a secret.*

Feeling like even *more* of a loser, she reburied her face, dropping it onto her enfolded arms on the sticky cafeteria table.

"What are you talking about, sweetie?" Bella scooched her metal chair closer to her. "Is this about cheeseburger boy? Oh no, *he's* not your latest crush, is he?"

Scottie stiffened and snapped her head up.

"I don't *always* have a crush," she protested.

"You're right," Amanda said supportively. "There were a couple days over the summer when you didn't like anybody."

"Right," Bella remembered. "When you and your parents were at that art auction in New York."

"And that was only because everybody there was old and wrinkly," Scottie groaned, dropping her head again. "I *am* ridiculously boy-crazy. And Amanda's right. *That's* why I can't get anybody interested in me, whereas Bella practically got her ears chewed off at Camp Hippie."

"Believe me," Bella rushed to say, "the ear chewing was awful, Scottie. You don't *want* the ear chewing."

Scottie peeked up at Amanda, whose expression said that she begged to differ.

Scottie was with her.

"I think I wouldn't mind it," she admitted miserably, "if it was perpetrated by The Guy."

"What guy?" Bella and Amanda blurted together.

"I don't know!" Scottie wailed, burying her face once more. "I didn't get his name."

Knowing her buds would be completely confused by now, Scottie told them the entire story, from the first instant she'd laid eyes on The Guy's oh-so-cute face to the moment that Scottie had, in so many words, asked him out.

"In my delusional state," Scottie said, prodding at her untouched chicken with her fork, "I thought I was being Amanda-esque. But no, I broke The Rules like two minutes into the game."

"No, you didn't!" Amanda exclaimed. "You had a totally chill conversation with the guy, then nicely offered to show him the ropes on the way to school. There's no way he could infer from that that you fell madly in like with him at first sight."

"Yeah," Bella said. "You didn't even bother to get his name. That's *very* chilled."

"Chill," Amanda corrected her sweetly. Then she turned back to Scottie.

"Bella's right. If you don't have his name, you can't write your future married name all over your notebooks," Amanda said, taking a giggly bite of salad. "You have to doodle, 'Mrs. Scottie Insert-Last-Name-Here.'"

"Which just doesn't have the same ring to it," Bella grinned. "Especially if you hyphenate. Scottie Shearer-Who-si-whatsis."

"Oh my God. You guys are more far gone than I am," Scottie laughed. For the first time since lunch had begun, she felt a little hungry. She took a bite of chicken, enjoying its peppery bite on her tongue. "So you really don't think I screwed up?"

"You did the opposite," Amanda declared. "You made the perfect inroad to girlfriend-hood."

"Really?!"

"Yup," Amanda said with a satisfied nod. "But it's going to take some time, Scottie. Because what you've embarked upon at *this* point is . . ."

"Don't say it," Scottie blurted. "Not the dreaded F-word."

"I'm saying it," Amanda insisted. "Friendship."

Scottie went through the rest of her day imagining what a "friend" would tell The Guy—*David? Henry? Owen?*—about the Stark School.

She had a feeling—from his scruffy hair and skinny build—that he'd be happy to hear that Stark was totally anti-rah-rah. They had exactly one good athletic team—the basketball team featuring Tay's BF John. The occasional pep rallies for said team were cheerleader-free. Instead, "school spirit" was evoked by the Post-Modern Dance Club, whose moves were sort of Mark Morris meets *Bring It On*.

She could also impress him with Stark's famous life drawing class.

* * *

In the wake of rigorous petitioning by every black-clad arthead in the school a few semesters ago, the art department's life drawing class now featured actual nudity. It also had black-out curtains on every window, not to mention a mile-long waiting list to get in, which was why Scottie was just taking plain old art this semester, charcoaling bowls of apples and pears, taking blurry black and white photos with a shoebox camera, and, best of all, knitting for credit.

During the long walk from her fifth period psychology class in the basement to twentieth-century lit on the top floor, Scottie tried to imagine what her school—almost as familiar to her as her own home— would look like to a newbie. Stark's main building (not including the hideous, linoleum-clad annex built in the 1970s that housed the cafeteria and gym) was more than a hundred years old and had tall wavy-glass windows, stone arches in the main hallways, and a dramatic swath of marble steps out front. It *was* kind of pretty, despite the clattery, peagreen lockers that'd been hauled in a few decades ago. If you forgot that a crush of cars, commerce, and cab drivers lurked just outside on Clark Street, you could almost imagine Stark was a romantic, New England boarding school.

Scottie pushed through the swingy double doors to emerge from the stairwell, imagining what it'd be like to be going home to a dorm room instead of a bread factory, and skidded to a halt.

Kate Calhoun and Edward Chang were wedged together into a narrow space between two banks of those pea-green lockers. Edward's hands were buried in Kate's blond hair and one of her ankles was wrapped around his. They were kissing with such intensity, they didn't even hear Scottie's small gasp. For a long, horrified moment, she stood transfixed as they writhed in each other's arms.

Not that she hadn't witnessed Edward and Kate spit-swapping before. They were Stark's king and queen of PDA and had been for an entire year—during which, it was widely known, they had done more than just make out.

Which was okay, because they were officially In Love.

Scottie had heard that at some high schools, this was uncool—being in love. Even being in *like* was dorky. Nobody went on dates, they just partied en masse. Nobody paired off, they just hooked up.

This struck Scottie as *so* much easier than the Stark School mandate, wherein couples went on real dates—with like, dinner and everything—then either settled quickly into boyfriend-girlfriend status, or parted ways.

The whole playing house thing struck Scottie as particularly weird, given that the rest of the school was completely anti-establishment. Stark was all about war protests, meat protests, and protests of the art department (until it agreed to the life drawing class, anyway). Monday mornings were spent scoping the halls for new tattoos and finding out who'd managed to sneak into which club or NOT-all-ages concert. At Stark, black was the new black, every year, without fail.

Sometimes it was just too exhausting trying to keep up with the hepcats.

It occurred to Scottie that maybe that was the reason people paired off. It was much easier to drop out of the rat race if you had someone to drop out *with*.

The only prob? Scottie sighed as she flattened herself against the wall to sidle around the still-macking Kate and Edward. *Now becoming someone's girlfriend has* become *the rat race. Only outties are single.*

The thought made Scottie skid to a halt on the hallway's overvarnished wood floor. The trauma of the Kate and Edward incident quickly faded as Scottie realized, *I think I know just what to tell The Guy about Stark World!*

With talking points squared away, Scottie only had to come up with an outfit for Friday. And after spending twentieth-century lit mentally flipping through the entire contents of her closet, she decided that she had a problem.

When the final bell rang, she almost ran to meet Amanda at their side-by-side lockers.

"You have to go shopping with me," Scottie ordered her breathlessly. "I have *nothing* to wear tomorrow."

"You have nothing to wear in front of your new *friend?*" Amanda said, arching an eyebrow. "The one who lives in your building? That you could potentially see on a daily basis? Whoa. I guess you're going to have to buy a whole new wardrobe."

"Oh, aren't you cute," Scottie said dryly. "C'mon. I just need one outfit. For the first date."

"If you're just *friends*, it's not a date," Amanda said primly.

"Why do you keep saying it like that?" Scottie glowered. *"Friends.* As if it's a sentence I have to serve."

"Or maybe that's how *you* see it," Amanda said. "Remember we're in the same psych class. I know what projection is. Scottie, you have to embrace the whole friendship thing or it'll never work."

She dumped some books into her locker and extracted a couple others, all the while, managing to clutch her cell phone.

Scottie glanced at Amanda's death grip on the cell. An impulse flickered through her mind—to ask Amanda if everything was okay with Toby.

The next moment, it flitted right back out. Of course everything was okay. Nobody was more okay than Amanda and Toby. They were one of those couples that inspired envy and awe. From almost the moment that they'd met, they'd seemed to speak the same language. It was like they'd had an instant arsenal of private jokes. Of common experiences. Of affection that welled from something deeper than the fact that Amanda was gorgeous and Toby was brilliant and they both had learning disabilities.

They just *got* each other.

The thought of it sent such a wave of yearning through Scottie that she snapped at Amanda.

"I *am* embracing him," she protested. "I mean it. The friendship thing. I'm just talking about a new outfit, that's all. Something fresh. Something that will make me feel confident and stylish and maybe even create the illusion of sproutage in certain upper regions of my body."

"Scottie," Amanda said, slamming her locker door shut and waving as she spotted Tay and John heading toward them from the other end of the hall. John waved back enthusiastically. "You met the guy in your most pilly lavender stretch pants. If he agreed to be seen with you in public after witnessing the lavender pants, then trust me, he's not a clothes-conscious kind of guy."

Scottie was still staring at Amanda, mouth indignantly open, when Tay and John landed at their side. John had barely come to a halt when he reached into his backpack and whipped out his French blue yarn, now woven into a respectable swatch of knit stitches.

"Check it out, Chicks!" he announced.

"John, that's awesome," Amanda cried. "OhmiGod, you're such a cool boyfriend. I don't think Toby would knit if I paid him."

"Isn't that ironic," John said, casting a sidelong glance at Tay. "I think *my* girlfriend would pay me to stop."

Tay turned to John in surprise.

"What?" she said. "I haven't said a word about your knitting."

"Exactly," John teased, stuffing his swatch back into his bag. "I thought you'd think it was cool. I'm just taking an interest in the stuff you like to do."

"Maybe *I* should try to join the basketball team," Tay said. Scottie detected just a hint of bite in her voice.

"Maybe you should," John responded sweetly. "You could kick Sam Tomlinson's butt."

Now it was Tay who was speechless. She looked like she didn't know whether to kiss John or kick him. Frankly, Scottie couldn't deal with the former—she'd had enough PDA for one day. So she jumped in.

"Tay," she said, "Amanda doesn't think I should get a new outfit for tomorrow."

"Walking to school with the new guy?" Tay said. "Bella told me all about it in Euro history. By the way, she can't hang with us this afternoon. She's going to some Hatha workshop with her parents. Anyway, why do you need a new outfit? I thought you guys were just going to be friends."

John snorted.

"Excuse me?!" Scottie sputtered.

"Sorry," John said, rolling his eyes. "I just thought that was kind of funny. You know, *you* wanting to be just-friends with a guy."

"Great," Scottie muttered with a scowl. "So nice to know that not only have my friends completely stereotyped me, their boyfriends have, too!"

As the words left her mouth, Scottie suddenly realized.

"Wait a minute," she said. "You're a boyfriend!"

"Yeah," John drawled, sidling up behind Tay. He wrapped his arms around her and rested his chin—scruffy with blond stubble—on top of her head.

"So tell me this from a boyfriend's perspective," Scottie posed. "If I *was* interested in being more than friends with The Guy—"

"What's the dude's name?" John said.

"Never mind," Tay and Amanda blurted together.

Scottie smiled at them gratefully before she went on.

"Do you think I should dress strategically?" she said. "Say with a new outfit from Abercrombie?"

"Nah, I don't think so," John said decisively. "You wear something that's still got creases and that new store smell and he's gonna be tipped off that you like him. Plus, he'll think, 'Well, if she got this new outfit just to impress me, then I'm not seeing the real her.' Hey! You know what you should do?"

"What?" Scottie and Tay said together.

• Chicks with Sticks

"You should wear your favorite *old* outfit," John declared. "That's the real you. Like these cargo pants of Tay-Tay's."

He hooked a finger into one of Tay's scruffed-up belt loops and pulled her closer.

"These aren't for your benefit, you know," Tay said. But she gave his cheek a sweet kiss before pushing his face gently away.

"Exactly why I like 'em," John said. "You've got nothing to prove."

"But *I* do!" Scottie lamented. "That's why I need a new outfit."

Amanda shook her head as she turned to lead their little group down the hall.

"Trust John. He's a boy. He's one of *them*," she said. Scottie spotted her giving her cell phone another glance before she slipped it into her purse. Then she pointed at John's backpack, from which peeked an errant squiggle of blue yarn, and added, "Even if he's also one of us."

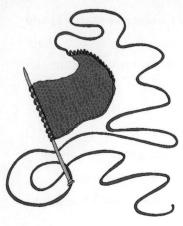

6 *(Work in seed stitch)

On Thursday night, Scottie could barely sleep.

Which was no surprise. The littlest things had always turned her into an insomniac—too-spicy Thai food; a particularly creepy ep of *Lost*; wondering if there'd *really* been no chemistry homework or if she'd just zoned out at the end of class . . .

When a biggie like the Friday Morning Walk reared its head, tossing, turning, and general neurosis were a given. Scottie was excited to see The Guy, but it was excitement swirled together with dread, fear, and loathing.

By the time her eyes snapped open at 4:45 A.M., the dread had pretty much taken over. She spent a full five minutes lying in the same fetal position in which she'd (sort of) slept. She listened to CC's sleepy purrs next to her, stared at the streetlight glowing murkily through her dirt-smudged windows, and, for a moment, literally wished that she could somehow do a *Freaky Friday*-like mind-body switch with Bella. She wanted to know what it felt like to live in Bella's head, to just feel no need for a boyfriend. To be absolved of the yearning. To know that beautiful, attentive, mature boyfriends dwelled somewhere in the future, and thus be perfectly content with her indie present.

Maybe it's all that yoga that makes her so patient, Scottie thought.

Instinctively, she reached for her own source of zen—the WIP on her nightstand. This wasn't Buttered Toast, with its skinny #3 needles and still-imperfect hem. No, this was a project made for a state of half-sleep—a stripey, roll-brimmed hat doing a lazy lap around a circular needle. Appropriately enough, Scottie was making it for Bella, whose birthday was coming up.

Scottie knitted a few stitches into the hat without even turning over in bed. She closed her eyes and felt her fingers work the push, the pull, the swish from needle to needle. She waited for the calm to seep from her nervous fingers up to her tight shoulders and finally, to her burning eyes.

But, only one row in, Scottie started to feel even more restless. Her fingers were twitchy on the yarn, instead of fluid. Her mind buzzed unpleasantly. She realized that her lips were pressed into a taut line destined to make her jaw ache if she didn't ease up. She slammed the WIP to the mattress, bouncing it so hard that CC woke up and squawked in protest.

Scottie skimmed her fingers briefly over CC's head to apologize, then swung herself out of bed. She decided if she couldn't fight the angst, she might as well join it in the blogosphere. She plopped herself into her desk chair, opened her laptop, and began surfing. She hit a few of her usuals: the American in Paris who always bragged about the antique knitting needles and precious Euro-yarn she found in romantic flea markets; the Indiana spinning guru with the grotesquely fat cat (pictured daily); the comic artist who catalogued her life in daily stick drawings.

Scottie felt her eyes drooping as she skimmed through each blog.

Well, what do you know, she thought grumpily. *Everyone's downright sunny this morning.*

Ooh La La had spent the previous afternoon finishing a delicate bolero jacket in a chic café. The spin guru had had a birthday party and photographed her cat in a goofy party hat. The comic artist drew an ice cream outing and called it *Simple Pleasures.*

So unsatisfying, Scottie complained in her sleepy mind. *C'mon, you guys. Gimme some agonizing. Some poetically sad memories. Is it too much to ask for just one broken heart?*

As she heard her inner whine, though, Scottie's finger paused on her computer's track pad. She cringed as she realized what she was *really* looking for—she wanted to comfort herself by reading about people who were worse off than her.

For an instant, she felt as petty as a paparazzo. But a moment later, she defended herself to the still night air of her bedroom.

Okay, I may be base, but I'm not the only one, she thought, her finger inching down to the mouse button. *Look at all those people who watch movies of the week and obsess over Brangelina? And besides, nobody knows what I'm reading. . . .*

Scottie began clicking her way from link to link, searching for some dark inside the light of her computer.

She'd found a few juicy hits—a man musing about mortality; a review of J. Lo's latest movie—when she spotted something in a queue of links that made her fuzzy brain perk up a little.

In a Sknit

Most knit blogs had perky titles, like *Purlina* or *KnitFaery*. This one looked just peevish enough to suit Scottie's mood.

She clicked.

Then her eyes went wider.

The blogger, who called herself T. C. Boil, lived in Chicago! Her logo was Chicago Picasso, the famous ribby sculpture in Daley Plaza, the one that Scottie had always thought looked like a dragon with pigtails.

T. C. Boil had Photoshopped the image, adding arms that were busy knitting a sweater. The sweater was hemmed with triangular shards, much like Scottie's tank top-in-progress.

I like the way this girl thinks, Scottie thought, scrolling down.

She clicked on the "100 things about me" list and flitted from 2) My parents got divorced when I was ten to 12) I secretly hate the sound of flip-flops to 23) I want to be a doctor when I grow up, but not a pediatrician like all the other girls.

Scottie also plucked out of the list that the blogger was fifteen years old, went to a private school on the north side of Chicago, was tattooed, and was a Cancer.

It was around this time that Scottie started to feel a prickle of uneasiness in her chest; a sick sense of recognition.

No way, she told herself as suspicion began to rise. *Hundreds of girls in this city have tattoos and private school creds.*

Still, she started reading the list more closely.

T.C. had a boyfriend and dark hair. She was sibling free but wished she wasn't. Her fantasy sibling was a brother, and younger, because she didn't want anybody bossing her around. She loved Addi Turbo needles and hated Crystal Palace ones. She loved hot dogs, olive and artichoke pizza, and cheese curls—the wrinkly, hard, compressed kind, not the air-puffed worms that make a film on the roof of your mouth.

Scottie's eyes were wide and her breathing was shallow now. She kept on reading the 100 things, but at this point, it was only for confirmation.

I commute between two neighborhoods (see #2), one self-consciously crunchy, the other self-consciously edgy.

Which pretty much nails down Andersonville and the Ukrainian Village, Scottie thought. *The neighborhoods where Tay's parents live.*

She skipped to the last screen-load.

76) Until recently, my best friend was a boy.

77) Now, he's not only *not* my best friend, we don't even speak.

78) My current best friends are girls. Three of them.

79) Nobody is more surprised by this than me.

80) I would do anything for them, even though . . .

81) They can really work my nerves sometimes.

82) My guidance counselor says I'm discovering "the beauty of vulnerability."

(Knit two together)

83) My guidance counselor kind of looks like a walrus.

84) But not in a bad way.

85) Beneath his crusty exoskeleton, I think he's all doughy and fluffy like a baby seal.

86) Also not in a bad way.

87) My boyfriend and I have been half-naked together.

88) The top half.

89) That's as naked as things are gonna get for a while.

90) I love him.

91) Which scares the pants off me.

92) Well, not literally. See #88.

93) He doesn't know about this blog, nor do my friends.

94) My guidance counselor *definitely* doesn't know about it.

95) Living in a city, I don't see a conflict between being intensely private . . . in public.

96) Hence the blog.

97) I think.

98) To tell the truth, it's a puzzle, even to me.

99) Maybe when I figure out *why* I blog, I'll tell people *about* the blog.

100) Either that, or I'll no longer have the need to blog and, *poof,* I'll be gone.

Scottie threw herself so forcefully back in her chair that it rolled several feet across the slick cement floor. While she shuffled herself back to her desk with her bare heels, she shook her head, stunned.

T.C. Boil is definitely Tay, Scottie thought. *Definitely, definitely. Unbelievably, but definitely.*

In her still hazy, dawn-just-breaking state, Scottie knew only one other thing.

Tay doesn't want me to read this blog. Or Amanda or Bella or John.

She clicked away from the "100 things" list, back to the blog's main page. A third of the screen was filled with the goofy, knitty Picasso.

The rest were words. Scottie's eyes flitted to the date at the top of the post.

It was yesterday's.

Then her eyes crept to the first sentence.

Still feeling weird about BF's foray into knitting.

Scottie gulped and swooped her cursor up to the red dot in the corner of the blog's window, knowing she really, really should zap *In a Sknit* back into the ether where she'd found it. She knew it was wrong to read Tay's innermost thoughts—even if she *had* posted them on the Internet.

Unless, Scottie's finger hesitated over the mouse button, *she* wanted *us to stumble upon it. Maybe this is Tay's way of saying things to the people in her life, without having to actually* say *them. It's the perfect solution for her, actually.*

Click-not.

Scottie's eyes crept, almost against her will, back down to Tay's blog entry.

Still feeling weird about BF's foray into knitting. On one level, it's super sweet. Like the time that we went to the screening of the Best. Movie. Ever. (*Napoleon Dynamite,*** of course.) And I saved the seats while he went for snacks. He came back with Good & Plenty and Coke, even though he prefers Sprite and hates Good & Plenty, much like everyone else on the planet except for S., whose taste buds are almost as sick-warped as mine—**

Scottie felt a shivery thrill. S! That was her!

So it was totally generous, right? But it was also selfless to the point of alarm. Self-less.

Who is **he? What kind of candy does** he **like?!**

Of course, I know what kind of candy he likes: anything with peanut butter. Or peanuts. Or even crunchy, peanut-flavored mystery substance. If he had one of those lethal peanut allergies, the boy would be dead right now.

So my question is—why not get Goobers? Or, okay, to be perfectly reasonable, Goobers and **Good & Plenty?**

(Knit two together)

Why is he all about me, me, me lately? It's sorta like dating a mirror. And if you knew me, you'd know that I look in the mirror as little as possible.

Scottie exhaled loudly and slumped back in her chair again.

The Chicks with Sticks had sleepovers at least twice a month. She'd seen Tay in her underwear and watched her spit toothpaste foam into the sink. She could spot Tay's lanky, lopey gait from a great distance. She'd even seen Tay cry once, a rage-filled, quick, hot burst of tears after a fight with her dad.

But Scottie had never seen Tay quite as rawly as she just had, in, of all things, her blog.

Scottie felt exhilarated and awful all at once. She was desperate to read more *In a Sknit* posts, and just as determined not to.

The sudden blare of her alarm clock made the decision for her. It was 6:30. Feeling breathless, Scottie jumped out of her chair and headed for her bedroom door. She wheeled around just before she reached it and ran back to her computer to quit out of *In a Sknit*. Then she bonked her alarm clock to turn it off, and ran to the bathroom.

It wasn't until she was rinsing shampoo out of her hair in the shower, and thus forced to stand still, that Scottie paused to let all that she'd read settle into her mind.

She remembered how Tay had scowled as John had cheerfully struggled with his blue yarn. She pictured John's finger hooked—Desperately? Possessively?—through Tay's belt loop.

But she also remembered Tay giving John that tender kiss in the Stark hallway. She envisioned Tay's face whenever John was around: her forehead unfurrowed and the defensive thrust of her hips melted away. The corners of her mouth softened, if not into a lovesick grin, then into an easy half-smile.

She looked like she was utterly at peace.

It was a vibe that Scottie felt *certain* that she herself didn't exude.

But she wanted to.

And maybe, just maybe, if she stopped scripting conversations, micromanaging her wardrobe, and worrying about wedgies and nose grease, it was something The Guy could help her attain.

Scottie began by breezing into the foyer wearing her favorite skinny, just-too-long jeans, a pink-and-brown baby T, and a retro satchel of brown, tooled leather that she'd scavenged from a vintage shop in Bucktown. She wasn't eagerly early or coyly late, but just on time.

The Guy was already there, waiting for her.

And yeah, Scottie's stomach fluttered when she first saw him. (His shaggy hair, after all, was still damp and just beginning to wave up over his thick eyebrows. And even from several feet away, his shampoo smelled delicious.) But mostly? Scottie's nervousness suddenly melted away! Maybe it was the pep talk she'd given herself in the shower. Or it was just some unexplainable gift from the universe. But a moment after landing in the foyer, she was all excitement, no dread. She grinned at The Guy.

"You ready?" she said.

His return grin was a little wobbly, but sweet.

"Almost," he said. "But first, you've got to tell me your name. I've been wondering . . ."

"Me, too!" Scottie laughed. "Maybe we should guess."

"I'll give you a hint," The Guy said. "It's not Rumpelstiltsken."

While Scottie laughed again, The Guy held out his hand.

"I'm Beck Snyder," he announced. "Nice to meet you."

"Nice to meet *you*," Scottie said. She felt another little flutter at the brief brush of Beck's warm palm against hers. Mentally, she tested the waters of his name—*Beck . . . Beck, Beck beckoning*—and found it perfect.

I don't even care if it's the same name as some rock star, she declared inwardly.

"So, uh . . ." Beck broke into her thoughts with a crooked smile. ". . . do you *really* want me to guess yours or are you gonna tell me?"

(Knit two together)

"Oh yeah!" Scottie blurted. "It's Scottie. Shearer."

"Scottie," Beck said. "That's different."

"It's my mom's maiden name," Scottie explained. "Well, sort of. Her name was Scott. When I arrived, they girlified it."

As Beck nodded, Scottie thought she detected a glint in his eye.

"No Scottie dog jokes," she warned.

Beck started.

"You were thinking of one, weren't you!" Scottie accused with a howl of laughter.

Beck's cheeks flushed and he smiled sheepishly. "We better get going," he said quickly. They pushed out of the bread factory doors and headed toward the L stop.

"I have this thing about being late," Beck explained as his pace picked up. "The thing being that I *can't* be. I'm totally compulsive that way. Which is weird, because in other areas of my life? We're talking truly slovenly behavior. When I was packing up my room in New York, I found an orange in an old school bag in my closet that had literally turned black and hard and wrinkly. Like a lump of coal."

"Gross!" Scottie sputtered.

"Um, yeah, it was," Beck breathed, "which, um, sort of makes me wonder why I brought it up."

Scottie glanced over at him as he trod along beside her. He was gazing intently at the sidewalk and his face was still a bit pink.

Oh my God, she realized. *He's doing it. He's doing the "Jesus loves you" ramble. We're totally even!*

Feeling even more buoyant, Scottie made an admission of her own.

"I have the same thing," she said. "About being late, I mean. I practically hyperventilate every time I'm late to school. It's just such an asinine reason to get detention, isn't it?"

"Exactly," Beck said. "But what's annoying is, I'm the same way if I'm like, meeting friends at a restaurant. I'm always the first one there."

"Because nobody else has this weird on-time fetish of ours," Scottie said, shaking her head with mock-sadness. She made a quick right onto Irving Park—forgetting that Beck didn't know where they were going—and crashed right into him.

"Oops, sorry," she breathed. The impact had been minimal, but it had taken her breath away anyway. Instantly, she decided that if she was going to achieve an at-peace-and-comfortable-around-a-guy vibe, she was going to have to avoid any physical contact with Beck.

Not wanting him to see her swooning, Scottie busied herself with asking Beck if he'd gotten an L card yet.

"Yup," he said, pulling his fare card out of his back pocket. "I've been using it to wander around the city, you know, in lieu of unpacking."

"I hear ya," Scottie laughed. She turned into the tiny box of a building that was the L station and they each *chunked* their cards into the turnstile.

As they began plodding up the stairs to the southbound track, Scottie asked, "Are you sad? You know, about moving here?"

Beck ducked his head.

"Yes and no," he said carefully. "It was, uh, pretty messed up, the circumstances that made my mom pick up and move."

"Really?"

Beck waited until they reached the platform to continue. He led Scottie through the early morning crowd until they found a pocket of airspace at the end of the platform. Then he leaned against the scuffed post of an overhead light and sighed.

"Really," he said finally. "Messed up *and* totally cliché. My mom left my dad."

"Oh . . . wow," Scottie whispered.

"Yeah, wow," Beck said, gazing bitterly at the sky. "The real wow is she didn't really have a good reason. I mean, nobody was cheating. Nobody was fighting. Things seemed to be pretty okay at my place, and believe me, I had a lot of dysfunctional families to compare with mine. A ton of my friends have divorced or otherwise screwed-up parents."

"So what was her reason?" Scottie said. Beck looked so miserable, she felt her own face crumpling into sympathetic pain.

"She jokes that she's having a midlife crisis," Beck shrugged. "As if it's funny! That she would leave her job, leave my dad, drag *me* away from my life, and move here. She said she was gonna wait until I left for college—I'm the youngest kid in the family—but she just couldn't. She had to follow her dream *now*."

"What dream?" Scottie croaked.

"She's a fashion designer," Beck said with a slightly curled lip. "She's good, too. Even if I'm mad at her, I have to admit it. She was designing for this big company. She was totally high up in the food chain—had her own line and everything. But suddenly, she decided that wasn't enough. She wanted to start her own house, with her name on it. And she wanted to do it somewhere where she could make a fresh start. Next thing I know, here we are. She's working out of our loft, trying to launch Hannah B. designs. The B. is for me."

Beck barked out a dry laugh and shook his head.

"I'm sorry," Scottie started to say, but suddenly, the train screeched to a halt in front of them, drowning her out. She'd been so wrapped up in Beck's story, she hadn't even been aware of the train rumbling into the station! As they joined the small crush of people clustered around the doors of the first car, Scottie gazed at the side of Beck's face. Half a dozen platitudes churned through her mind, but none of them felt nearly meaningful enough to actually say.

In the moment before the train doors opened, Beck turned and caught her looking. Their eyes locked on each other's for a moment and Scottie went breathless again.

Whooosh.

The doors opened. The clump of commuters squirmed with impatience as they waited for a few passengers to get off the train. The moment the doors were clear, they surged forward, carrying Scottie and Beck with them.

Miraculously, Scottie spotted two open seats at the far end of the train. Without thinking, she grabbed Beck's forearm and dragged him toward the seats. They flung themselves into them.

Beck turned to Scottie.

"Thank you," he said.

"Oh, it was nothing," Scottie said. "I'm glad we got a seat though. It's a good fifteen minutes before we get to Stark."

"No, I meant—"

Beck hesitated and swallowed. Scottie stared at his Adam's apple as it bobbled up and down.

"I meant, how you were looking at me a minute ago," Beck said. "I meant, thank you for being sorry."

Scottie almost choked.

How did he—It's like he read my—

Scottie couldn't finish even her silent sentences, she was so taken aback.

"You're welcome," she said quietly.

"The thing is," Beck said, turning to peer out the window as the train lurched into forward motion, "I wasn't *completely* upset about leaving New York. I started a new school three years ago, when I hit high school. I was in a public school up until then, but my parents decided I needed a blazer with a crest on it if I was gonna get into a decent college."

"Ew," Scottie said. Beck was wearing some very cool, not too baggy workman's pants and a long-sleeved T with sporty stripes running down the sleeves. He didn't look like he had a preppy bone in his body.

"Yeah," Beck groaned. "I was terrified that everyone was gonna be named George and Muffy and talk about nothing but sailing and summer houses and stuff. But actually, a lot of the people were cool. I was kind of . . ."

Beck shook his head and winced.

". . . I can't believe I'm saying this, but I was kinda popular," he said. "It was dumb luck, really. My locker was next to the 'right guy's' locker, and he was dating the 'right girl,' and next thing you know, I'm being invited to all the 'right parties.'"

"That doesn't sound so bad, actually," Scottie said. "I mean, everybody knows they've got the best chips and dip at the 'right parties.'"

"Heh." Beck looked at her and rolled his eyes. "Try the best vodka. It was quite the scene."

Scottie bit her lip.

Is "the scene" good or bad? she wondered.

"At first it was fun, I've gotta admit," Beck said, perhaps reading Scottie's expression. His gaze drifted back out the window. "But I sort of felt like I was on trial. I passed the first test, apparently. I was cool enough to join the clique. But that wasn't enough. After I was in, I had to keep proving I was worthy. I had to somehow just *know* that the Nellie McKay everybody was grooving to last month was suddenly over, and now it was time to move on to Arcade Fire. I had to know which places were cool and which were out. And the irony was, I was never really angling for popularity to begin with. I'm more of a few-good-friends kind of guy. My thinking has always been that everybody being into a certain something—a book or a band or whatever—makes it *less* special, not more."

"I know just what you mean!" Scottie blurted.

Beck looked at her with a hint if skepticism. Scottie knew she must sound like quite the yes-girl. So, she decided to show him what she meant.

"With me," she said, flapping open her satchel, "the book or the band is . . . this."

She pulled out Buttered Toast, carefully gripping the needle points so none of the slippery cotton would pop off.

"You knit?" Beck said. "I hear knitting is very hot these days."

"Exactly!" Scottie said. "But I've got to say, when I started knitting

•• Chicks with Sticks

a year ago? It wasn't. It was a little weird and sorta dowdy. And it was . . .
it was . . ."

"It was all yours," Beck said quietly.

Scottie didn't want to say it yet again, so she answered in her mind:
Exactly. She looked at him shyly. "Well, it belonged to me and my three
best friends," she said. "Now our Stitch 'n Bitch is overrun. It's good, I
guess. But it's also making me feel itchy."

Scottie fingered the newly knitted jags at the hem of Buttered Toast.

"I guess that's why nothing I knit feels quite right lately," she said.

"Maybe it's time to move on to something else?" Beck suggested.

Scottie looked up sharply.

No! she wanted to shout.

But just on its tail, was a, *Maybe sorta.*

She shrugged, trying to downplay the sudden confusion roiling in
her mind. Luckily, the L saved her.

"Our stop," Scottie said, nodding at the blocky ARMITAGE sign just
rolling into view. "The school's just about a five minute walk away—
Oh no!"

"What?!" Beck said.

"This whole ride was supposed to be me telling you about Stark,"
Scottie said. "And I didn't tell you *anything*."

"We've still got five minutes," Beck said with a smiley shrug. "Tell
you what, you can give me the Cliffs Notes version on the walk to
school. But on Monday's ride I expect you to work it, Shearer."

Scottie giggled—so much that it took her a second to realize that
the train had come to a complete stop. And the doors had opened! They
had only about three seconds to make a leap for the platform.

"Ack! Come on!" She squealed. Clutching her still-flapping satchel
under one arm and her Work in Progress in the other, she popped out of
her seat. Beck was just ahead of her, still smelling wonderfully sham-
pooey. Scottie watched his shoulder blades bobble beneath his T-shirt
and was suddenly aware of how tall he was. And how cutely skinny. And—

(Knit two together)

Shoomp.

"Whoa!" Scottie squeaked. The L doors had closed the second she'd cleared them, almost nicking her arm.

As the train began to chug away, Scottie smiled at Beck and swiped the back of her hand over her forehead in cartoony relief.

"Whew!" she yelled over the clatter of the train.

That's when she felt the tug.

Scottie looked down. She saw Buttered Toast, edging away from her, clamped between the L doors! The circular needle was wedged crossways on the other side of the doors, locked in place as firmly as a latch.

It took a long second for Scottie to realize what was happening. The train was *stealing* her WIP!

"No!" she cried in confusion. "No way!"

She glanced quickly at Beck. He was all action.

"Just pull it!" he ordered her. "Maybe you can yank it out."

From Scottie's vantage point, this looked hopeless. But she had to try. She yanked at the little tail at the bottom corner of the tank—the remnant of the project's very first stitch.

Pop-pop-pop-pop.

Buttered Toast began to unravel! Of course, Scottie couldn't hear the little loops disengaging from their anchors. She could only see them. It was the fastest frogging in history! As the train carried Buttered Toast away from her, Scottie clutched desperately at the string, watching it lengthen and lengthen until it became a ridiculously long tether.

She was dimly aware of passengers' faces skimming by as the rest of the train pulled out of the stop. At first, they were confused. Then they were *amused*. Some of them even pointed.

"Scottie, you have to drop the yarn!" Beck cried.

Scottie's grip only tightened as she looked over at him. She could tell he was trying hard not to laugh. She looked back at the fluttery, butter-colored yarn, getting longer by the millisecond as the train picked up speed. It dawned on her that she actually *didn't* have the strength to yank a hurtling L-train to a halt with a bit of yarn.

And *she* laughed.

No, she howled.

"Good-bye, sweet WIP!" she screamed before she threw her end of the yarn into the air. As the last car on the train passed by, leaving in its wake that familiar pocket of soft, echoey thunder, Scottie pointed at her yarn, trailing along beside it.

"I think it's a good tenth of a mile long!" she laughed.

"You're right," Beck said, shaking his head and laughing along with her. "Your version of knitting? It *is* weird."

"Shut up," Scottie giggled, lightly pounding him on the arm and jutting out her lower lip. "Buttered Toast has been hijacked. I'm in mourning."

"And *I'm* thinking," Beck said, still smiling that little smile as he headed for the streetbound stairs, "that this is the strangest first day of school I've ever had."

7 ✦ (Agitate to felt)

"I think it's a sign," Bella said that night, looking troubled. She was sitting on the floor at the foot of Amanda's bed, a tub of squishy red licorice chunks by her knee. She leaned her head back against the mattress, as if the weightiness of her thoughts had suddenly made it too heavy to hold upright.

"Sign of what?" Scottie sputtered from her spot on the plush carpeting a few feet away. "A scourge of yarn-eating trains sweeping the city?"

"That'd make a good movie," Tay remarked without looking up. She was sprawled in the shabby chic easy chair in the corner of Amanda's bedroom, squinting at the pinkie of the glove she was knitting. She was trying to work the tiny tube with too-slick double-pointed needles. The sticks kept slipping out of their loops and disappearing beneath the chair's cushion.

Scottie was not knitting. She was lying on her stomach, crunching tortilla chips. Every few weeks, the Chicks with Sticks staged what had come to be called the Sacred Sleepovers. Tonight's S.S.O., at Amanda's condo thirty-four stories above Michigan Avenue, was just beginning.

Like any sacred thing, the S.S.O.'s had unassailable rituals. They weren't written down or anything, but every Chick knew the rules:

1) The hosting of sleepovers happened in alphabetical order. The first ever S.S.O. happened at Amanda's house, thus Bella's came next, then Scottie's, then Tay's.

2) Before the S.S.O. everyone gathered at a previously agreed upon food establishment for the choosing of snacks. Each Chick chose (at least) one snack. In deference to Bella, half of the snacks had to be vegetarian.

3) Upon arrival at the designated Chick's home, everyone immediately changed into pajamas.

4) At some point in the evening, a DVD would be played. The hosting Chick got to choose the movie.

5) Chicks with boyfriends were allowed to call them to say good night, but no other contact with the boyfriends was allowed.

6) If dinner was required in addition to copious snacks, it was takeout. But breakfast was homemade by the Chicks.

7) Before heading home in the morning, the Chicks had to *pen* into their calendars the date of the next sleepover.

Scottie had shown up at Amanda's place super-excited. An S.S.O., she'd thought, was the perfect setting for some deep and affirmational analysis of Scottie's morning with The-Guy-Now-Known-as-Beck.

Now about that affirmational part, Scottie grumbled to herself as she gazed at Bella's furrowed forehead.

Out loud, she admitted, "Yes, it's bizarre that the train stole my WIP but I don't think it's a sign. Or if it is, it's a sign of something *good.* That tank top was plaguing me."

"Tscha," Amanda volunteered. She'd just slipped through the bedroom door, carrying a tray of frosty, fruity drinks, complete with pineapple garnishes on toothpicks. She plunked the tray onto her desk and grabbed one of the smoothies, taking a noisy slurp. "You frogged Buttered Toast so much, she was shaggy, the poor thing."

"I don't know," Bella said. "If it was a dream, your WIP-snatching would be fraught with symbolism. It'd be your subconscious telling you, 'Good-bye, knitting, hello, boyfriend.'"

Bella chased the word with a quick bite of licorice, as if she had to cancel out a bad taste.

Scottie scowled and looked at Amanda.

"Okay, I *know* what you're thinking," she glowered.

She had to have been thinking the same thing that *Scottie* was thinking. She was remembering their very first psych class only a few weeks ago. Their teacher, Dr. Fishman, had stood in front of the class, creakily rocking his short, paunchy self from his toes to his heels and back to his toes. He'd clasped his chubby fingers on top of his round, protruding belly and regarded the twenty or so kids before him with a single raised eyebrow.

In any other class? This could easily have been written off as a classic scare tactic. The *mess-with-me-and-I-will-make-your-report-card-beg-for-mercy* evil gaze.

But in this class—intro to psychology—Dr. Fishman's fish-eye made everyone squirm.

Everyone except Tom Castellucci, who always wedged his barrel-shaped body into the farthest-back desk possible, and could be counted on to bark out something obnoxious at least once per class.

"Are you reading our minds, right now?" Tom guffawed, patting his mop of black hair with a meaty hand. "Listen, can you tell us what Amanda Scott's thinking about? She's thinking about me, isn't she? The girl is hot for me."

Amanda twisted in her seat, shot off a "You're vomitrocious," and turned back to the front of the room before Scottie even had a chance to register Tom's obnoxism.

She's had plenty of practice after all, Scottie thought. She knew that it was stupid to feel envious of being a sex object to gross Tom Castellucci, but she was envying it nevertheless.

Dr. Fishman stopped rocking and smiled smugly.

•• Chicks with Sticks

"It happens every year," he said. "I receive students who have reached the age of sixteen. Ten years of very expensive education under their belts. Yet they are ignorant as to the definition of the word *psychologist*. I can see that—"

Dr. Fishman glanced at his roll sheet.

"—Mr. Castellucci has confused *psychologist*—that is, a professional trained to study and analyze behavior—with a *psychic*, or charlatan mind reader."

The students' squirming had taken on a giggly tenor. Amanda looked especially pleased as she peeked back at Tom, sniffing in disgust.

"I will do my best to disavow you of such misinformation over the course of the semester," Dr. Fishman continued, the smug smile holding steady. "Mr. Castellucci makes it clear that we have far to go, students. Expect the maximum amount of homework."

The giggles turned to grumbles, and a few whispered threats to kick Tom's butt the moment the bell rang.

"The homework begins tonight as you sleep," Dr. Fishman said loudly, cutting off the pre-riot murmurs more effectively than Scottie would have predicted, given his nebbishy presence. "It will continue for the rest of the semester."

Wait a minute, Scottie thought. *As we sleep?*

"Much of what we shall study this session," Dr. Fishman declared, "exists in the crevices of the cerebral cortex. Lurking there are neuroses and psychoses caused, in some cases, by chemical imbalances in the brain, and in others, by traumas of the past. Life's events and their impact are often tucked away into the subconscious.

"So how can we dig into our own psyches?" Dr. Fishman went on, tapping, not his temple the way most people would, but the back of his skull, where his thinning hair met his neck. "One avenue wends through our dreams. Travel that path and you might be amazed at the insights you'll find, that is, if you bother to write them down before they evaporate like so much morning breath."

(Knit two together)

"Ew," Amanda whispered, grimacing at Scottie in the desk next to hers.

"You will each purchase a notebook," Dr. Fishman pronounced, padding around his desk to pick up a piece of chalk. "You will keep this notebook next to your bed or beneath your pillow or nested atop the undoubtedly mountainous pile of dirty laundry at the foot of your mattress. I don't care. The point is that every morning, before you rise, you are to record every detail you can remember from your dreams.

"Every other Friday," Dr. Fishman said, "you will turn this notebook in to your teacher, complete with a one-page analysis of a dream of your choice."

Oh my God! Scottie thought in a sudden panic. *Psych is going to be all about revealing our sordid secrets. I'm so switching to computer programming.*

"Your dreams, of course," Dr. Fishman added, "will be kept strictly confidential. Nor will they be read with much interest on my part. It is the agility of your analyses that I will be grading."

Okay, never mind, Scottie sighed. *I think.*

"Now, because remembering one's dreams does not come easily to everyone, I will write down some helpful hints. I expect each of you to copy these tips down and study them before retiring this evening."

As Fish-Eye turned to the board to scribble a list of things like *Go over your dream in your mind before opening your eyes* and *Get eight hours of sleep to promote R.E.M.* Scottie raised her eyebrows at Amanda.

"This'll be different," she whispered.

Amanda replied with a little glint in her eyes. "Who knows what creepy things we'll find—"

She tapped the back of her head with exaggerated goofiness.

"—back there."

"The question is," Scottie had whispered back, "do I want to know?"

Now, at the S.S.O., with Amanda gazing at her suspiciously over the top of her smoothie glass, Scottie protested.

"Amanda, this isn't something we can analyze like a dream in psych class," she said. "It *wasn't* a dream. It was just a random WIP-snatching. Chance. Totally insignificant.

"Everything's significant, Scottie," Bella said seriously.

"The only significant thing is the impact it made on my wallet," Scottie said. "I put two balls of Takhi cotton and my favorite circular needle into that thing. Now if you want to analyze something, can we get back to that thing Beck said to me? 'On Monday's ride I expect you to work it, Shearer.' So on one hand, he *seemed* to be eager to see me again. But then he called me 'Shearer,' which is kind of a buddy-buddy thing to call me, right? Not an okay-we're-starting-off-as-friends-but-underneath-I-find-you-really-attractive thing."

"Inconclusive," Amanda said, taking another loud sip.

"But Buttered Toast isn't!" Bella insisted. She unslouched from her perch against the bed and knelt in front of Scottie, looking at her intently. "When have you ever been that uninspired by a Work in Progress, Scottie?"

Scottie shrugged and skimmed quickly though a mental list of her Works Finished. Her very first project—the rough-around-the-edges scarf gartered out of three shades of blue—still gave her warm fuzzies. And then there was Squash Blossom, a beautiful orange sweater that she'd wear every day if she could. She adored her copper poncho and fuzzy green monster slippers (the left was Oscar the Grouch; the right, Mike Wazowski), the flowery eye pillow she'd made her mom, her chunky mittens with matching hat and scarf . . . she loved them all.

"I guess this is the first time I've been this restless," Scottie admitted. "But Bella, that doesn't mean I'm gonna chuck knitting. I couldn't even if I *did* want to."

"See?" Bella wailed. "You're making it sound like you've been given a life sentence or something. Where's the joy, Scottie? *Where is the joy?*"

She waved her skinny arms in the air like a bohemian televangelist,

(Knit two together)

which only made Scottie collapse onto the carpet, screaming with laughter.

"Looks like joy to me," Tay said dryly. She grabbed one of the smoothies off Amanda's tray and took a slurp.

"Not to be ungrateful, but this tastes suspiciously healthy," Tay said to Amanda. "Have you forgotten the cardinal law of the S.S.O? All food must be artificially flavored, colored, or hydrogenated within an inch of its life. Where's the junk in pineapple smoothies?"

"It's spiked with coconut sorbet," Amanda announced with a devilish smile. "Believe me, there's definitely some high fructose corn syrup going on in there. You can thank my mom later."

All three of the girls raised their eyebrows at her.

"Okay, my mom asked Theresa to whip them up for us," Amanda admitted with an eye roll. Theresa was the Scotts' housekeeper/nanny. The nanny part was for Amanda's little brother, Trey. "But hello, we weren't talking about me—"

"And your bourgeois ways," Tay teased with another appreciative slurp of smoothie.

Amanda pretended to flick something out of her nose at Tay.

"Aigh!" Tay screamed, jumping out of her chair.

"I'm sorry," Amanda said calmly. "I thought you said 'booger ways.'"

"Wah-ha-ha!" Now it was Tay who flopped onto the floor. Scottie didn't think she'd ever seen her laugh so hard.

"See!" Bella said, frowning at Scottie as their friends howled. "Booger jokes! They're clearly under the influence of gross boys. The same thing'll happen to you if you get a boyfriend, Scottie. Be forewarned."

"Yeah," Scottie giggled. "I didn't know disgusto-humor was part of the girlfriend job description. I'm gonna have to rethink my goals."

"And return to the knit!" Bella cried. She scurried on her knees over to Amanda's desk. With one hand, she snatched herself a smoothie. With the other, she grabbed Amanda's sleek, titanium laptop. While

Amanda and Tay giggled away between sips of smoothie, Bella started surfing.

"Let's find you a cool new pattern," she said to Scottie. "That'll get you reinvigorated."

Scottie sidled up next to her as Bella hopped from one knitting site to the next, looking for inspiration. She'd just finished a quick scan of Stockinette's candy-colored site and was getting ready to move on, when Scottie spotted a button lurking in the site's busy right-hand column.

"What's that?" she said.

Bella clicked.

A new site materialized with a banner of rainbow-colored yarn balls, shimmering like stars. A headline read:

YarnCon Chicago! October 14th–15th

Workshops. Lectures. Purl-a-thons. Book signings.

And miles of Yarn!

Come share the joy of knitting with

knitters from all over the Midwest. Register Now!

"*There's* the joy!" Bella exclaimed. She was so excited, she knocked over her licorice tub, spilling the cherry-red chunks over the carpet like squishy rubies.

"Scottie, we've *got* to go to this. Think of all the new stuff you'll learn. All the cool people you'll meet. You'll totally find a new knitting path, I know it."

"It does look pretty amazing," Scottie breathed. Leaning over Bella's lap, she began clicking around on the site herself. "Risdie's one of the sponsors. Sweet!"

"We'll all go, right?" Bella said, looking over at Amanda and Tay who'd finally chortled their last.

"Sure," Amanda nodded, wiping a bit of smeared mascara from

(Knit two together)

beneath her eye. "I bet there'll be some cool freeformers there. I'll have to rope in Polly and Regan."

Tay looked skeptical.

"I don't think Polly and Regan are gonna go for it," Tay said. "Doesn't it seem awfully joiny?"

Scottie looked balefully at Tay, then turned to Amanda.

"Denial is a very sad thing, is it not?" she asked her, shaking her head sorrowfully.

"Here she is, a member of Chicks with Sticks," Amanda said. "A fervent pilgrim of the Sacred Sleepover. And yet, she thinketh that she is not . . . what was the crude term she used?"

"Joiny!" Bella yelled.

"Isn't it time for the movie?" Tay scowled. "Even the sappy romantic comedy Amanda inevitably chose for tonight is better than your mockery."

"You know it!" Amanda crowed. "We're watching *Serendipity.*"

"Oh God," Tay said, slapping her forehead. But Scottie could see a smile twitching at the corners of her thin lips.

And she was the only one who knew why.

68) I have a bit of a thing for John Cusack.

Scottie was much more interested in returning to the topic of Beck Snyder than popping in the movie, but she decided that it could wait. She was feeling more lighthearted than she had in days.

That's what hanging with the Chicks did for Scottie. Time with them had a way of intensifying the positive and diffusing the negative in her angsty mind. Her friends made her feel like all her maybes could easily turn into yeses.

It was because they could see beneath Scottie's skin, to her true self. They saw Scottie's faults. (They called her on them without fail, in fact.) And yet—they still thought she was pretty fabulous. *They* thought she deserved a boyfriend, even if no boy had gotten around to recognizing it yet.

Somehow—in much the same way this life-buoy called YarnCon had materialized in Amanda's computer—Scottie felt that Chicks' Luck was going to make love happen for her, too.

I just have to figure out how to make that luck last beyond the S.S.O., Scottie told herself wistfully.

"Hey, I have something that's going to make Tay happy," Amanda piped up, interrupting Scottie's brood. "That is, in addition to the rapture of watching Kate Beckinsale fall in *love* with John Cusack."

"Yich," Tay squirmed.

Yeah, right. Scottie grinned

"Not only are my parents *not* entertaining any stodgy clients tonight, thus keeping us in exile in my bedroom," Amanda announced with great fanfare, "but they aren't even here! They've gone to some party. And Trey is sleeping over at a friend's house. So, we have the joint to ourselves, which means . . ."

"Movie's on the giant screen TV in the media room!" Tay said, raising a fist in the air. "Yes!"

"I still can't believe you have an entire media room," Bella said, taking a sip of smoothie, "when I don't even have basic cable."

"Well, you have a yoga room at your place," Amanda countered. "And we definitely don't have one of those."

"Oh, you can never be too sure," Scottie joked. To Tay and Bella she said, "One time, when we were seven and I was over here to play, I went looking for the bathroom and discovered a room that I never even knew existed."

"My mother's lair," Amanda growled.

"Her dressing room," Scottie corrected her. "I've never seen anything like it. All pink and powdery and—wait, did you say your parents already left?"

"Yessss," Amanda said carefully.

"So let's show Tay and Bella," Scottie begged.

Amanda held up her hands and shook her head.

(Knit two together)

"Tay's allergic to pink, remember?" she said.

"I'll take it over this pinkie," Tay said. Very carefully, she set the glove she was struggling with on the arm of the chair and got to her feet.

"Adventure!" Scottie cried.

Giggling like little kids, they all scurried out of the bedroom, slurping at their smoothies as they went. Amanda led them down the hallway past Trey's room, Theresa's room, *and* the guest room, then into the breezeway overlooking the condo's massive living room. Its floor-to-ceiling windows looked as if they were draped with black velvet. That was because they faced Lake Michigan. During sunny days, those windows glimmered and danced with sunlight reflected off the water. But at night, the water beyond the shoreline seemed to swallow all light, going vast and inky. Scottie shivered as Amanda led them into another hallway.

"We are entering," Tay said in a throaty, creepy voice, "the Twilight Zone. Where all the women look like Barbie, and the men like Ken. Maybe when we walk through the door, we'll find that our jammies have been magically transformed into Chanel suits."

"Okay, we're turning back," Amanda said, grinding to a halt at her parents' bedroom door. "If I show you the lair, you guys are never gonna let me live it down."

"Oh please," Tay said. "I was just kidding. We all know *I'm* in no position to make fun of anyone's parents. My dad just bought a BMW sports car, for God's sake."

"*Ew,*" her three friends said together.

"The midlife crisis of a divorced dad," Amanda sighed. "Never pretty. Okay, you get to come in."

The dressing room was behind narrow glass doors hung with gauzy white fabric that matched the Scotts' white-on-white-on-still-more-white bedroom. But inside the dressing room? The only thing that was white was the Kleenex. Everything else was pink. The chaise lounge and vanity, the floor-to-ceiling bank of drawers, the padded hangers in the room-length closet, even the little knobs on the shoe trees—all were peppermint, mauve, and fuchsia. The air *smelled* pink.

"Oh. My. God," Tay said, pinching her nose. "I think a hundred sachets crawled in here and died."

Bella draped herself on the chaise lounge and put the back of her hand to her forehead.

"I'm having a fainting spell!" she said in a breathy Southern accent. "Fetch me my smelling salts!"

"I know," Amanda giggled, flapping one of the gauzy doors a bit to circulate air. "Would you believe my mom told me this is her favorite room in the house? It's the only place that's hers and hers alone."

"It's her sanctuary," Bella said, propping herself on her elbows. "I get that. That's cool. Not so many parents are self-aware enough to make a refuge for themselves like this."

"I guess you're right," Amanda said. One of the closet's sliding doors was half-open. She slipped inside and began flipping slowly through her mother's silky, expensive outfits. "Doesn't it seem kind of sad, though? That my mom's refuge is a *closet?*"

"It's a very *nice* closet," Bella noted, touching a fingertip to each of the half-dozen crystal perfume bottles on the vanity.

"And *this* is a very nice dress," Scottie cried, stepping past Amanda to extract a glittery champagne-colored sheath from the closet. The dress was so bedazzled, it felt like it weighed about ten pounds. It was strappy and low-cut. And it was still dangling its tag. "It's a Valentino!"

"Well, you know the holidays are coming up." Amanda shrugged. "There're balls and stuff."

"Wow," Tay said, shaking her head. "What's it feel like to be Cinderella?"

"She won't know unless she tries it on," Scottie goaded, waving the dress in front of Amanda so it rustled and clicked enticingly.

"I'm not trying it on," Amanda scoffed. "It's a *mom* dress!"

(Knit two together)

"Excuse me, but in *our* worlds?" Scottie protested, pointing at Bella and Tay. "This is not a mom dress. Moms wear painty overalls."

"Or Birkenstocks," Bella said.

"My mom's all about those blowsy linen things from J.Jill," Tay added.

Amanda looked at the dress and scowled.

"It's a Valentino," Tay said. "Even I know that you live for that crap, Amanda. Try it on. Live a little."

"Ooh," Bella cried, bouncing off the chaise and pulling an insanely high heel out of one of the cubbies that lined the closet. The shoe was pointy-toed, spike-heeled, and gold. "Try it on with these."

"Bella!" Amanda sputtered. "You're always saying that high heels are a misogynist plot to keep women unbalanced, dependent upon men, and out of touch with nature."

"Wait, I don't get that last one," Scottie said.

"Because you can't walk in the grass when you're wearing spike heels," Bella explained. "You'll sink." She thrust the shoe out to Amanda. "And it's all true," she declared, "but that doesn't mean they're not pretty. You can try them on for fun. I just don't approve of you wearing them in public."

"C'mon, Amanda," Scottie said. "How can you resist? You even wear the same size as your mom." She pointed at Amanda's chest. "Y'know, since the whole *blossoming.*"

"Shut up!" Amanda giggled, crossing her arms over herself and turning bright red. She snatched the dress out of Scottie's hand and untied the drawstring of her crisp cotton pajama bottoms at the same time. "Okay, I'll try it on. But after I do your little dare, we are proceeding directly to *Serendipity.*"

"With microwave popcorn," Tay insisted as Amanda slithered into the skinny sheath. "The artificially buttered kind."

"Duh," Amanda said. Scottie helped her zip the dress up and Bella arranged the gold shoes on the floor so Amanda could step into them.

"Wait!" Scottie cried. "Before anyone looks at her . . ."

She ran over to the vanity and grabbed a shimmery hair clip off a tray of accessories. Then she opened Mrs. Scott's jewelry box. It didn't take her long to locate a pair of delicate earrings—sprays of hair-thin gold chains, each anchored with a tiny diamond—and a matching necklace.

"Put these on," she ordered, handing the jewelry to Amanda. Then Scottie herself swept Amanda's dark, glossy hair up into a twist at the back of her head, fastening it with the hair clip.

"Okay!" Scottie cried. "Now . . . feast your eyes!"

Amanda turned toward the full length mirror in the dressing room's corner. The other girls stood back to take Amanda in, from her sleek chignon to her pointy gold toes.

"Whoa," Tay whispered. "I was right about Barbie living here."

"But . . . in a good way," Bella said. "I know it's not very P.C. of me to say, but Amanda, you look hot."

Scottie was speechless. It wasn't like she hadn't always known how beautiful Amanda was. Or that she had the body of a *Friends* character. But seeing her in that dress, looking more *ideal* than Scottie could ever hope to look herself—it just about broke her heart.

That's what boys fall in love with, Scottie thought, looking at Amanda's sharply defined cheeks; her faint freckles; her slim, muscular arms. Scottie was so transfixed by her friend's perfection that it took her a moment to realize that Amanda—still staring at her reflection—was crying. Silent rivulets were streaming down her cheeks.

"Amanda?" Scottie said.

Amanda barely acknowledged her. She seemed to be speaking to herself in the mirror when she rasped, "I don't want this."

"Well . . ." Scottie glanced at Tay and Bella, who looked as bewildered as she felt. "That's okay. Just take the dress off."

"'Cuz maybe if I didn't look like this," Amanda went on, fresh tears welling in her eyes, "Toby would act like I was normal. We'd go back to the way we were."

"Oh no!" Scottie said, grabbing Amanda's hand. "You guys didn't break up, did you? Why didn't you tell us?"

"No, we're still together," Amanda shrugged. "But lately, things have been different."

Finally a sob escaped her. Standing stiffly in her fancy dress, Amanda put her hands over her face and scrubbed at her eyes with her fingertips.

"Come on," Tay ordered her, grabbing her elbow and leading her to the chaise lounge. Amanda hobbled over and sank to a grateful seat on the couch, out of view of the mirror. She kicked off the gold shoes and curled her feet beneath her.

"Now tell us what's going on," Tay said, more gently than Tay usually said anything. Scottie swiped a Kleenex out of the dispenser on the vanity and handed it to Amanda, while Bella knelt on the floor next to the chaise and laid her head in Amanda's lap.

"Well . . ." Amanda said after blowing her nose, "I feel dumb being a drama queen about it, because it might be nothing, but, I don't know, I can just tell that something's shifted."

"What do you mean?"

"Toby and I used to talk all the time," Amanda snuffled. "We sort of had an unofficial schedule. He would always call me at lunchtime, just for a second, to say hi. Then at 3:35, he'd call again, to see how school went. And I would always call him at ten when he got done with band practice. We woke up half an hour early in the mornings just so we could call each other and chat before we had to get up.

"But lately, the talking? It's just not like it used to be. It's more like checking in. And it's not happening nearly as much."

"Well . . ." Bella proposed, "maybe that's how things get when you've been together for a long time like you guys."

"Maybe," Amanda said sadly. "But then how do you explain the fact that he's totally attentive when it's date night. *Especially* if he wants me to come hear his band play. Or go to a party with him. Or meet his friends for dinner."

"Um . . ."

Scottie, Bella, and Tay exchanged furtive glances. What *did* that mean?

"I'll tell you what I think," Amanda said, the tears starting again. She grabbed a handful of shimmery dress and said, "I'm a trophy! Toby's more interested in having me as arm candy than a real girlfriend."

"What?" Scottie blurted. "That's crazy. Toby's not like that!"

"Maybe he didn't used to be," Amanda sniffed, "but he's changed. He used to be sort of nerdy-cute."

"The best kind of cute." Bella sighed.

"Yeah." Amanda nodded. "But now, I'm kind of scared that Toby's become Just Cute. I remember when we first met, we went to hear some jazz at this little club in Hyde Park. And all these kids from U of C kept coming up to him, y'know, just to say hi or talk about a class or whatever. And Toby was totally shy back to them. It was like, he couldn't really believe people *liked* him; that he was just another guy to them, y'know, instead of the weird kid with the L.D. that he'd been in high school."

Amanda looked up at Scottie for a quick moment before returning her gaze to the wad of tissue in her hands. Even though Amanda was handling her own learning disability better than ever, Scottie had watched her battle its demons ever since the second grade. She knew as well as Amanda that the scars never completely went away, even if all was bright and shiny on the outside.

"So what's different now?" Scottie asked, even though she thought she already knew the answer.

"I guess it finally sunk in," Amanda said. "He's not weird anymore. He's this good-looking, cool guy in a band with a . . . with a . . ."

"With a hot girlfriend," Tay provided sympathetically.

Amanda gave a shuddery sniffle.

"Toby's life is so full of all these cool guy trappings," she said, "that I don't think I'm *me* to him anymore. I'm just one of the trappings."

(Knit two together)

"But maybe not," Bella proposed. "Why don't you ask him what's going on? Maybe you're wrong. Either way, open communication is very important in a relationship."

"Exactly why I can't ask him," Amanda cried. "Lately, we're either doing the polite 'check-in' or we're on a date, surrounded by people. He's right there, but . . . he's kinda *not* there. Not the way he used to be."

Scottie widened her eyes at Tay and Bella. An uncomfortable silence filled the dressing room. Suddenly, the powdery scent of Mrs. Scott's countless sachets felt oppressive.

Or maybe Scottie just felt itchy because she so hated not knowing what to say.

Of course I don't, Scottie thought. *What do I know about relationships? Here I thought Amanda's and Toby's was perfect. If they can't make it work, what chance do I possibly have with Beck?!*

8 *(Slip remaining stitch)

On the Sunday after the S.S.O, Scottie woke up at nine, her gut already growling.

Must have stretched out my stomach Friday night, she thought, remembering the stuffed pizza the Chicks had ordered to drown out Amanda's sorrows after her big meltdown.

It was too early to call her buds to propose an insta-brunch. And she knew that her own kitchen was pretty much bare, beyond a bunch of leftover takeout and empty cereal boxes.

Cereal . . . Scottie thought. Visions of sugar-crusted puffs of refined flour drowning in 2 percent milk danced through her head. She wanted artificially colored marshmallows. Pseudo-graham crackers. Choco-puffs. Basically, the kind of stuff you couldn't buy at the yuppified, whole wheaty supermarket her dad shopped at every Sunday night. (Now that her parents had given up their no-carb kick, they were on an all-organic, all the time kick.)

This moment called for a Jewel run. Jewel was the perfect supermarket—just three blocks away and crammed with any processed food your heart could desire. Pushing CC off her chest, Scottie hauled herself out of bed.

Normally, she would have just skimmed a toothbrush through her mouth and shuffled right out the door. But just as she was pulling on her usual Sunday morning wear—the infamous lavender stretch pants—Scottie remembered Beck.

Beck, who lived in this very building—and had already witnessed The Horrible Stretch Pants once. Automatically, Scottie peeled them back off.

There's no way I'm gonna run into him again, she grumbled as she headed back to the bathroom, where she sulkily put on mascara, blushed up her pale cheeks, and glossed her lips. *Just the fact that I'm making the effort means there is* no way *I'll run into him. But if I do* wear the Stretch Pants, *I definitely* will *run into him. Fate is a total jerk that way.*

Ten minutes later, her stomach complaining loudly now, Scottie was at her parents' bedroom door wearing her second-favorite pair of jeans (since Beck had already seen her favorites on Friday), and a very-Sunday-but-cute assemblage of layered tank tops.

Scottie tapped the door and poked her head in. Her parents were sitting up in bed. Her dad was slurping at a cup of coffee, surrounded by sections of the *New York Times* and *Chicago Tribune*, and her mom was already sketching in a large notebook.

Which reminds me, Scottie thought with a grimace. *I totally forgot to write last night's dream in my dream journal.*

A wispy image of the dream glimmered behind her eyes. Had it been about Alice? She thought she remembered seeing Alice's wild, black curls. She remembered smelling soup. Or did she? The last dream remnants slipped away as Scottie's dad said, "Hi, sweetie! To what do we owe the pleasure of seeing you before noon?"

Scottie said good-bye to the dream (and to any chance of an A in psych) and waved at her parents.

"You've deprived your offspring of provisions," she announced. "I'm making a Jewel run. Want anything?"

"Hmmm, do they have organic yogurt there?" Mom murmured, glancing up from her sketch for a moment. She had a conté crayon smudge on her nose.

"I'm thinking, no." Scottie shrugged.

• • Chicks with Sticks

"Maybe just some eggs then," her mom requested. "The cage-free kind. Oh, and coffee! About five pounds? Just the generic brand. Nothing fancy."

"Five pounds?!?" Scottie balked. "Mom, I know you're in paint-till-you-drop mode, but that sounds like a lot of caffeine, even for you."

"I'm not going to *drink* it," her mom scoffed. "That's what the shade-grown Peruvian beans are for."

"Your mother's going to paint with it," Scottie's dad explained. "She's experimenting with organic materials. Do you know yesterday, she sent me out for dirt? I had to go ask the neighbors if I could borrow some from their flower boxes."

"Do you ever get the feeling that we're a little too urban in this family?" Scottie said through a yawn. "I mean if we have to seek out sources for *dirt* . . ."

"Then again, you have twenty-four-hour access to Lucky Charms," her mom pointed out. "Not that I condone you eating that kind of thing, Scottie."

"I think they're making whole grain Lucky Charms now," Scottie quipped. "See you, guys."

She grabbed some cash out of the jar in the kitchen reserved for take-out funds, gave CC a good-bye pat, and headed out the door.

She was so busy wedging her keys and cash into her not-exactly-roomy jeans pockets as she walked down the hall that, at first, she didn't see him.

Luckily, she looked up the instant before she turned out of the long corridor into the elevator vestibule. And then she froze. Because there he was. Beck! Sitting on the floor of the hallway, his wrists propped on top of his hunched-up knees, staring at the ceiling.

Um, fate? Scottie thought as she tried not to hyperventilate. *I'm sorry I called you a big jerk.*

Beck reached out toward the bike that was propped on the wall next to him and gave one of the pedals a spin.

Okay, he's acting kind of weird, Scottie thought, *which I find inexplicably adorable.*

Before she could chicken out and make a break for the elevator, she forced the single syllable out of her mouth.

"Beck?"

Whoa, that was loud!

Beck jumped. Scottie cringed as she tiptoed toward him.

"I always forget how echoey these hallways can be," she said. Beck hopped to his feet.

"Oh, uh, that's okay," he said, making a quick, self-conscious swipe at his wind-buffeted hair. "I didn't realize we lived on the same floor."

"Me either," Scottie said. She suppressed a nervous laugh as she continued, "So, um . . . what are you doing out here in the hallway?"

Beck thumped himself lightly on the forehead and rolled his eyes.

"I forgot my key," he sighed. "And my mom is out, scoping the early morning flea markets for fabric. So now I've got no way to eat my breakfast."

He gestured at a white and red bag plunked next to his bike. Scottie caught her breath. The bag was from Jewel! Through the thin plastic, Scottie could spot a cereal box and a jug of milk.

Fate, Scottie thought, biting her lip to keep from grinning too hard, *I owe you a big apology.*

"Y'know," Beck sighed, "in New York, you forget your key, you just call the super. Here, there's no recourse. Chicago's a tough town, I tell ya."

Scottie laughed.

"I was just going to grab some breakfast, too," she heard herself saying, even as she realized that the grumbling in her stomach had mysteriously disappeared.

"Oh yeah?" Beck said. He looked down at his feet for a quick beat, then said, "Well, if you don't mind some lowly Golden Grahams and two percent milk, you could have some of mine."

Fate? I adore you!

Scottie tried to sound breezy as she said, "I think I can live with that. Tell you what. Wait here for a sec?"

"Where would I go?" Beck shrugged, sliding back down the wall.

"Good point." Scottie giggled.

Scottie waited until she was back in her loft to do her happy dance, biting her lip to keep from squealing with joy. Then she got to work. Grabbing one of her dad's canvas grocery bags, she started packing—two bowls, two spoons, a knife, the last banana from the fruit bowl on the counter, and a handful of the sugar packets that her parents kept handy for their art openings. Then she filled two silver thermoses with the coffee her dad had brewed that morning.

Good old shade-grown Peruvian beans, Scottie thought with an inner cackle. On a paper napkin, she scribbled a note to her parents.

Ran into a friend. We went 4 breakfast. Will get yr coffee latr? xoxo Scottie.

Back with Beck, Scottie thrust one of the fragrant thermoses into his hand and said, "I want to take you to one of my favorite breakfast spots in the city."

"Changed your mind about the Golden Grahams, huh?" Beck said, jumping back to his feet. "I guess I can't blame you. You were probably hoping for something a little fancier."

"Oh no," Scottie insisted. "Bring the goods!"

She led him to the elevator, and pressed the button for the top floor. When they emerged, Scottie looked around to make sure nobody was there, then tugged open the door to the supply closet in a shadowy corner of the vestibule. Beck slipped into the closet behind her and they gazed together at a vertical swath of thick metal rungs poking out of the wall. At the top of the ladder was a small, square hatch.

"When you said you wanted to go to your favorite breakfast spot," Beck teased, "I kind of thought we'd be leaving the building."

Scottie just grinned, slung her bag over her shoulder, and started climbing. When she reached the hatch door, she punched four numbers into a combination lock next to the handle. The door gave a little pop and she pushed it open.

"Hey!" Beck said from below her. "Nobody told *me* the combination to the roof door when we moved in."

"That's because you're not supposed to know it," Scottie said, peering down at him. "We're breaking and exiting, dude. Be cool."

"Wow!" Beck said. "Scottie, you're . . ."

"I'm what?" Scottie said, suddenly feeling a rivulet of cold sweat tickle down her ribs.

I'm a dork? I'm a delinquent? I'm in possession of a butt that looks really weird from your angle down there on the floor?

"You're a surprise," Beck said quietly.

Okay, I really don't understand boy-speak. Because being a "surprise"? I don't know if that's good or bad.

To her *own* surprise, Scottie found herself asking Beck to clarify.

"Well . . ." She gripped her ladder rung so tightly that her knuckles ached. "Do you like surprises?"

Beck smiled a bit rakishly.

"Life would be pretty boring without 'em, wouldn't it?"

That doesn't really answer my question, Scottie sighed. She had the urge to push for *further* clarification, but it suddenly occurred to her that she was dangling off a ladder.

Not exactly the cozy, coffeehouse setting I'd pictured for my first date with Beck, she thought, stifling a snort. She crawled onto the roof and dusted off her hands as Beck clambered up behind her.

"Whoa!" he exclaimed as he emerged from the hatch. The roof of the bread factory was draped in tar paper. The sticky-looking black stuff covered every surface, swooping up to frame skylights, rolling over drainpipes, and creeping up the low brick wall at the roof's edges.

"It's like a lava spill up here!" Beck cried, bouncing across the tar paper's spongy surface.

"Except we're on top of the volcano," Scottie said, "not down below. Check out the view!"

As Beck gazed out at the sea of rooftops, treetops, and train tracks below them, Scottie drank in the Sunday morning quiet—interrupted only by the occasional *whoosh* of a car or the plastic clatter of someone taking their trash out to the alley. Her lungs filled with green, pre-autumn air and her muscles softened in a way that only happened during her rare forays up to the roof.

She actually hadn't been up here since a lonely Sunday in July, when Tay had been working her summer job at Northwestern Hospital, Amanda was at the beach with her family, and Bella was at Camp Hippie. Scottie had sat there and gazed at the shimmer of the rooftops, working round after round of gossamer alpaca into the sleeves of a shrug. It had ended up being one of the sweetest days of her summer.

Now, as Scottie remembered that feeling, she forgot to feel jittery in Beck's presence. She didn't try to analyze the way his arms had slackened and his eyelids had gone heavy as he took in the view. She didn't need to. Somehow, she just knew what he was thinking.

"It's not New York," Scottie said, joining him at the almost-edge of the roof. "But it's cool in a different way, isn't it?"

"Definitely," Beck whispered. "It's a weird kind of silence on a roof, isn't it? It's different up here."

"I was thinking the same thing."

Scottie became pleasantly hyperaware of Beck next to her. His arm was probably eight inches away from hers, yet she could *feel* it there. She so wanted to peek over at him but was scared of what she'd broadcast if she did. She knew what she was thinking, at least: *Ooh! We're having a Moment! Kiss me!*

Which would be wrong on a dozen different levels. For all Scottie knew, the only thing intoxicating Beck up here were the tar fumes burning off the roof in the morning sun. So she kept her eyes on the landscape.

"That's where my friend Bella lives," she said, pointing to a clump of brick three-flats nesting in the shadow of Wrigley Field.

"Must be a Cubs fan," Beck said.

"She's so far from being a big-haired Cubs fan that you wouldn't even believe it!" Scottie snorted. "Well, she's got big hair, but it's not *that* kind of big. She's completely crunchy. I guess her parents bought their place years ago, when nobody wanted to live this far north of the loop and it was really cheap. My parents moved here when I was a baby, too. They're *very* proud of their urban pioneer thing."

"And it worked on you," Beck joked. "You're this street-smart thug now, stealing lock combinations, making unauthorized trips to the roof..."

Beck pointed at a rickety folding chair propped in a corner of the roof, angled westward for sunset-viewing.

"That yours?"

"Uh-huh." Scottie shrugged. She didn't want to tell him that she'd found it in the alley, because *that* would just perpetuate the street-smart myth. In truth, it didn't exactly take a lot of guts to nick a chair someone had already thrown out.

"You must come up here a lot," Beck said. Scottie could feel him looking at her now. Her cheeks burned.

"Not too much, actually," Scottie said. She hesitated for a moment before finally turning to look at Beck full on. He looked back at her, right into her eyes, and Scottie wondered if he liked her blue, the way she dug his hazel.

"I want to keep this place special, you know?" Scottie admitted. "So I don't come up too often. That would be like eating ice cream every day."

"Yeah?" Beck's smile was crooked—half shy, half flirty.

"Yeah." Scottie bit her lip. "The only thing is, I *would* eat ice cream every day if I could."

"I hear ya." Beck's smile was wide now. "But at the moment? Two percent milk is sounding just as good."

"Oh! I forgot about breakfast," Scottie blurted. Suddenly, she was starving again. Feeling giddy, she headed over to her chair.

"Since you're the 'guest,'" Scottie said, laying her bowls and spoons out on the roof's lip, "you may sit in the chair."

"I may be the guest," Beck said, "but *you're* the girl. *You* get the chair."

"Oh, so we're doing the gender role thing?" Scottie teased. "I guess that means you expect *me* to make breakfast."

"Hey, I'll do the coffee," Beck defended himself with a grin. He pulled out the thermoses and milk while Scottie poured two giant mounds of Golden Grahams into the bowls.

"I'm guessing you want sugar?" Beck said, pulling out a big handful of the little white packets.

"Four," Scottie said. "And about an inch of milk."

"So, you're basically drinking hot coffee ice cream," Beck said with a wince.

"Oh, and I suppose you, being a *guy* and all," Scottie teased, "you drink your coffee black?"

"Yeah," Beck said, shaking a lock of hair out of his eyes. "Black with cream."

"Uh, that's not black."

"It's the *new* black," Beck said. "You forget I come from a fashion family. I'm allowed to bend the rules."

"I'll consider myself warned." Scottie laughed as she settled into her folding chair. Beck sat on the low wall next to her, placing their coffees on the floor between their feet.

And then a sweet silence—save the steady crunching of their break-fast—took hold again. Scottie couldn't believe this was happening. She was filling her empty stomach and a beautiful boy was beside her. All her plaintive desires seemed to be melting away!

But eventually, of course, it had to end.

When the cereal was gone, Scottie and Beck had nowhere to pour their grainy dregs of milk, so they just tipped the bowls to their mouths and drank up, giggling because they felt like little kids.

Beck stood up and stretched, his T-shirt sliding up enough to expose a sliver of pale, taut stomach. He looked down at Scottie, who again realized how tall he was. He must have been close to six feet.

"So what are you doing with the rest of your Sunday?" Beck wondered casually.

Scottie froze.

Oh my God, she thought. *He's about to ask me out. That is, if I have no other plans. Which, of course, I don't. But if I have no other plans, does that make me a loser? And either way, we just sort of had a date, didn't we? An accidental, totally non-official one, anyway. So should I leave him wanting more? But, hello, if he asks me out, I'm not gonna say no for no reason!!! Oh God, Oh God, awkward silence happening. Say! Something!*

"What are *you* doing?" Scottie said.

"Well, I might start by breaking into my apartment," Beck said, "if my mom's not back yet. Better go check."

"Oh. Oh yeah," Scottie said. She suddenly felt tired. The easy bliss of breakfast was over and she was once again finding herself powerless to interpret Beck's signals.

If he's even sending any!

"Your mom's probably worried," Scottie blurted. "I mean, by your abandoned bike and all."

"Eh, I don't think so," Beck said. "Let's just say, this isn't the first time I've locked myself out of the house. I think I'm destined to be an absent-minded professor someday."

"Oh, so you're the next Einstein?" Scottie said with a smile. "I don't know, Beck. I don't think you've got the hair for it."

"You're just saying that because I have bike helmet head," Beck said, helping Scottie pack up the cereal bowls and thermoses. "Believe me, my hair can get very, very big. That's my theory, actually. My bedhead requires so much energy, it's sapping my brain. Thus, forgotten keys. Forgotten homework. Forgotten cello on the subway. . . ."

"You left a cello on the subway?!" Scottie screamed.

"It was fourth grade," Beck protested. He began to walk back toward the roof hatch. "I'd had a very rough day. Some kid gave me a bloody nose on the playground."

"Awwww," Scottie said. "Why?"

"Because I was a dweeb who played the cello!" Beck sputtered. "Clearly the dude had never heard of Yo-Yo Ma. Anyway, I was lugging the thing home on the subway, my stop snuck up on me, I dashed and . . . sayonara, Stradivarius."

"Just like my poor knitting project," Scottie said.

"Exactly," Beck said. Crooked smile. Crinkly eyes. "Clearly, neither of us can be trusted on a train. The next time we hang out, we've gotta come up with some other form of transit."

The next time we hang out!

Scottie exhaled so loudly that she was sure he heard it. But, for this moment, anyway, she didn't care. *The next time we hang out!*

She grinned at Beck.

"Well, have you ever left anything important in a taxi?" she asked him.

They were paused in front of the hatch now, soaking in the last moments of rooftop vibe.

Beck gazed at the clouds and listed, "Two wallets, one set of keys, and a history notebook just before midterms."

"Ouch," Scottie said. "Okay, I guess we go on foot, then. I mean, what can you lose walking down the street?"

"If childhood memory serves," Beck said, his crooked smile back, "countless mittens."

"Now *that* I can help you with," Scottie pronounced. "I'm a knitter, remember? I'll just make you some mittens with a long string that you can thread through your coat sleeves."

"That sounds like the height of sophistication," Beck said.

"Oh, it's *very* cool," Scottie assured him. Then she started.

"Wait," she gasped. "I can't knit you mittens! I totally forgot about The Curse of the Boyf—"

Suddenly, Scottie cut herself off. As she clamped her lips shut, she felt all the warmth of the morning drain out of her.

I did not just say that. I did not just allude to the Curse of the Boyfriend Sweater.

Which was, of course, the widely documented certainty that if you ever knitted anything for your boyfriend, he would break up with you before the last stitch was sewn.

But here's the thing. He's not my boyfriend!!!!

"What was that?" Beck was looking at her through a yawn, his smile lazy. "Curse of the what? Is there some serial mitten thief lurking around Chicago that I don't know about? Damn. First the bad bagels. Now I have to worry about the safety of my outerwear."

Scottie's laugh was a quick—relieved—bark.

He didn't hear me.

She tossed her hand and said, "Nah, nothing to worry about. I *will* knit you those mittens. What are friends for?"

Now they were back in the elevator, and Scottie was feeling, miraculously, like she'd done everything right. She hadn't thrown herself at Beck. She hadn't acted like a *complete* dork. She'd even enjoyed herself!

That is, when I wasn't feeling so crushy that I thought I might throw up.

When they landed in their second-floor hallway, a woman was at Beck's loft door, struggling to hold a few bulging bags with one hand and wheel his bike inside with the other. Scottie felt Beck stiffen beside her.

"Mom?" he called out.

Beck's mother glanced up. Even from a distance, Scottie could see that she had the same poochy mouth as Beck, and the same wavy, dark hair, though hers was streaked with cherry-red highlights and pulled into a couple of loose pigtails. She was wearing layered tank-tops, just like Scottie's, but hers looked way more filmy and expensive. Her plum-colored skirt was long and billowy, with asymmetrical tucks nipping it in here and there. And on her feet? Green, suede athletic shoes.

"Did you lock yourself out again?" she said with a rueful smile.

"Yup."

Beck grimaced slightly at Scottie, then began to walk toward the loft.

Okay, was that good-bye?

Beck's mom was clearly wondering the same thing. Shooting a quick, questioning glance at her son, she propped the bike against the doorjamb and took a few steps toward Scottie.

"Hi," she called out. Her voice was a little nasal, with a touch of New York twang. "I'm Hannah, Beck's mother."

"Hi," Scottie called, waving stiffly. All this shouting through the echoey hallway was embarrassing.

"Want some brunch?" Hannah offered bluntly. "On the way home from the flea market, I accidentally found Chinatown! I got some dim sum goodies to go and of course I got way more than Beck and I could possibly eat."

Scottie laughed, but Beck just shuffled his feet and muttered, "We ate already."

Scottie thought she saw Hannah wilt, just a little. But maybe it was her imagination, because the woman's mouth just kept on going.

"Sure, sure, you ate already, but darling," she said to Beck, "we both know that you're gonna get one whiff of these red bean buns and you're gonna be ready for the second course."

She grinned at Scottie.

"I first took him to Chinatown in New York when he was a year old," she said. "He didn't care about chicken fingers or peanut butter and jelly. The kid wanted Sichuan spare ribs."

"Mom!" Beck huffed. He crossed his arms and cast another baleful glance in Scottie's direction.

(Knit two together)

She felt his pain. Why couldn't parents just keep the toddler years stored away on videotapes where they belonged? Suddenly, Scottie spotted an opportunity for a subject change and pounced on it, sure that Beck would be grateful to her.

"That's a really pretty fabric," she said, coming closer and pointing at a poof of shimmery orange stuff poking out of one of Hannah's bags. "What is it? Silk charmeuse?"

Hannah raised her eyebrows.

"The girl knows her fabric," she said to Beck. "I like her!"

"Scottie's a knitter, Mom," Beck said, two spots of red bursting onto his cheeks. "So yeah, she knows fabric."

"No way!" Hannah yelled with a grin. Scottie jumped. It occurred to her that if Beck's mom had been sixteen Scottie would have wanted to be friends with her.

"Knitting is so hot right now," Hannah said.

"Yeah, I've heard that," Scottie said, shooting a secret smile at Beck. He smiled back.

"Awww, come on in," Hannah said, throwing an arm around Scottie's shoulders (and banging her with a clunky bangle bracelet while she was at it). "It's nice to see a fresh face around here. I've been working so hard, I've been terrible company for Beck."

Scottie looked at Beck, her eyebrows raised. He fidgeted for a minute, glanced from his mother to Scottie, and shrugged.

"Yeah, come on in," he repeated in a flat voice that Scottie couldn't quite interpret. Her instincts were telling her to head home. The whole roof moment? It was over. Beck's *mother* was here now.

But on the other hand, Scottie was craving that daily dose of ice cream. She wanted a little more of Beck. One more stab at that easiness they'd had on the roof. One more chance to lock eyes with him and feel like they had a connection.

So Scottie stayed.

9 • (Pass slipped stitch over)

Bella opened her apartment door looking wary. But as soon as she saw Scottie, she cracked a wide grin.

"I thought you might have been Sergio," she said. "I'm so glad it's you!"

Scottie started to slump through the door, but halfway through, she froze and gaped at Bella.

"Wait a minute," she said. "Sergio the foreign exchange student from Italy?"

"Yeah," Bella said. She slumped her body against the door, so weary she apparently had to hang on to the knob lest she wilt to the floor.

Scottie blinked hard.

"The Sergio who looks like he stepped out of a Prada ad?" she yelled at Bella.

"I guess so."

"Has Sergio shown up at your doorstep before?!"

Bella hooked her free arm through Scottie's and drew her inside. She shut the door and leaned back against it.

"No, but he's been calling and calling," Bella said. "I did some Internet research and I've heard that Italian boys are like this. You give them a speck of encouragement and they won't leave you alone!"

"Bella," Scottie said. "Half the girls at school have been, like, lying down at Sergio's beautiful feet. What did *you* do?"

"He asked me for directions to the counselors' office," Bella said with a shrug. "And, well, you know, his English isn't so great and I didn't want him to get lost. So I walked him there, said good-bye, and went to class. Now he's in love with me. Ugh!"

"Oh my God," Scottie wailed. "Now I'm more depressed than ever."

She stumbled into Bella's flat and waved hello to Bella's parents, who were cuddled up on the couch watching a movie and munching on something that looked like congealed twigs. As always, they looked like a cutely odd couple. Bella's mom was tall, angular, and gawky like her daughter. She had blond, wavy hair that hung almost to her waist. Meanwhile, Bella's dad was this stocky African-American guy with a shaved head and a goatee, his plump cheeks always scrunched into a smile.

"Scottie!" he called out. "What a nice surprise."

"Hey, sweetie," Bella's mom echoed. She pointed a bare toe at a plate of the twiggy things on the coffee table. "Want a wheatberry treat?"

"No thanks," Scottie sighed. "I feel kinda sick actually. I just had Golden Grahams for breakfast and dim sum for elevenses."

Bella scrutinized Scottie's miserable face. As she did, she straightened up and let go of the doorknob. Scottie felt like she was watching one of those accelerated nature films, where a night-drooped plant unfurls at the first hint of sun. Bella went from too weak to stand to caretaker in about thirty seconds.

Still gazing at Scottie, she declared, "Scottie doesn't need wheatberries, Mom. She needs hot chocolate."

Wrapping an arm around Scottie's shoulders, she led her to the kitchen in the back of the flat. Scottie loved the Brearleys' kitchen, with its saffron walls and ancient icebox. The wheatberries and soy that Bella's parents were always cooking tasted pretty awful, but somehow they left the kitchen swimming in spicy, yummy aromas. They lingered most in the orange, yellow, and green pillows piled onto the woody window seat.

This is where Bella led her. She plunked Scottie down, grabbed some milk out of the fridge, then got on her hands and knees in front of a small cabinet.

"I hide the non-carob cocoa back here," Bella told Scottie. "That way, my parents can sort of be in denial that refined sugar and non-organic cocoa beans and stuff are in the house."

"Say no more," Scottie said with a wan smile. "My parents have been on a whole-grain kick of their own lately. Now that they're post-sushi-obsession and pre-who-knows-what? And they call *us* flaky."

Scottie kicked off her shoes and pulled her knees up beneath her chin as Bella poured the milk into a banged-up saucepan. Scottie leaned her head back against the cool window, listening to the flutter of the wind chimes that hung on the Brearleys' back porch. Bella's cute-but-psycho cat, Eden, darted into the room, hopped up to the window seat, and began gnawing on the hem of Scottie's jeans. Since he usually went for her toes, this was quite a behavioral improvement.

Scottie actually began to feel a little better. That was, until Bella folded herself into lotus position on the floor in front of her and propped her pretty face on her fists.

"So," she said. "Tell me what happened."

"What happened is . . ."

The tears came quickly.

"What happened is," Scottie choked out, "I blew it. I just blew it!"

"Blew what?" Bella cried.

"Blew it with Beck," Scottie said.

Bella hopped up as quickly as she'd sat down and grabbed a napkin off the kitchen table. She handed it to Scottie who blew her nose loudly, only to burst into tears anew.

More napkins and a cup of hot chocolate later, Scottie had choked out the first part of the story.

"So we had this dreamy morning on the roof," she said, "and then I met his *mom*."

"Oh no," Bella said. "Was she awful?"

"No!" Scottie said. "She's the coolest, actually. Only Beck's mad at her."

Frowning with confusion and concern, Bella reached over and dug behind one of the window-seat pillows. Gently, she pulled out a fuzzy scarf-in-progress and started knitting.

"Okay," she said, "tell me everything."

Scottie had liked Beck and Hannah's loft from the start. In her own apartment, work was tucked away until it was Ready. Scottie's yarn stash and WIPs were sealed in plastic boxes and stacked against her bedroom wall. Her mother's palettes and paintings hid behind a mammoth canvas curtain that might as well have been a safe door. It was understood that Mom's Creation was meant to be heard (at least its soundtrack was) not seen.

"No feedback until I finish," she always said when Scottie's dad wheedled for a peek.

Hannah's loft, on the other hand, could barely contain her ideas. The dining room table was covered with sketches. Lengths of fabric were draped on the back of every chair. Three mannequins were stationed around the room like party guests, each dressed in patchworked dresses fluttering with dozens of loose, white threads. Tacked to one wall were more sketches and along another was a work table littered with conical spools of thread, more fabric, and two different sewing machines.

"Forgive the mess," Hannah said, bustling over to the coffee table, where she began stacking the Chinese take-out boxes. "I haven't gotten the hang of the whole 'live-work' space. It's pretty much just work-work."

"Maybe," Beck muttered, "if you'd kept your job in New York . . ."

He was standing in the middle of the loft with his arms crossed. He suddenly looked very small to Scottie and it wasn't just the vastness of the loft creating an optical illusion. In the brief trip from the roof to the second floor, Beck had gone from expansive and elastic to a knot of hunched shoulders, entangled forearms, and legs pulled taut.

Hannah halted her frenetic unpacking for a moment and shot Beck a quick glare, but instead of saying something to him, she turned to Scottie.

"So you're a knitter," she announced. "Do you write your own patterns?"

"Not really," Scottie said with a shrug. "I mean, I don't write original patterns, but I do doctor up *other* people's patterns. Keeps me from getting restless. I guess. Although lately, that doesn't seem to be working."

"See!" Hannah pointed at Scottie, apparently not noticing that a take-out box was dangling off her thumb by its wire handle. "See, that's just what happened with me. So now you're feeling a need for more, right?"

"Well . . . yeah," Scottie said, glancing at Beck. He was still all crisscrossed, but he was also looking at her with some wary interest.

"I'm going to this big knitting extravaganza soon," she volunteered. "YarnCon. There'll be workshops and lectures and stuff like that. I'm hoping it'll boot me out of this rut."

"Exactly," Hannah said. "That's the why behind Hannah B. I just wasn't *feeling* the designs I was doing in New York. I needed to shake things up and find my own voice."

She turned to Beck.

"I just wish you got that, honey," she said.

"Mom!" Beck glanced at Scottie. "I *do* get that. I'm just wondering, why, y'know, finding your voice had to mean ditching Dad and New York."

Hannah opened her mouth to respond, but Beck cut her off by turning to Scottie.

"Dim sum?" he said hopefully.

Scottie nodded, relieved at the subject change.

"You're right," Hannah said, giving her head a little shake and seeming to shake off the argument with it. "Let's eat."

Scottie followed Beck to the L-shaped couch in the far corner of the loft. She was about to sink into it when Beck and Hannah both yelled, "Wait!"

Beck snatched a delicate-looking dress off the cushion before Scottie squished it.

"Ooh!" Scottie said, catching the hem of the dress before Beck could sling it over the back to the couch. "This is beautiful!"

"See!" Hannah said, pointing this time at Beck. "I should have this girl bring some friends over for a focus group."

She turned to Scottie.

"But since I've got you here now, Scottie, tell me what you think this dress needs."

"But. . ." Scottie said, *"you're* the designer. How could I know?"

"Whatever," Beck whispered. He flipped open a take-out box, pulled out a doughy little dumpling, and popped it into his mouth. He offered the box to Scottie.

"Thanks," she whispered as she took a dumpling.

"No, really," Hannah said. "It's not quite right and I need a real teenager's opinion. Please?"

With her cheek full of dim sum, Scottie looked from Hannah to Beck. She couldn't help feeling like this was a test.

This is harder than psych class, Scottie thought. Still chewing desperately, she picked up the dress.

The fabric was the color of eggplant, bisected at an empire waist by some soft yellow cord. The cord swooped up in a graceful arch that exactly echoed the swoop-down of the deep, U-shaped neck. The three-quarter sleeves were edged with the same corn-floss piping, but the hem of the circular skirt fluttered into layers with no clear beginning or end.

Barely realizing it, Scottie got to her feet and draped the dress across her front. She peered down at it. She *loved* it.

"I could just see this with a pair of cowboy boots," she breathed.

"Really!" Hannah said. She aimed a chopstick at the fluttery hem. "So you like it? You don't think it needs, oh, something? To really make it pop?"

It's perfect, Scottie wanted to say. But somehow, she knew this was the wrong answer. Beck was looking at her with a clenched jaw, another dumpling poised—and apparently forgotten—in front of his mouth.

"I would add some trim," Scottie declared, not quite knowing where she was going with this. "On the . . . wrists."

And suddenly, Scottie *did* know where she was going with it.

"You know, maybe some rustic lace knitted out of thin cord," she proposed excitedly. "It would give the dress some texture, without taking away from its lines."

Scottie bit her lip and looked up.

Beck actually looked mildly impressed! If still a bit wary. And Hannah?

Hannah's face was glowing.

"Oh my God," she exclaimed. "You're so right! Some chunky, boho lace, maybe sort of tapering toward the wrist bone?"

"That's *exactly* what I was thinking," Scottie said.

"Let's see," Hannah said, brushing aside a couple Chinese boxes to dig out a notebook and colored pencil. "Where could I get my hands on some lace? I'll check my supplier in New Jersey, but I've never seen anything like this in their stock. And the tailoring's gonna kill me . . . it'd be better if I could get it custom-made. But . . ."

As Hannah muttered to herself, Scottie sat back down next to Beck, her eyebrows raised.

"So that's it?" she whispered. "She's gonna change the whole design just because of something *I* said? I'm kind of freaking out."

"Don't," Beck whispered back. "That's how my mom makes all her decisions—instantly. Especially the big ones. She's always saying 'You gotta go with your gut.' That's how we ended up here."

"Man," Scottie breathed. "That's gotta be a little hard to live with."

"Well . . . " Beck suddenly looked away. He swiped a chopstick off the coffee table and began drumming idly on his knee.

"Yeah, it is," he admitted. "But you know . . ."

Beck peeked over at her, before quickly returning his attention to the beat of his chopstick. "Sometimes the Epiphanies have a way of turning out all right."

While Scottie tried not to melt into a puddle right there on the couch, Beck did himself one better.

"Besides," he said, "yours really was a good idea. If I had any interest at all in, y'know, dresses, I think I'd dig the lace cuffs."

Scottie threw back her head and laughed out loud.

"Scottie!"

Scottie clapped her hand over her mouth. She'd almost forgotten that Hannah was still there, muttering through her calculations and raking her blunt-nailed fingers through her pigtails.

"Um, yes?" Scottie said, while Beck laughed softly beside her. Hannah's eyes flashed on Beck for a moment, but then she refocused on Scottie.

"You're probably part of a, what do ya call 'em, a stitch and bitch?" Hannah said. "You know, a group who get together to knit?"

"Yeah, actually," Scottie said. "But we don't call ourselves a Stitch 'n Bitch. We're—"

"Chicks with Sticks," Beck said before crunching into a sticky sesame ball.

Scottie turned to him, her mouth hanging open.

"How did you know that?" she squeaked.

"Um," Beck's bulging cheeks went pink. With his mouth still full, he blurted, "I might have asked around at school. When I saw you guys knitting in the cafeteria."

Oh. My. God. The guy is totally stalking me.

Scottie felt like she'd just won the lottery! But she ordered herself not to whoop or dance around or engage in any other types of lottery-winning behavior. She only allowed (well, couldn't help) a giant grin as she nodded.

"That's us," she told Hannah. "Me and my friends Amanda, Bella, and Tay."

"I *love* it!" Hannah cried. "Oh my God—Epiphany."

"Here we go," Beck sighed under his breath. Hannah didn't seem to hear him—she was too excited about her Epiphany.

Scottie braced herself.

"Scottie," Hannah said, tossing her notebook on the coffee table and clasping her hands beneath her pointy chin. "Have you worked with lace before?"

"Oh sure." Scottie blurted before she could think twice about it. "Love it."

"Then I'd like to offer you and your friends a job," Hannah proposed. "It would be temporary—just for the next month while I finish this round of samples to show my investors. But I'd like *you* guys to design and knit the lace for this dress—and all the others in the line."

Hannah sprung off the couch and dashed across the loft so fast that her long skirt flapped behind her. Scottie trailed behind as Hannah pointed at a series of sketches on the wall. Scottie saw more eggplant and gold, some deep blues and bottle greens, some cute little knickers paired with ankle boots, and a couple A-line skirts.

"I'm calling it 'Isn't It Romantic,'" Hannah announced. "And it's for juniors! So how cool would it be to have actual teenagers collaborating on it with me? We'll get photos of you knitting . . . work it into the marketing plan. OhmiGod, the press will eat it up!"

Wait a minute? Press? A job?

Scottie peeked over her shoulder. Beck's silence was coming at her like blast of cold air.

Scottie didn't even have to think about her next step.

"You know," she said to Hannah, "I'm pretty slammed at school right now. I don't think I really have the time."

"Realleeeee?" Hannah said, slumping against the wall. "Cuz, I gotta say, Scottie, I think this could be a really good opportunity for you girls. I mean, especially if you're interested in design. . . ."

Scottie blurted it out before she could stop herself.

"Amanda's the one who wants to be a fashion designer," she said. "Ever since she started knitting, that's been, like, *it* for her. She's found her purpose in life."

"So you guys should do this!" Hannah cried. "I can pay you each twelve-fifty an hour. And even beyond that, it makes sense on like twenty-five different levels. Really, Scottie, I think it's an offer you can't refuse."

"So . . . I didn't," Scottie told Bella. She was cross-legged in the kitchen window seat, miserably hugging an orange, satin pillow to her chest. "I mean, I told Hannah I would check with you guys, but, basically, I said yes."

"Okay," Bella said carefully. Her fingers, which had been flying through her scarf, came to a rest as she stopped to think.

"So let's look at the positives and negatives," Bella said. "Positive, this would be a really neat thing to do. It would give Amanda exposure to a real designer. It would give me extra yarn money. And it would get *you* closer to Beck. Cuz we'd be working at the loft, right?"

"That thought had crossed my mind," Scottie said dryly.

"Negative," Bella said. "Beck's mad at his mom. And now you're hooking up with Hannah in the very enterprise that has already turned his life upside down."

Scottie squeezed the pillow so hard, she was surprised the seams didn't pop.

"When you put it that way," she wailed, "it sounds even worse."

"Oh!" Bella cried. She dropped her knitting, plopped onto the window seat, and grabbed both of Scottie's hands. Scottie let herself droop until her forehead was resting on Bella's shoulder.

• • Chicks with Sticks

Scottie could vaguely remember a time when such intimacy would have made her squirm; when she and her friends exchanged only stiff-legged, notched-at-the-waist hugs or tiny back pats. But in Bella's world, there was no sense in walking with her friends if it wasn't arm-in-arm. Her hugs were big, breezy, and constant.

Now Scottie found comfort in all that contact. She always seemed to see things more clearly in Bella's embrace.

Well, almost always. Now, even with Bella's fingers fluttering over her back, Scottie felt nothing but agitation.

"What should I do?" she croaked.

"You have to do what's right for you," Bella whispered. "Amanda will understand."

"So, I'll tell Hannah we can't do it," Scottie declared, pulling back to look into Bella's green eyes. "Then Beck won't think I've taken her side."

"On the other hand," Bella said as Eden sproinged into her lap with an aggressive *mrawr*, "if Beck really likes you, he should understand if you *do* decide to do it. Because it'd be a really big deal for Amanda—not to mention you, Scottie. I haven't seen you this excited about a knitty project in a while."

"That's just like you, B," Scottie said with a sad smile, "to go all Obi-Wan on me."

"Who?" Bella said distractedly. Eden was using his claws to crawl his way up to her shoulders and Bella was busy fighting him off.

"Doesn't matter," Scottie said, reaching out to pull Eden off of Bella's poor, pilled sweater. As she set the cat on the floor, he *mrawred* irritably, then stomped over to his food bowl to crunch sulkily through a snack. "The point is, you're right. On both counts. As the great Hannah B. says, *I gotta go with my gut.*"

The problem was, all Scottie's gut could seem to do was roil aimlessly. No matter how hard she searched her soul Sunday night, all she found was indigestion from all the funky things she'd eaten that day.

By bedtime, she was so desperate, she slipped her dream journal beneath her pillow.

Maybe I'll wake up remembering a dream that gives me all the answers, Scottie told herself hopefully. *That can't only happen in the movies, can it?*

Apparently, it could. Because when Scottie woke up the next day, all she could remember were the hours she'd tossed and turned in a state of anxious half-sleep. After slogging through her morning routine, she showed up—still unenlightened—in the Bread Factory's foyer at 7:40.

Since Beck wasn't there yet, Scottie dug a compact out of her Suki to do one last mirror check. Simultaneously, she despaired at the faint gray hollows beneath her eyes and pressed her lips together to make them more poochy. Then she leaned against the bank of mailboxes to wait.

Five minutes later, it was time to leave and he still hadn't arrived.

Don't panic, she told herself. *It's only 7:45 on the dot.*

And Beck's compulsive on-timeness? She shoved it out of her head. Until 7:49.

Then she felt her lip start to tremble.

No, she berated herself. *You're not allowed to cry. First of all, a boy I've known for about thirty seconds cannot possibly be cry-worthy. That's crazy—even if I did fall in like with him at first sight. I'm probably just hormonal.*

And second, Beck's probably gonna walk through that door in a minute. If I'm crying, he'll *think I'm hormonal, on top of being a back-stabber.*

She bit her bottom lip to steady it, not caring that she was messing up her lip gloss. She twisted toward the mailboxes to rest her forehead against their cool, slate-green metal. As she turned, a wad of flyers in the junk mail trough sliced at her hand. One of the flyers hit at the perfect angle to produce a paper cut alongside her fingernail.

"Damn," Scottie whispered. She put her stinging index finger into her mouth. With her free hand, she poked irritably at the flyers to tuck them back into the trough. Instead, they fell out, accordioning on the floor as if to spite her.

Scottie scowled and scooped them up. Before she could shove them back into place, though, a familiar logo jumped out at her. She gasped.

The sheaf of flyers? They were take-out menus—for Raja India.

It's a sign, Bella's voice squeaked in Scottie's head.

Feeling her face crumple, Scottie looked at her watch.

7:56. Beck wasn't showing up.

Her mind churning with questions, Scottie headed out the door toward the L stop by herself.

Maybe this time I should believe Bella, she thought. *This cannot be good.*

But Scottie held it together that morning in school. She *had* to. If she let her emotional guard down for an instant, she would burst into tears. Then minutes later (fate virtually guaranteed this) she would run into Beck in the hall, her face red, squashy, and tear-streaked.

That's all I need, Scottie thought as she grimly worked through a problem set in her first period pre-calc class, *for Beck to see my gross, crying face.*

Now it was Tay's voice she heard in her head.

"Oh, please," she said. *"If the guy can't hack your crying face or your stupid lavender stretch pants, who needs him? Besides, you know that's not what you're really worried about."*

The lead in Scottie's mechanical pencil snapped. The Tay-in-her-head was right. What Scottie was *really* worried about was that Beck would think she was a rat. The question was, which kind of rat? One who double-crossed her crush by helping out his mom? Or one who double-crossed her best friend by *not* taking the job?

Which is it gonna be?! Scottie wondered. She was gripping her blunted pencil so hard, her paper cut throbbed.

But she couldn't come up with an answer. Tay's voice had disappeared from her head. And her gut? It was still silent.

By lunchtime, Scottie was starving. Her body was, anyway. She could hear her stomach rumbling and feel a pinprick behind her eyes that told her a low-blood-sugar headache was heading her way.

Yet, in the cafeteria line, nothing appealed to her. Not even the super-mayonnaisey tuna sandwiches on squishy white bread that she could usually count on to be super-comforting.

Now they only promised tuna breath.

Finally, because the lunch line was backing up behind her, Scottie grabbed some French fries and a bowl of chili and headed for the Chicks' usual table. As soon as she sat down, she yanked her knitting out of her Suki. Since Buttered Toast was, well, toast, she'd started a lacy scarf over the weekend. The pattern was filled with tons of tiny eyelets and curving rows of purls. It was the kind of knitting you couldn't just zip through while watching *The OC*. It required counting and concentration.

As she spotted Bella and Amanda walking together toward their table, Scottie speared her first loop and dove into the complicated WIP. By the time her friends sat down, she was halfway into her knit zone. Her filmy little swatch had become as good as a brick wall.

"Hey," Amanda said, sitting down next to Scottie in a breeze of Kiehl's cucumber. Bella sat across the table holding a foil-wrapped packet. She unwrapped it to reveal a whole-wheat pita, bulging with veggies and fuzzy-looking alfalfa sprouts.

"Hi," Scottie murmured, not meeting Amanda's eyes.

"So guess what?" Amanda said. "Toby and I had a great chat this morning. It was almost like old times."

"That's fabulous!" Scottie said, glancing up from her knitting for an instant.

"Yeah," Amanda said. "I hope so. Maybe we just went through a little phase. And maybe it doesn't matter that we didn't have a date this weekend. I mean, he had tons of band practice because they've got a gig coming up. And of course, *I* had an S.S.O. to attend!"

"I'm *sure* it's all good," Scottie said, maybe a little too emphatically. "You and Toby love each other! That's all that matters."

"Yeah, I guess so. . . ." Amanda said, crunching thoughtfully on a carrot slice.

"Of course it does," Scottie insisted. And then she felt it—a lurching sensation that seemed almost physical.

It was her gut. Her gut was finally talking to her. It was saying, *Amanda has Toby, phase or no phase. She's also beautiful. And she has endless amounts of pocket money! She doesn't* need *this gig with Hannah.*

Not nearly as much as I need—or at least, want—Beck.

And just like that, Scottie knew what to do. She just had to figure how to do it.

"What're you working on?" Bella piped up.

"I'm doing that thing we saw online," Scottie said. "The super-wide scarf with all the lace. It's really hard."

"That's why they call it *Charlotte's Noose*," Amanda said.

"Tell me about it," Scottie said with an exaggerated sigh.

Across the table, Bella was looking at her pointedly. Scottie could feel it.

"Well, I guess you found some inspiration!" Bella said hopefully. "Then maybe you don't need—"

"Yeah," Scottie said, glancing quickly at Amanda. "Maybe I don't."

Bella looked from Scottie to Amanda, then nervously took a big bite of her veggie sandwich.

"Don't need what?" Amanda said. She'd been busy tossing vinaigrette into her grilled chicken salad, but she'd clearly detected the flicker of secrecy traveling between Scottie and Bella. "What's going on?"

"Nothing," Scottie said quickly.

"Well, excuse me for asking," Amanda said, looking hurt as she stabbed a cherry tomato with her fork.

"Sorry, it's just . . . Bella helped me yesterday when I was drama queening over Beck," Scottie said. "I did something that kind of rubbed him the wrong way, and of course, I freaked."

"Ohhh," Amanda said, patting Scottie's shoulder. "What was the drama? Tell."

(Knit two together)

"Eh, it's not worth going into," Scottie said with a shrug. "The point is, I know what to do about it now."

Scottie's eyes skimmed over Bella's questioning gaze to do a sweep of the cafeteria. Even though the school year was only a few weeks old, most people had already settled into habitual roosts. Jocks were stationed next to the food, for easy access to seconds and thirds. The theater geeks lined an open space in the middle of the room so they could bounce into it for impromptu, *Fame*-style dance routines. Poets and other broody types were hunched in the corners of the room, communing with their Moleskine journals. And A-list hotties—the hard-partying crowd that Amanda *used* to do lunch with—sat beneath the windows where the sun could best illuminate their highlighted locks and flawless complexions.

But where was Beck?

There he is!

He was sitting in the middle of it all, not with a clique but with two other seniors. Scottie couldn't quite type the guys except to say they seemed Beckish. They were more skinny than buff with shaggy hair, slouchy-hip clothes, and easy smiles.

Scottie felt her heart thump with nervous excitement. She turned to Bella and Amanda.

"Yup, I know what to do, now," she repeated. "I'll be back in a bit, 'kay?"

"Well, I can't promise your fries will be here when you get back," Amanda joked.

Scottie smiled absent-mindedly. In her mind, she was already crossing the vast cafeteria; she was already tapping Beck on the shoulder.

10 *(Weave in ends)

Except when it was *real?* When Scottie was actually traversing that long stretch of linoleum and reaching out to touch Beck's sharp shoulder blade? It wasn't nearly as dreamy as her fantasy. In fact, Scottie had the sudden urge to throw up.

Good thing I didn't eat those French fries, she thought as Beck turned and looked at her, his eyebrows raised.

"Can I talk to you?" Scottie asked. She hated how tremulous it came out.

Beck seemed to hesitate for a moment, but then he glanced behind her. Scottie figured he was sizing up the chasm of cafeteria she'd just crossed to get to him.

His eyebrows went down and he shrugged.

"Sure," he said quietly. He glanced at his new buds as he got to his feet. "Uh, I'm gonna take off, you guys."

"With a half a burrito left?!" One of the boys gawked, pointing at Beck's tray.

Scottie saw the two boys exchange a meaningful glance.

Okay, what does that *mean?* she thought. It was all she could do to interpret Beck's boy-speak. She couldn't even try to translate some other guy's.

Beck didn't seem interested in his friends' covert communiqués either. He grabbed his tray to take it over to the dishwashing window.

"Dude," the same guy squeaked. "You don't just *throw away* half a burrito! Leave it here. I'll finish it!"

"Sure," Beck said again. Then he turned to Scottie.

"Where do you wanna go?"

"Oh, um, well we could go out to the courtyard," she said.

"Sure," Beck said.

Okay, I think he's said "sure" about five times in the last two minutes, Scottie realized. *Is being overly agreeable a bad sign?*

As Scottie followed Beck toward the exit doors, she peeked over at Bella and Amanda. Of course, they were watching her. Amanda looked totally confused, but she waved and smiled sweetly. Bella smiled, too, but it was a wavery one, tinged with concern.

Scottie looked away quickly and ducked through the doors, focusing on the back of Beck's head to try to blot out Bella's worried eyes.

Outside, Scottie pointed to one of the benches that lined the dry, grassy courtyard behind the school.

"You wanna sit?" she asked.

"I'd rather walk, actually," Beck said. The courtyard led to a flight of stone stairs, and they led to the track and field. Both were packed with Starkers in P.E. but a little gravel walking path that wound around the track was mostly unoccupied. "I'm kind of restless. I don't know why."

Scottie was silent for a second, but as they headed down the steps, she figured *Well, if I've come this far . . .*

"Maybe you're restless because you're mad at me," she said quietly.

"Why would I be mad at you?" Beck said. He stopped halfway down the stairs and turned to frown at her.

"Because—I told your mom I'd do this knitty thing for her," Scottie said. "And you're not exactly thrilled with your mom these days."

Beck stared at Scottie for a second, then continued down the steps.

"No, I'm not thrilled with my mom," he said carefully. "But that doesn't have anything to do with you, Scottie."

• • Chicks with Sticks

Scottie followed him.

"Then why didn't you show up this morning?" she asked. "Weren't we supposed to go to school together?"

"I overslept," Beck said defensively.

"Oh."

"Okay," he blurted. "I guess I sort of overslept on purpose. Which is stupid, I know. I mean, you doing this thing for my mom should be *fine*. It's a job. It's a great opportunity for you and for your friend. She's the one with the learning disability, right?"

"Um, yeah," Scottie said. They landed on the walking path and began a loop around the playing fields. Beck was looking at the ground, his sneakers scuffing through the gravel with a rhythmic crunch.

Usually Scottie loved that sound, because it meant she was off the beaten path—tiptoeing over railroad ties to take a shortcut, slipping into an unpaved part of Lincoln Park, being on vacation on the pebble-strewn south shore of Lake Michigan . . .

But now the crunch felt like the tick-tock of a clock. Scottie had the duration of this walk to make things right with Beck. She felt a breathless fizz of pre-panic as she opened her mouth to speak.

"Listen," she half-whispered. "I don't want things to be weird between us."

Beck looked at her seriously.

"Me either," he said. "Because . . . Scottie? I *do* like surprises."

Scottie inhaled with a happy shudder. For *once*, she got Beck's boy-speak! He liked her, too!

This should only have made it easier for Scottie to move on to the Hannah issue. But when she opened her mouth, her throat suddenly felt dry and croaky.

Just say what you wanted to say, she ordered herself. *The gut finally spoke and it said one word—BECK. So just tell him!*

"Beck," she said, "I've decided that I'm not—"

"I want you to take the job," Beck interrupted in a red-faced rush.

(Knit two together)

"What?" they blurted together. Now Scottie was feeling an inner fizz of a different kind. She skidded to a halt and turned to face Beck.

"Yeah, at first I was all, 'Okay, I've met this really cool person and my mother swoops in and, like, *steals* her,'" Beck said, seeming a little breathless himself. "Pretty dumb, huh?"

"No!" Scottie said. "I can totally understand why you'd feel that way."

"And you don't even know my mother," Beck said. "She's got this way of . . . sucking people in."

"Oh, I can't relate at all," Scottie joked. "My mom is only this art goddess that everyone adores. I call her 'The Creator.'"

She wished she could tell Beck that maybe his mom wouldn't *always* be completely annoying; that it was possible for a person to actually *enjoy* having an artistic mom, once you got over the flakiness and the constant takeout.

But Beck was looking a little too intense for such a tangent. And besides, the last thing Scottie wanted to be talking about was their *mothers*.

Once again, Beck was so on the same page.

"Listen, whatever's going on with me and my mom doesn't matter," Beck said. "And I thought it was really cool that you wanted to take that gig for Amanda—that that was the first thing you thought of."

"Yeah," Scottie said, feeling a poke of guilt. After all, a few minutes ago, her gut had told her to forget about Amanda! "I guess it was."

"See, that's what I like about you," Beck said, suddenly going pink as they resumed their walk. "You're really, I don't know, selfless. I mean, that first day we met? You didn't know anything about me. I could have been some total perv or a dumb pothead or something. Yet, you just jumped in and offered me a walk to school, not to mention a Stark 101 tutorial."

"Yeah, and a lot of good that did ya," Scottie said. "I spent so much time TPing the L stop with yarn that I didn't give you any dirt. You were on your own, navigating the no-flush third-floor bathrooms, the putrid gym uniforms, and the dead bunny painted on the cafeteria wall."

• • Chicks with Sticks

"Well, you meant well, anyway," Beck said with a little laugh.

The thing is, I didn't, Scottie thought. *I was just trying to pounce on you in your vulnerable state and make you my insta-boyfriend.*

Between her Amanda-based guilt and her Beck-based guilt, Scottie was starting to feel pummeled from all sides. Maybe that was why it was so easy to swerve into irrationality.

You know what? she realized. *Beck's right! I pounced knowing nothing about him except that he was unbearably cute!*

Before she could stop herself, she blurted out, "You're *not* a pothead, are you?"

"No," Beck said with one of those crooked smiles.

"Or a perv?"

"Scottie—no!" he said with a laugh. "I'm kind of a film geek, I'll admit to that. I think I miss the Film Forum more than my old apartment. But other than that, I guess I'm relatively normal. Boring even."

"No," Scottie contradicted him. "Not boring."

"Well, not to belabor the issue," Beck said, scraping to a halt again, "but you barely know me. How do you know I'm not a total snore?"

They'd stopped beneath a canopy of tree branches at the far end of the track. After the blaze of the noon sun, not to mention all of Scottie's guilt, the quick blanket of shade felt wonderful. As her eyes adjusted to the dimness, the details of Beck's face went blurry. She couldn't see the hazel in his irises anymore. The waves of his hair became just a dark halo and his thick eyebrows, just slashes.

Maybe that was why Scottie felt she could say anything she wanted to him. With that breezy blanket wrapped around her like armor, she could be brave.

"I just know," she said, her voice a little raspy. "I knew that first moment that we met, that you were, well, a very interesting person. To me, anyway."

"Are you saying you're . . . interested in me?" Beck said.

From some other boy, like Tom Castellucci, the words would have been a smarmy bit of flirtation, tossed out without a thought, or any real intention.

But from Beck, it was an earnest question. Scottie's face flushed. If not for the cool shade, she might have melted right into her hand-knitted socks. She couldn't bring herself to answer Beck's question out loud, so she just nodded, her eyes on his scuffed leather sneakers.

The sneakers crunched in the gravel as Beck took a step toward her.

"Do you want to go out with me sometime?" he asked quietly.

This made Scottie look up.

"You mean, on a date?" she blurted, before she could bite the words back.

"Um, yeah," Beck stammered. He shoved his hands into his jeans pockets, pressing his shoulders up so far, they grazed the ends of his shaggy hair. "I've heard that's the way people do things around here. Y'know, dinner. Movies. One milkshake, two straws, that sort of thing."

"You want to go for milkshakes?" Scottie said dumbly. She was so stunned, she'd only heard the last bit of what he'd said.

"Um, no, not actually," Beck said with a lame laugh. "I was thinking we could go see *Annie Hall*? It's, you know, early, pre-skank Woody Allen. It's playing at the Music Box all week."

Beck took a deep breath and exhaled audibly.

Now it was Scottie's turn to go red and start stammering.

She'd always imagined what this would be like, the moment that some boy asked her out on an actual date. In fact, she'd dreamed up several responses. In one, Scottie didn't miss a beat, breezily answering, "Sure, that sounds fun!"

In another, she was coy and confident, smiling with closed lips and breathing, "Oh . . . why not?"

There was also the beatific, "I'd love to."

But Scottie's favorite—and most remote—fantasy had her gently and suavely surprising the boy with a kiss.

That was the scenario that Scottie had replayed in her mind the most. Of course, she'd never, *ever* intended to actually do it! But apparently, now that Scottie's gut had had a taste of power? It seemed to have taken over! Suddenly, Scottie found herself puckering up and aiming for Beck's lips.

Or trying to anyway. But when a guy is a good eight inches taller than you, it's kind of hard to plant a gentle, suave, surprise kiss on him. Scottie had to grip each of Beck's shoulders and stand on tiptoe to crane for his mouth.

Unfortunately, Beck was just as surprised by Scottie's pounce as she was, and all that gripping and craning knocked him off balance. Scottie—teetering on her tiptoes—was *already* off balance. After a millisecond of gazing, panicked, into each other's eyes, they both toppled over into the mulchy dirt next to the path! Along the way, Scottie's forehead thunked into Beck's chin.

"Ow!" Beck said as the back of his head hit the dirt. Gracelessly, Scottie landed next to him. She rolled onto her back and stared up at the treetops, shocked at herself and too mortified to look at Beck.

"Oh my God," she groaned, still looking at the sky. "I'm so sorry. That was so—"

Desperate? Presumptuous? Completely and utterly spazzy?!

"—um, dumb. Of me. I mean, I don't know what I was thinking. Are you okay?"

Beck sat up and rubbed his chin. Now he was in Scottie's line of vision, so she had no choice but to look at him. He seemed to be trying hard—*really* hard—not to laugh.

"You know what *I* think you were thinking?" he broached.

Scottie sat up, picked a few dead leaves out of her hair, and looked at him miserably. Her head was hurting, but she couldn't tell if it was the thunk or the humiliation at fault.

"I think you'd *really* like to see *Annie Hall* this weekend," Beck declared with a big grin.

Scottie rolled her eyes before slapping her hand over them.

Listening to Beck chuckle, she groaned. "You're right. I do. I mean, I did. If you've, uh, changed your mind, I understand."

Beck didn't answer.

Oh my God, he's considering it! Scottie cringed. *Okay, maybe he'll just leave before I open my eyes. Then I won't have to watch him go. And I can sit here and try to figure out a way to* never *run into him at the bread factory agai—*

Scottie jumped as Beck's fingers closed around her wrist. Gently he pulled her hand away from her face. Her eyes snapped open.

Beck's face was remarkably close to hers. By now, she'd adjusted to the gloom beneath the trees, and she could see the scrunchy lines around his eyes, the way his hair fuzzed a little at the temples, an almost-dimple she'd never noticed in his cheek. . . .

"It looks like what we've got here," Beck said, a shy smile making that almost-dimple go a little deeper, "is mutual interest."

"Looks that way," Scottie whispered. She felt a smile of her own breaking through her embarrassment.

"So, maybe," Beck said, taking a deep breath, "we should try this again."

He angled his head downward. His eyes closed.

He was going to *kiss* her.

And then he did.

Beck's lips were just as soft as Scottie had imagined. One of his hands rose to cradle the back of her head as the other alighted on her cheek. All the while, he never stopped kissing her. Scottie wrapped her arms around his slim waist and thought, *You'd never know he just ate a burrito. He tastes like honey.*

After that, she didn't think anything at all, because the moment was too warm and wonderful to analyze.

For once.

Scottie wasn't sure how long they sat there in the shade and kissed. But by the time she and Beck started walking back to the school, the Starkers on the playing field were plodding gratefully to the locker room.

And Beck was holding her hand.

And Scottie, it appeared, had her first boyfriend.

KNITCHICK16: I STILL can't get over it.

HALO2CHAMP: Dude, it's been like 9 hours since The Most Legendary Kiss of All Time. R u planning on getting over it any time soon?

Scottie laughed out loud, then fished a mint Milano out of the bag propped on her desk next to her. Between walking home from school with Beck (followed by more kissing) and settling in for a jammie-clad evening of giddy IM'ing, she'd made a celebratory Jewel run. In addition to the cookies, she'd bought a giant box of Golden Grahams.

KNITCHICK16: No! This part is too fun. I'm still tingly.

HALO2CHAMP: Tell me u did not just use the word TINGLY. Maybe you should e Bella instead of me. She's a tingly kind of gal. Me? Not so much.

KNITCHICK16: C'mon, Tay. TRY and tell me u didn't feel like this after u kissed John the first time!

HALO2CHAMP: My tingles are my biz.

KNITCHICK16: Whatevs. So R u going 2 do it?

HALO2CHAMP: Do what?!?

KNITCHICK16: Are you going to do the lace-knitting thing for Hannah with me, Bella, and Amanda?

KNITCHICK16: Why, what did you THINK I meant?

HALO2CHAMP: OK, that would also fall into the category of MY BIZ. Anyway, the answer to both questions is no.

KNITCHICK16: Oh, Tay. Pleeeeeeeeeease? Hannah really wants all 4 of us.

HALO2CHAMP: SO not my thing! Besides, now that you're in lurve with Beck, u R gonna spend all your time there macking with him, leaving the rest of us 2 toil. This must be how those kids in sweat-shops feel.

KNITCHICK16: All macking (hee!) will take place off-duty. Hel-lo. His MOTHER will B there.

HALO2CHAMP: Oh, forgot.

HALO2CHAMP: Still not doing it tho. I'm NOT a lace kind of girl. Besides, I'm making myself a Ribby Cardi. It's already kicking my butt. I don't need more knitty headaches.

KNITCHICK16: Thanx a lot. Guess John'll b happy. He'll have u all 2 himself.

The moment Scottie clicked the SEND button, her hand flew to her mouth.

What did I just say?

Cringing, she dropped her half-nibbled cookie back into the bag. Regret was washing over her—and growing worse as the pause between her SEND and the bubbly chime of Tay's reply grew longer . . . and longer. Finally—

HALO2CHAMP: Maybe I will do it.

KNITCHICK16: Are u sure? I don't want 2 guilt u into it.

HALO2CHAMP: Nah. Fact is, I could use a little girl time, sans John. I mean, I lurve spending time w him, but John + knitting is weird-ing me out a little.

KNITCHICK16: I know.

KNITCHICK16: I mean, u were pretty edgy at Joe last week.

HALO2CHAMP: I know. I suck.

KNITCHICK16: No you don't!!!! I'm having the same issue with my sister. She actually called from NY this afternoon, wanting 2 know if she *really* had 2 worry about gauge. Thinks swatches R beneath her.

HALO2CHAMP: Ah, remember when we thought we were above

swatches? Then I made that Booga bag that could double as a duvet cover.

HALO2CHAMP: Anyway, u r right. That's annoying.

KNITCHICK16: If I didn't have a BOYFRIEND in my life, I'd be REALLY annoyed. But y'know, the tingles really soothe my pain. I can honestly say that I'm 95% happy right now!

HALO2CHAMP: Whoa, you're already using the BF word?

KNITCHICK16: Hello? Have you not heard about the kissing? The hand-holding? The date? The TINGLES?

HALO2CHAMP: I heard, I heard! Enuf with the tingles already!

KNITCHICK16: My point is—clearly, this is a boyfriend/girlfriend sitch.

HALO2CHAMP: Hey, as long as u guys r on the same page, fine by me.

Well, *duh*, Scottie thought, rolling her eyes. *We are so on the same page. That goes without saying.*

HALO2CHAMP: But dude, if you guys keep moving this fast, you're gonna b eloping by Thanksgiving.

KNITCHICK16: Would that b so wrong? ;-)

HALO2CHAMP: Just don't expect me 2 wear a bridesmaid dress. Or ANY dress, for that matter. Btw, what's with the 95% happy? Aren't u 100% happy, now that you're in lurve?

Scottie sighed.

Maybe I'd be at 100 percent, she thought, *if I felt like I deserved it.*

But she couldn't get around the fact that she'd been most un-Chick-like today, not once, but twice. She'd tossed aside Amanda's fashion design dreams (or tried to, anyway) in favor of *her* dream for a boyfriend. And just now, she'd used what she'd learned from *In a Sknit* against Tay.

(Knit two together)

It only made Scottie feel worse that both scenarios had somehow twisted in her favor. She'd gotten to accept Hannah's job offer *and* snag her son. She'd manipulated Tay into joining the lace brigade, and Tay had no idea what had given Scottie the upper hand.

And she'd done it *all* in the name of a boy, which would have disappointed Bella horribly—if she'd known.

But she didn't know. None of the Chicks did. Scottie had managed to emerge from this crazy day with all her friendships still solid, and a boyfriend to boot. She was having so much cake and eating it, too, her mint Milanos felt like overkill. Crunching the cookie bag closed, she tossed it into her desk drawer. As she slammed the drawer shut, she wondered what she'd do if she had a second chance; if she could turn back the clock and do it all differently.

Would she?

HALO2CHAMP: Hello????? U still there?

The fact was, Scottie *couldn't* take any of her actions back, even if she wanted to. So she did her best to shake off her guilt—and neatly dodged Tay's question.

KNITCHICK2: Whattup with the "lurve?"
HALO2CHAMP: Duh, it's a Woody Allen reference, in honor of your "Annie Hall" date! You should start studying up on that kind of thing, y'know. Now that u r dating a film geek.
KNITCHICK16: I'm dating a film geek. I'M DATING. I still can't get over it.
HALO2CHAMP: OMG, isn't this where we started? You're outta control. See your tingly (ew) self 2morrow.
KNITCHICK16: Kewl. Don't forget, we start at Hannah's on Sunday.
HALO2CHAMP: Okaaaaaay. Buh-bye.

Scottie felt drained when she logged off. Without the burbles and chimes of the e-chat, her room felt eerily silent. She pressed at the paper cut next to her nail. Had it only been that morning that she'd gotten it?! The cut still stung a bit, but it was already starting to heal.

Or maybe I just can't feel it, because being in lurve means no more pain! Scottie giggled to herself.

But it was a nervous laugh. Because part of her still couldn't wrap her brain around all this. Even with Beck's kisses still vivid in her mind, even after all the exultant IM'ing, Scottie couldn't quite believe that she really had a boyfriend.

Nudging nervously at her cut again, she shot a rueful glance at her still-blank dream diary on her nightstand.

Well, at least I know today wasn't a dream, she thought. *Otherwise I wouldn't have remembered it.*

Scottie had a sudden urge to dial Beck's number, which she'd keyed into her cell's address book only a few hours ago. Just to say hi.

That's it. Just to say hi—and make sure he hasn't changed his mind, Scottie thought. *Or realized that he only kissed me in a fit of post-move dementia. Or met that tattooed girl in 4-H and liked her better.*

Scottie was being ridiculous, she knew. She was also poking at her paper cut so much it was starting to bleed! As she dashed to the bathroom to grab a Band-Aid, she argued with herself.

You can't call him! she insisted. *How desperate would that be? The relationship is practically fetal! Must play it cool.*

She nodded firmly as she returned to her bedroom. CC scampered into the room after her. Scottie scooped her up gratefully.

My cat and some knitting, she told herself, plunking CC onto her bed. *That's what I need to get my mind off Beck.*

Scottie swiped Bella's half-finished hat off her nightstand and pulled a basket of yarn scraps out of her stash. She flopped onto the bed next to CC and began to paw through the countless bits of wool swimming around the basket, trying to decide what color stripe to add to the hat next.

Five minutes later, she was still pondering. She rolled her eyes and tossed her scrap basket to the floor.

Okay, until I talk to Beck, she sighed, *I'm clearly useless.*

She fished her cell phone out of her Suki. Her stomach fluttered as she scrolled through her contact list. There was BECK near the top, nestled between AMANDA and BELLA.

As Scottie hovered her bandaged finger over the SEND button, her paper cut throbbed painfully.

Is it another sign? Scottie wondered. *Am I screwing this up before I even begin?*

She had no idea what to do. But she knew who would. She returned to her phone's contact list and scrolled up.

AMANDA.

She was just about to hit SEND when her computer burbled. Someone was IM'ing.

She frowned.

That's probably Jordan, e'ing to ask me the difference between merino and alpaca or something equally annoying.

Scottie grabbed her laptop, propped it against her pillows, then flopped stomach-down on the bed. Lazily, she dragged her cursor over to her IM window.

*DUSTMEMORIES: **Hey Scottie. It's me, Beck!**

When people talked about their eyes bugging out of their head, Scottie'd always thought they were exaggerating. But now—with her freshly minted BF winking at her from her iBook monitor—she could almost feel her eyeballs bulging.

"No way!" she screamed, bouncing up to her hands and knees on the mattress.

•• Chicks with Sticks

A distant, male voice responded.

"Scottie?! What's wrong!"

Scottie froze and clapped a hand over her mouth, imagining for one irrational instant that it was Beck responding to her bellow—right through the sixteen or so brick walls between their two lofts.

In the next moment—when she heard the *swish-swish-swish* of her dad's suede slippers making their way across the apartment—Scottie, of course, realized that it was her parents who'd heard her.

For about the thousandth time, Scottie cursed the open-air layout of her loft.

"I'm *fine,* Dad," she called into the empty space above her bedroom wall. "I just read something surprising, that's all."

"Well, sweetie. . ." Her dad opened her bedroom door and peered at her blearily over his lime-green reading glasses. "It's after ten. Could you try to keep the outbursts to a minimum?"

"I have a better idea," Scottie proposed. "Let's call the drywall guy tomorrow. He could seal off my bedroom walls and then I wouldn't bother you a bit with my, um, outbursts."

"Scottie, we've talked about this," her dad sighed. "That would interrupt—"

"—the aesthetic flow of the loft," Scottie finished wearily. "I know, I know."

"So what's so earthshaking in there?" her dad wondered, nodding at her laptop.

Scottie gasped and snatched up the computer. She'd almost forgotten! *DUSTMEMORIES was still flashing expectantly in her IM window.

"Urgent IM, Dad," she said briskly, hopping off the bed and sitting down in her desk chair. "Sorry I freaked you out. But I've really gotta answer this."

"Whatevs," her dad said with a grin, before blowing her a goodnight kiss.

(Knit two together) 139

Oh no, Scottie groaned. *Don't tell me my parents are gonna go through a slanguage phase. I've really got to stop letting them watch UPN with me.*

Shaking her head, she propped her laptop on the desk and began to type.

KNITCHICK16: Hi there. How's ur evening?

Scottie sighed as she hit the ENTER button. She loved how IM could make you sound breezy even when your fingers were trembling and you were eying the wastepaper basket, just in case your mint Milanos decided to make a reappearance.

*DUSTMEMORIES: Hey. I was about 2 give up on u.
KNITCHICK16: Sorry, I was

Just being a complete spaz? Scottie offered in her head.

KNITCHICK16: in the middle of a yarn emergency.
*DUSTMEMORIES: Sounds ugly.
KNITCHICK16: Well, it's not like my new WIP was eaten by a train or anything, so I think I'll live.
*DUSTMEMORIES: Okay, though I DID just laugh out loud, I refuse 2 write LOL. I hate the LOL.

Scottie's mouth dropped open. She swiveled in her desk chair and looked at her cat, who was purring and licking at a paw.

"Ceece, if I wasn't in lurve before, I totally am now."

CC looked bored and switched paws.

Scottie shrugged.

"Oh well," she said. "I shouldn't expect you to understand. Now that you're fixed and all."

CC gave her a squint, spun around on the duvet, and curled up for a nap, her tail pointed straight at Scottie.

"She's never gonna forgive me for that operation," Scottie murmured, grinning as she wrote her reply.

KNITCHICK16: Say no more. I'm very anti-LOL.
*DUSTMEMORIES: So with all the, uh, stuff going on 2day, I realized we didn't make an Annie Hall plan.
*DUSTMEMORIES: What's your rents' policy on weeknight dates?

Scottie bit her lower lip and shook her head wildly to keep from shouting out again.

So I don't even have to wait for the weekend to see him? she screamed inside. *OhmiGod, I'm so glad I played it cool. Well, sort of cool, anyway. Okay, I was a total spaz, but thanks to the timing gods, Beck has no idea.*

As for her parents' dating policy? *Scottie* had no idea. The pathetic truth was that the subject hadn't ever come up. But Scottie wasn't about to tell Beck *that!*

KNITCHICK16: My parents have a crazy home-by-sundown system. Which pretty much means I spend the winter getting in trouble. The sun's been known 2 set at 4:30 on certain days in January.
*DUSTMEMORIES: Okay, I'm literally crying now. Tears are raining upon my keyboard.

Scottie laughed quietly as she typed.

KNITCHICK16: Sorry. The truth hurts.
KNITCHICK16: Anyway, the sun doesn't set THAT early these days.

Scottie held her breath as she waited for the chortle of Beck's reply.

*DUSTMEMORIES: So want 2 go 2 an early show on Wednesday? There's one at 5:30 . . .

Scottie grinned. She didn't even have to sift through her scripted date responses to know just what she wanted to say.

KNITCHICK16: I'd love to.
*DUSTMEMORIES: Cool! See you in the a.m.? You still have some 'splaining 2 do about that dead rabbit on the cafeteria wall. I was forced to get a vegetarian burrito 4 lunch 2day.
KNITCHICK16: I promise 2 leave my WIP at home so we can talk. See u in the a.m.
*DUSTMEMORIES: K. Good night.
KNITCHICK16: Buh-bye.

Scottie stared at the blinking *DUSTMEMORIES until it disappeared with a watery *plunk*. Then she slapped her hands on both cheeks and drummed her bare toes on the floor! She was so happy, she thought she might explode.

Suddenly she was ravenous, too. She flung open her desk drawer and grabbed her bag of cookies. Clamping one of the Milanos between her teeth, she danced over to her bed and did a giddy backward flop onto it. She flopped so hard that she catapulted her hat in progress onto the floor, and nearly toppled CC as well.

Eow! the kitty squawked, sounding a lot like her mother, Monkey.

"Just the opposite, Ceece," Scottie murmured happily. Her throbbing finger, her smarting conscience—they'd all flown out of her mind to the tune of a computerized raindrop.

"It wasn't a dream," Scottie whispered, hugging her kitten to her chest. "Today really happened. I'm never gonna be the same again."

11 * (Work sts in patt as set)

"Scottie, you *always* do this," Amanda said the next morning at school. She and Scottie were doing their pre-school root through their lockers while Bella sat on the floor at their feet, working her magic on a yarnover-filled shawl. While Amanda juggled her lipstick and cell phone, Scottie scarfed down a pudding cup that she'd just fished out of her bag lunch.

"I always do what?" Scottie protested after she'd swallowed a chocolatey spoonful.

"Totally spaz out," Amanda said, pooching her lips to sweep on a coat of pinky-beige lipstick. As she pulled a tube of clear gloss out of her makeup case, she and Bella exchanged a knowing grin.

"Okay, *how* am I still spazzing?" Scottie sputtered. "For once in my life, I'm feeling totally together. Hello? Did I not just walk to school with my new boyfriend? Do I not have a date with said boyfriend tomorrow night?"

"And are you not eating chocolate pudding for breakfast?" Bella said from her perch on the floor. She was gazing—with a combination of disapproval and yearning—at Scottie's snack pack.

"Um," Scottie mumbled through another mouthful of pudding, "yesh."

"Because you were too giddy about walking to school with Beck this morning to eat at home," Amanda said, smugly lining her lips with a gold-tipped pencil. "You couldn't eat anything. But now that he's gone, you're ravenous."

Scottie stared at Amanda for a moment before groaning.

"You're right," she wailed, before taking another quick bite of pudding. "I'm *such* a spaz. Do you think everybody can tell, you guys? Do you think *Beck* can tell?"

"How could he?" Bella said. "The spazzy you is the only you he knows. He probably just thinks you have a really fast metabolism or something."

"Um, thanks, I guess," Scottie sighed.

"Relax," Amanda breezed, zipping up her makeup bag and tossing it into her purse. "First of all, Beck is clearly smitten with you."

"Really?" Scottie glowed. She blushed as she scraped at the sides of her pudding cup to get every last morsel. "You really think so?"

Amanda only rolled her eyes at Scottie's shameless fish-for-a-compliment and added, "And second, spazzing is totally normal at this point in a relationship. I lost five pounds when Toby and I first started dating."

She gave her cell phone a frown before she turned the ringer off in preparation for class and slipped it into her purse. "Of course, that poundage is all back now."

Now it was Scottie and Bella who were exchanging glances.

"Um," Scottie said guiltily, "did you talk to To—"

"No," Amanda cut her off. She began rummaging in her purse for something else. "No, he didn't call this morning, but that's because he had a big exam today. He probably pulled an all-nighter studying. It's no biggie."

"Right," Scottie said, a touch too enthusiastically. "No biggie."

Although now that she herself had a boyfriend, she didn't really buy that. When it came to Beck, *everything* seemed like a biggie. Every chat. Every brush of their hands against one another as they walked to and from the L stop. Every kiss . . .

Scottie went melty as she reminisced—only for about the dozenth time—about her latest encounter with Beck's lips that morning in the foyer. It had been so natural, Scottie felt like she'd been kissing for weeks.

And after all the months I wasted worrying about my first spit-swap! Scottie thought with an eye-roll. *Like . . . how would I know which way to angle my head? And what if I was breathing through my nose (my mouth being obviously occupied) and it whistled?! What was I supposed to do then? And then there was the whole breath question. Would it be better to pop mints constantly to make sure I was minty fresh at all times? Or would that be too wonkish—*

"Oh. My. God!"

Amanda's disgusted voice booted Scottie out of her daydream so soundly that she yelped.

"What?!" she cried, her eyes still out-of-focus from all the kissing imagery. "I wasn't spazzing, I swear!"

Of course, when her vision *did* unfuzz? Scottie realized that Amanda wasn't even looking at her. She was staring at her Palm Pilot, her just-glossed mouth hanging open.

"I can't believe I forgot. . . ." she muttered.

"Uh-oh," Bella said, stashing her WIP in her backpack and springing to her feet. "Did you forget about a test or something? Do you want help with some last-minute cramming?"

"No, no," Amanda sighed. Her outrage had quickly turned into weariness. "This is an after-school thing. Ugh! I don't know why I agreed . . ."

"Amanda!" Scottie said, wild with curiosity. "What *is* it?"

She neatly swiped Amanda's Palm out of her hand and looked at the screen.

5–7 P.M. TABLE DUTY @ BENEFIT.

"Okay, still confused." Scottie shrugged, handing the Palm back to Amanda.

"It's one of my mom's ridiculous pre-debutante things," Amanda wailed. "In order to *earn* my place as a member of Chicago society I have to do community service."

"Well, that doesn't sound so bad," Bella chirped. "Hey, maybe you could go put together a stitch 'n bitch in a nursing home. An ElderFrogs! That would be nice!"

"No, no," Amanda said, waving off Bella's brainstorm. "Bellissima, the country club isn't interested in community service that actually *serves*. It's just an excuse to have a party. A benefit party, yeah. But after all the invitations, decorations, and canapés have been paid for, there's hardly anything left for the cause of the week."

"So you have to go to this party, I take it?" Scottie said.

"I have to *work* at the party," Amanda said. "Which means sitting behind a table, wearing an uncomfortable dress, smiling until my cheeks go numb, and handing out the goodie bags."

"Goodie bags?!" Bella exclaimed.

"Oh yes," Amanda sighed. "Those who give, like to get."

"Oh," Bella said, sounding completely confused.

"This was *so* not what I was in the mood for tonight," Amanda complained. "I was dreaming about Ethel's chocolates, my WIP, the couch, and my new *Sex and the City* box set."

"Poor you," Bella sighed. "I still don't understand why you have to do this debutante thing when you hate it so much."

"Oh, I don't *have* to," Amanda snarked. "The only thing that'll happen if I don't is every one of my female ancestors will come back to haunt me in their moldy old white dresses. *Plus* my mom will never let me hear the end of it. *And* my dad will cut me out of the trust fund. That's all. All because I refused to go to a few parties in long white gloves."

"Well, when you put it that way," Scottie said with a wry smile, "tonight doesn't seem that bad, right? I mean, being haunted by dead debutantes definitely sounds worse than giving out goodie bags."

"I guess so," Amanda sighed. But she still looked miserable. *So mis-*

erable, that Scottie's Beck-based euphoria actually receded for a moment. She felt Amanda's sadness—over Toby and over this ridiculous party—in her gut.

"Hey," she blurted before she could change her mind, "do you want company at this benefit thing?"

Amanda and Bella both stopped in their tracks and stared at her.

"What?" Amanda gaped.

"I'm saying," Scottie said, trying to sound breezy, "I could go with you tonight. I'm not as entertaining as Carrie Bradshaw, but—"

"Are you kidding?" Amanda squealed, cutting Scottie off with a big hug. "You're totally throwing yourself on your sword for me! Are you *sure* you want to do this?"

"Jeez," Scottie laughed, loving Amanda's glee. "You act like we're going to war. It's just a party. How bad can it be?"

She should have *known* not to ask.

After school, Scottie and Amanda went straight to Amanda's condo and announced their plan to Mrs. Scott—who responded to the news as if someone had offered her a hunk of stinky gefilte fish on a sheet of newspaper.

"But Amanda, darling," she said, following the girls as they hustled into Amanda's bedroom. Her arms were folded over her chest and one perfect, blond eyebrow was jutting into her Botoxed forehead. "As much as I'd love to have Scottie join us, we had your party outfit fitted months ago. What ever will Scottie wear?"

"I thought of that!" Amanda said proudly, marching to the closet. "She can wear that suit you got me at Nieman-Marcus. The one I outgrew before I could wear it."

Amanda fished around in her crammed closet for a moment before pulling out a plastic-wrapped A-line skirt and a jacket with a mandarin collar.

"Gee, let me guess where you outgrew it," Scottie said, pointing morosely at the barely-darted chest of the jacket.

"Whatever," Amanda burbled, thrusting the painfully tasteful, chocolate brown ensemble at Scottie. "It'll look cute on you. And since it doesn't fit me anymore, you can keep it."

"Cool," Scottie said. "My parents are having some folks from the Mayflower Society over to the loft for tea next weekend. This'll be *perfect*."

While she and Amanda doubled over laughing, Mrs. Scott's face went stony. Well, ston*ier*.

"Amanda," she barked. "I'm very glad that Scottie is willing to keep you company at the benefit. Lord *knows* you've been complaining about it enough. But I can *not* have the two of you chortling your way through the party. It would be insulting not only to the guests, but also to the cause."

"Oh," Scottie said, straining to swallow her giggles. "Um, I forgot to ask. What is the cause?"

"We're raising funds for a monument in Lincoln Park," Mrs. Scott said, brushing an invisible speck of lint off her sleeve.

"A monument to what?"

Amanda answered this time.

"As a matter of fact," she said, a chuckle barely contained in her voice, "it's to the Chicagoan descendants of people who came over on the Mayflower!"

"Oh!" Scottie squeaked. She clamped her jaw shut and frowned as hard as she could, but with one look at Amanda's already-tearing eyes, she lost it.

The girls laughed so hard they fell into each other's arms.

"Girls!" Mrs. Scott said sternly. "If you can't get a hold of yourselves, I'm afraid Scottie will have to go home."

"No!" Amanda cried. "We'll keep it together, Mom, I promise. Deb's honor."

Amanda held up three fingers and contorted her face into a semblance of seriousness until, apparently satisfied, Mrs. Scott left the room. Only when she'd *clicked, clicked, clicked* her way down the hallway to get ready for the party herself did Scottie begin giggling again.

"Deb's honor?" she snorted. "Hello, you *have* no deb's honor."

"But my mother doesn't know that, does she?" Amanda said with a smug grin. "She still thinks my genes will shine through."

"If mine do," Scottie groaned, "people are gonna be mighty confused."

She pulled her face into a haughty mask and looked down her nose at Amanda.

"Scottie *Shearer*, did you say?" she warbled in the upper-crusty accent of an American aristocrat. "How *interesting*. I didn't know they had *Jews* on the Mayflower!"

"Stop!" Amanda shrieked, gripping her sides as she collapsed into another fit of giggles. "You're so gonna get me in trouble."

"And you love it," Scottie giggled. "Gimme the zoot suit. Let's get ready."

Of course, once Scottie had strapped herself into her suit, pantyhose, pinchy-toed pumps, and more makeup than she'd ever worn in her life, she was feeling a *lot* less giggly. The girls' arrival at the party—held in a completely fussed-out ballroom at the Drake Hotel and mostly populated by white-haired people sipping gimlets—knocked the last of the humor out of her.

In fact, the first thing she glimpsed as she and Amanda wandered the fringes of the room made her gasp in horror.

"What's that thing?!" she whisper-screamed in Amanda's ear, pointing fearfully at a dowager strolling past them.

"What's *what*?" Amanda replied in alarm.

"The thing wrapped around that woman's neck," Scottie said. "It's some *animal* eating its own tail."

"Oh yeah," Amanda said, sounding bored now. "The self-cannibalizing fox. Or mink or chinchilla or whatever. It's called a stole and they're back in vogue, apparently. Never went *out* of vogue for ladies in their eighties. They're totally gross, but get used to it. You'll see a lot of 'em tonight."

"Ew," Scottie complained, averting her eyes from the grisly scarf. "You think she's never heard of PETA? Or even faux fur?"

"Channeling Bella, are you?" Amanda said sweetly. "Well, here's the thing. When you're worth half a billion dollars like Mrs. Fox Stole over there? You don't have to worry about PETA. You don't have to worry about *anything*."

Amanda was right. Scottie had never seen a more self-satisfied expression than the one on Mrs. Fox Stole's finely powdered face.

"And guess what else I know about her," Amanda said with a weary shake of her head. "She always takes *two* goodie bags from these things."

"No way!" Scottie breathed.

"Oh, you wouldn't believe," Amanda said. She sighed, swiped a couple smoked salmon puffs off a passing tray, and handed one to Scottie. "That's one of the reasons I hate these things. The smugness is suffocating!"

"*Tscha,*" Scottie said. She shifted uncomfortably from one high-heeled foot to the other and ate her salmon puff carefully, terrified that she'd dribble phylo down her front.

"The other thing I hate," Amanda said, "is not being able to knit. People-watching is *much* more satisfying with a pair of sticks in your hands, isn't it?"

"Wait a minute," Scottie said. "You never said anything about not knitting!"

She popped open her purse and thrust it beneath Amanda's nose. In it, she'd stuffed three balls of yarn and a sheaf of needles in addition to her own needles, and her WIP, Charlotte's Noose.

"No way!" Amanda shouted, before slapping a hand over her mouth. Even her hand couldn't hide her grin, though.

Scottie put on her haughty aristocrat accent again.

"I assume," she purred, "that this, how do you put it, *goodie bag* table is draped in the finest linens?"

"But, of course," Amanda replied with a giggle.

"Then let us make haste to it, and begin stitching and bitching undercover!"

The girls quickly cruised the buffets, filling a dainty glass plate with all the sweets it would hold. Then they stationed themselves behind the goodie bag table next to the ballroom's main entrance. The long table was filled with boxy gold bags that were fastened with gold net ribbons. More importantly, it was also covered in a voluminous white and gold tablecloth.

"So, what'll it be?" Scottie asked, giving Amanda a peek into her bag.

"Hmm!" Amanda said as she pawed through Scottie's wares. Finally, she plucked out a puff of cotton-candy-colored tendrils. "I'll take this baby-weight stuff and some number threes. I can do some lace swatches to practice for our gig with Hannah B!"

Scottie felt her cheeks flush as she remembered, with a stab of shame, how ready she'd been to chuck the lace job that Amanda was so excited about.

And even if giving out goodie bags and watching foxes chase themselves around the necks of wrinkled millionaires *was* a penance of sorts, Scottie felt like she needed to do more.

"Hannah's going to *adore* you, you know," she said pulling out her WIP.

"Oh really," Amanda said as she quickly cast a series of baby-fine loops onto her needle. "What makes you so sure?"

"Well," Scottie began as she dug into her own filmy project, "she definitely doesn't go by the book. And neither do you."

"Got that right," Amanda said, poking fun at her learning disability with a devilish smile.

"I meant *knitting* books," Scottie laughed, elbowing Amanda's arm.

(Knit two together)

"Hey!" Amanda protested as she dropped a stitch.

"Ex-*cuse* me?"

Amanda and Scottie both gasped before reluctantly glancing up. Standing before them were a silver-haired man and woman. They were one of those couples who'd probably been together so long, they looked more like brother and sister than husband and wife. They were both the same size—shrunken—and they had matching pink-rimmed eyes and flushed cheeks.

They're even swaying in the same direction, Scottie marveled, angling her head as the couple tilted decidedly leftward.

"I think the proper way to addresh ush, young lady," the man slurred, "ish with a 'Good evening.' Not 'Hey!'"

"Not only are the martinis here too weak," his wife muttered to him, barely trying to conceal her barb, "but the *help* is rude! Is *this* what passes for a debutante these days?"

"Unfortunately for both of us," Amanda snapped, "yes."

She grabbed a goodie bag off the table and thrust it roughly into the woman's hands. Then she tilted her own head, flashed a dazzling smile, and bobbed her head politely.

"Now thank you for coming to the Mayflower Memorial Benefit," she recited sweetly. "We appreciate your support tremendously. Look for acknowledgment of your generous gesture in the country club's next newsletter!"

The old man's scowl melted into a boozy smile, but his wife was unmoved. She peeked into her goodie bag.

"A Cross pen," she scoffed. "*What* do we need another Cross pen for? Come along, dear. The Stoningtons' cocktail party starts in twenty minutes."

Scottie and Amanda both gaped as the couple teetered their way out of the ballroom.

"Please, God!" Amanda cried, rolling her eyes heavenward. "May I never turn into that!"

"How on earth could you turn into that?" Scottie sputtered.

"It's like the deb thing," Amanda sighed, immediately returning to the solace of her sticks. "It's in the genes. Look at my mom!"

"Look at your knitty hands!" Scottie protested. "Amanda, you *are* the anti-deb. If you're gonna be like anyone when you grow up, it's badass Hannah Snyder. *She* says whatever she thinks, too."

Amanda cringed and peeked out the ballroom door. The boozy couple was waiting for an elevator, still tilting and still scowling.

"I guess that wasn't very deblike behavior," she agreed with a small, satisfied smile. "Except for that dumb thank-you my mom made me memorize."

"See!" Scottie said. "You've already got the *cojones* to make it in the fashion world."

"Well, so do you!" Amanda flung back at her.

"Yeah, right," Scottie said, giving her strictly-by-the-book shawl a baleful look. "I'm a knitter, not a Creator. I thought we established that from the beginning."

"Well, that doesn't mean your knitting isn't special," Amanda shrugged. As she said this, she whipped her way through a seemingly effortless combo of knits, purls, and yarnovers.

"I guess," Scottie said, fingering one of the goodie bags' gold bows idly. "As special as something can be when half of Stark and even my *sister* can do it."

"Scottie!" Amanda huffed. She was about to launch into lecture mode, but out of the corner of her eye, she saw a pack of goodie bag seekers approaching. "Dag. Hang on a sec."

Amanda dropped her knitting to the carpeted floor and rose to her feet in one seamless move.

"Good evening," she cooed. She handed one bag to a tall, blond drink of water whose collarbones jutted so sharply they made Scottie wince. Looking bored, the woman passed the bag to her much-older husband and sauntered out of the room. The next bag was for a woman in head-to-toe Chanel and the last was for a lady with a *ferret* around her neck. This rodent, at least, wasn't eating its own tail. Instead its tail was wrapped around its neck like a noose, while its head flopped sickeningly on the woman's bosom.

Scottie shuddered as Amanda zipped through her "generous gesture" spiel. The moment the people left the ballroom, Amanda sat back down and said, "Where was I?"

"Um," Scottie said with a shrug, "knitting being special?"

"That's right," Amanda said, scooping her lace off the floor and diving right back in. "So, you might not be a freeformer or a pattern writer. That doesn't mean you're not a mastermind."

"Of what?" Scottie snorted.

"Hello?" Amanda said. "Never Mind the Frogs, for one? The Chicks with Sticks, for another! Where would we be if you hadn't been so *incredibly* stubborn about shoving us all together last year?"

"Gee, you make it sound so romantic," Scottie joked.

She knit a couple stitches before she plunked Charlotte's Noose back into her lap and added, "Besides, that wasn't me. I thought we all agreed, it was fate that brought us together."

"Yeah, well sometimes fate needs a little help," Amanda said brusquely. "And now, here you are doing it again with Beck."

"Beck?" Scottie squeaked.

"C'mon," Amanda said. "You *made* that happen. You made a totally-against-the-Rules play for the guy and it worked. Now you're both in lurve."

"*You've* been talking to Tay," Scottie laughed.

"Of course," Amanda said. She reached across the table and grabbed a chocolate truffle off the girls' dessert plate. "That's what we do, isn't it? We're all up in each other's biz. Thank gawd! If not for that, I'd be doing goodie bag duty all by myself."

Scottie looked at Amanda, open-mouthed.

"Which is my way of saying thank you," Amanda said, popping the chocolate into her mouth and grinning at Scottie. "You saved me from a world of misery tonight!"

Scottie smiled and looked shyly at her lap, where Charlotte's Noose looked a lot more pretty and appealing than it had a few minutes earlier.

Wouldn't you know it, she thought, gratefully picking her sticks back up. *I came here to make everything all right for Amanda, and* she *ended up doing it for me!*

12 +(Make I-cord)

"I cannot believe I've never seen that movie before!" Scottie cried. "It was amazing."

It was Wednesday night and she and Beck had just emerged from the Music Box. Scottie was still brimming with confidence after the pep talk Amanda had given her the night before. And thus far, she was having a fabulous time. She hadn't even worried at all—well, much—about trying not to be spazzy.

"You know," Scottie pointed out, propping her purse on a newspaper box so she could stash her half-full box of Good & Plenty into it, "it's really rare that a movie is so fabulous that I forget to finish my candy."

Of course, the fact that Beck had held her hand through half the movie had played a part in this, too.

"I can't believe you like Good & Plenty," Beck said. "It's so gross!"

Well, now I know Tay'll like him, Scottie thought with a grin. *He's no yes-boy.*

To Beck, she retorted flirtily, "It's a classic."

"No," Beck said, turning to gaze admiringly at the Music Box's vertical marquee, each retro letter lit so bright you could see the sign from six blocks away. "This movie theater is a classic. Did you see they show old movies every Saturday morning at eleven? I'm *so* there."

"Wow, you really *are* a film geek," Scottie said.

"How else am I gonna be the next Pauline Kael, if I'm not?" Beck said, still gazing at the marquee.

"Who?!"

"Oh," Beck said, looking at Scottie. "She was this film critic for *The New Yorker*. I used to ask my dad to read her reviews to me instead of bedtime stories."

"You did not!" Scottie laughed.

"Sad, but true," Beck replied. "My parents love to tell the story about how they took me to my first movie, and during the entire dinner afterward at the Carnegie Deli, I kept talking about how I would have made the film different."

"What was it?" Scottie said.

"*Lady and the Tramp,*" Beck laughed. "So of course, they got me a little video camera, thinking I'd be the next Spielberg."

"Just like my sister," Scottie said with a little grimace.

"Yeah, except I was never very interested in making movies," Beck said. Scottie had to admit, she felt a bit of relief at that.

All I'd need, she thought, *is for Beck to find out that Jordan's the next Zach Braff. And suddenly my sister would seem so much more interesting than my knitty self.*

"Really, I just like to *talk* about movies," Beck went on. He started to walk lazily down the sidewalk toward Irving Park, the street that led to the bread factory. "And I write about them. I was the film critic for my high school paper in New York. I think I might start doing it for *Starkers*, too."

"So, you've already discovered our school's little webzine," Scottie said. "I'm impressed. That's pretty underground. Especially since they did that exposé, 'Inside the Teacher's Lounge.'"

"Yeah, that's when they started writing under pseudonyms," Beck said admiringly. "Or so I heard from my friends from the cafeteria."

"Wait a minute," Scottie said, skidding to a halt. "Don't tell me those burrito brothers are Strindberg and Beckett?"

Strindberg and Beckett were the names the *Starkers'* founders had given themselves. They were the 'zine's most notoriously funny scribes. Rumor had it that they'd spent the summer interning at *The Onion*. But nobody could confirm the rumor because nobody would own up to being Strindberg and Beckett.

"Hey, don't ask me," Beck said. "The guys aren't talking. All I know is they told me they'd somehow procured a secret e-mail address to *Starkers'* editor-in-chief and I should send in a review. It's all very covert."

"Oooh," Scottie giggled. "Intrigue."

"Totally," Beck smirked. "I shouldn't even be telling you! For all I know, your knowledge puts you in grave danger."

"If anybody leaves a horse's head in my locker," Scottie joked back, "I'll know to follow the scent of burritos to the perp."

"A *Godfather* reference," Beck cried, pounding a fist on his chest. "Be still my heart."

"Hey, just because I never saw *Annie Hall* doesn't mean I'm completely film-ignorant," Scottie said defensively.

The fact that she'd accidentally Netflixed *The Godfather* because she'd thought it was a Sofia Coppola movie, instead of one by Sofia's dad? Scottie decided to leave that part out. In fact, she was racking her brain for a subject-change when the street lights lining Southport Avenue blazed to life. Scottie and Beck both jumped. Beck gazed at the sky. It was blue-gray and darkening quickly.

"Does this count as sundown?" he said, sounding disappointed.

"Oh no," Scottie said. "My parents and I negotiated on that. 'Sundown' means the sun is so gone, it's become moon. The sky has to be *black*."

"Now *that's* an impressive con," Beck said. "You could be a lawyer."

"What?" Scottie huffed. "It's a perfectly reasonable interpretation of sundown."

"Hey, I'm not gonna argue," Beck said. He stopped on the corner, his almost-dimple deepening. "Not when it benefits me. Coffee?"

Scottie looked up. Beck had stopped in front of Mandrake's, a hole-in-the-wall coffeehouse that was so old, its front window had gone sepia.

The window was lined with dying plants and stacks of faded board games. Beyond that was an assemblage of rickety, mismatched tables and an olive-green metal bookshelf full of graphic novels and comic books.

"This happens to be one of my favorite coffeehouses in all of Chicago," Scottie sighed, "other than Joe, of course."

"Of course it is," Beck laughed, pushing through the humidity-warped door. "I think you'd have an allergic reaction if you ever stepped foot in a Starbucks. How do you do that? Be so cool without even trying?"

"Me?" Scottie blurted, feeling her cheeks flame up. "I'm not cool. I'm like the least trendy person there is!"

"Exactly," Beck said. "But you don't make this big statement about it. You just are who you are. I really—"

Now it was Beck who was going pink.

"Well, let's just say," he said, his voice suddenly going a bit gravelly, "that's a very attractive quality."

Scottie felt very balloony all of a sudden—like she was floating beneath Mandrakes' pressed-tin ceiling, watching this conversation take place from a distance. Because it couldn't really be happening to *her*, could it? There couldn't be a totally cute boy telling *her* how attractive she was.

Could there?

"So I'm assuming you want your usual coffee with four sugars and a cup of milk?" Beck quipped, though he was still scratchy-voiced and flush-cheeked.

Suddenly, Scottie swooped back down from the ceiling. This moment was too wonderful to enjoy from afar.

"Nope!" she announced giddily. "I'm gonna have ice cream with espresso."

Beck laughed.

"The girl likes her sugar," he said.

And once they'd settled into a cozy table with a Sorry game and a waiter hovering nearby, Beck added, "Of course, I like sugar, too."

He ordered hot chocolate.

(Knit two together)

This moment could not be any more perfect, Scottie thought, melting back into her chair.

"Hey," she proposed. "Let's play that game, like when Diane Keaton and Woody Allen are in Central Park? And they make up stories about all the people they see?"

"Oh, watch out," Beck said. "I'm good at this one."

He twisted in his seat and looked furtively at a woman sketching in a corner. Her hair was twisted into a frazzled topknot and she was wearing mismatched socks.

"Well, clearly she's making architectural drawings for her new performance space," Beck said, "a bomb shelter slash puppet theater."

"What about these guys?" Scottie said, nodding at a couple checking out baked goods at the counter. The girl was built as powerfully as a rugby player and her boyfriend was so willowy, he looked like the blast of the air from the cappuccino machine might knock him over.

"They're on again, off again," Beck pronounced. "He's giving her a second chance even though she accidentally concussed his Chihuahua. Girl doesn't know her own strength."

"Well, I have a theory about the barista," Scottie said, nodding at the scruffy guy bustling behind the counter with a perpetual frown. "He spends his nights sizing all of us up, just like we're doing. If he likes the looks of you, you get a madeleine with your coffee. If he doesn't— biscotti."

Just then, their server brought over their treats. Wedged onto the rim of Scottie's ice cream bowl was a fluffy, yellow madeleine. On the saucer of Beck's hot chocolate—an almond biscotti.

Beck's eyes widened.

"No way," he whispered. "What did I do?"

Scottie slapped a hand over her mouth and laughed guiltily.

"Beck!" she snorted. "I was just kidding. I've been here a million times. The madeleine versus biscotti thing? It's totally random, I promise."

"Ooh, you're good," Beck laughed, taking a devilish bite out of his biscotti. "But I bet I'm better. Let's see. . . ."

As he twisted to eye the front door, Scottie poured her espresso over her ice cream. While she studiously stirred up her dessert to meld the coffee and cream, Beck found his next prospect.

"Okay, she's cleverly disguised herself as a yoga student," he said, "hence the mat. But in truth she's a Wiccan priestess, picking up some hazelnut-flavored coffee for her latest potion."

Scottie giggled, took a big bite of caffeinated ice cream, and looked up at the to-go counter to check out the girl Beck was describing. Then she gasped so hard, the ice cream went straight down her windpipe!

As Scottie sputtered and struggled loudly for air, the girl glanced over, shoving aside the hank of honey dreadlocks that had been hiding her face so she could see.

"Scottie!" Bella cried. She waved wildly. Still-coughing, Scottie waved back. Through teary eyes, Scottie saw Bella swipe up a tall paper cup, stuff a few dollars into the tip jar, and begin walking over.

"Sweetie, what happened to you?" Bella said. She alighted behind Scottie's chair and began pounding her on the back. Beck stood up looking pink and awkward, but Bella didn't seem to notice.

"You must be Beck," she said between thumps. "I'm Bella."

"Oh . . . hi!" Beck stammered. "I . . . I didn't recognize you at first." He glanced down at Scottie, his eyes flashing a question.

Did I just inadvertently dis one of your best friends?

Scottie quickly and subtly shook her head at Beck. After all, Wiccans were cool these days, right? Like a lot of subcultures that were once considered freaky. Like folks with tattoos and . . . knitters!

Still, Scottie felt all kinds of weird as she finally caught her breath and stood up to give Bella a hello hug.

"How was yoga?" she asked.

"Oh, you know," Bella said with a shrug and an edgy glance at Beck.

"The same old vinyasa. I usually stop here on the way home for a soy milk and honey. I love this place, don't you?"

"It's the best," Scottie sighed, hoping Bella would understand that this was code language for *Beck is the best!*

"Bella, you want to play Sorry with us?" Beck said, motioning to the board game on their table. "Sorry's always better with more than two people."

It was all Scottie could do not to throw her arms around Beck right there.

Okay, not only does he take me to the most romantic movie of all time? But now he's reaching out to my friend? I luuuurve him.

Bella, though, didn't seem to share the sentiment. After taking an awkward sip of soy, she shook her head hard.

"I couldn't," she said. "You guys are on a date."

"It's okay," Scottie laughed, sitting down again and pointing to their table's extra chair. "We can tell you about this awesome movie we just saw."

Scottie was loving the way all those "we's" rolled off her tongue.

"Oh, I've seen *Annie Hall* a million times," Bella said. "I love that scene where Woody's all, 'Do I love you? I *lurve* you. I loave you. I luff you!' Isn't it weird that he turned out to be this creep who married his stepdaughter?"

Scottie couldn't answer. She was too busy clenching her teeth to fight the flush that *had* to have been creeping up from her collar to her face.

Once again, psychic Bella hits her mark, Scottie thought in horror. *I've only been "lurving" all night long.*

Bella frowned at Scottie. Clearly, she could tell that Scottie was freaking.

"What did I say?" she stage-whispered.

"Nothing!" Scottie blurted. "I lurved that scene, too. I mean, loved it."

"Oh, yeah, but nothing's funnier than the lobster scene," Beck piped up. "Y'know, where the lobsters escape in the beach house?"

Suddenly, Scottie felt his fingertips graze hers under the table. Her

•• Chicks with Sticks

cheeks heated up again, but this time in a good way. It was while they'd laughed hysterically at the movie's lobster scene that Beck had reached over the nubby theater seat armrest to hold her hand.

"Oh," Bella said, her face falling. "I'm vegetarian. I'm not so into lobster humor."

"Oh," Beck said. "Er, sorry."

"That's okay," Bella said flatly. "You didn't know."

The pause after that was long and awkward. Scottie finally broke it by peering out the window.

"I think we're approaching black sky out there," she said, taking another quick bite of ice cream. "We better go. See you tomorrow, Bellissima?"

"Oh yeah," Bella said, perking up. "By the way, do you have a cable needle I can borrow? Tay's got mine."

"I'll bring it to school." Scottie grinned. But as Bella headed to the door, Scottie's smile faded. On one level, she loved running into Bella while she was with Beck. Bella had borne witness to Scottie's first date bliss. And, of course, everyone knew that introducing the BF to the BFFs was completely crucial.

But Scottie couldn't get around the fact that if she *hadn't* been with Beck tonight when she'd run into Bella, she and Bella would have fallen immediately into gossip mode. They would have offered each other sips of their coffees, and whipped out their yarn for a few minutes of knitting before doing a double-cheeked kiss good-night.

In the presence of Boy, things had definitely been a little weird.

Maybe this is why Tay wishes John would keep his needles to himself; why she wants to keep her friends and boyfriend separate but equal, Scottie thought. *Maybe this having-a-boyfriend thing is more complicated than I thought.*

Of course, the next morning at school? When all the Chicks had gathered around Scottie's locker for serious dishing? Scottie couldn't find a dark side to her evening if she tried.

"So in the elevator vestibule after we got back to the building," she burbled, "we kissed for, like, fifteen minutes without stopping."

"But no ear-chewing, right?" Bella said fearfully. She was looking especially crunchy this morning, in one of her blowsiest skirts and a trio of copper neck-rings that clanked around her clavicle.

"Maybe a little on the neck," Scottie whispered with a giggle.

"TMI," Tay groaned. She crossed her arms over her chest and did her signature slouch—flat stomach pooched out, shoulders hunched, chin down. "You guys are gross."

"Hey, I'm not nearly as bad as Amanda," Scottie defended herself. "I mean, do any of us *really* need to know that Toby has extremely ticklish knees?"

"No!" Bella and Tay both blurted.

"Hey, hey," Amanda said, her face a bit stiff. "Enough about Toby's knees. Let's talk about Toby's band! They're playing their first gig at a U of C party this weekend. He *really* wants us all to come."

"Really?" Tay said, her eyebrows raised. "Toby wants *us* to come?"

"Yeah," Amanda said, frowning at her buds. "Why is that so hard to believe?"

Tay shrugged.

"Don't get me wrong," she said. "I dig Toby. It just seems like he always wants to hang out with *his* crowd."

"Just because he's so swamped with school and stuff," Scottie said quickly. "I mean, any free time he has, he wants to spend with you."

"You and his friends," Bella added.

And even though it was true, Scottie cringed for Amanda, who was blowing a strand of hair out of her face and rolling her eyes.

"Okay, you're right," she said. "It's *me* who wants you to come to the party. Toby's gonna be playing most of the night. It'd be so much more fun if I could hang with you guys while he's up there."

Amanda's face was still tensed up and she was picking nervously at the frayed wire sprouting off one of her spiral-bound notebooks.

Scottie exchanged a quick glance with Bella and Tay. Once again, Amanda was a Chick in Need, and there was no question about what they should do.

"Of course, we'll go!" Bella cried.

"It's pretty much guaranteed that there won't be any fox stoles there, right?" Scottie joked.

"And, it'd be cool to hear Toby's music," Tay chimed in. "What's his band called again?"

"Beaker's Revenge," Amanda said flatly. "It's a Muppet reference."

"I love those old Muppet shows," Scottie said. "I used to watch the reruns on PBS."

"Pigs-igs-igs!" Tay said in a deep, reverberating voice.

Scottie cackled and responded, "In-in-in!"

"Space-ace-ace!" they yelled together.

Tay had unslouched and uncrossed her arms. She was looking positively unscowly.

"Yeah, it'll be cool," she said to Amanda. "A little Chick time *without* the burden of a chick flick."

"Oh please," Amanda said, relaxing enough to pop open her locker and start gathering goods for her morning classes. "You got completely teary at the end of *Serendipity*, Tay-Tay. Don't think I didn't see that."

"Don't call me Tay-Tay," Tay grumbled. "I'm gonna have to give it to John for that one."

I wonder when Beck will make up a pet name for me? Scottie thought dreamily. She *chunked* open her own locker—and a folded square of paper tumbled out onto the floor.

"What's that?!" Bella cried.

Bewildered, Scottie scooped up the note. It couldn't be from Beck, she thought. He'd *just* dropped her off at her locker and headed to his own.

She unfolded the torn-off bit of notebook paper. It looked like a quick scrawl.

(Knit two together)

Scottie. I'm glad you liked the lobster scene, too. Maybe we can get together again Saturday? —B

Scottie did a little dance of joy as she looked up at her friends.

"He must have slipped it into my locker when he dropped me off," Scottie cried. "He wants to go out again!"

"Whoa," Tay said. "Even John waited the requisite three days before he asked me out for date number two. Heavy."

Actually, Scottie felt nothing but light. Maybe now she was allowed to believe this was all really happening. Maybe now she could really say the word *boyfriend* without feeling like an impostor. Maybe the other shoe *wasn't* going to drop.

"This is so perfect," she swooned. "We'll all go to the party on Friday, and on Saturday night—*date* night—I'll actually have a date."

Suddenly Amanda's face crumpled.

"Oh, no, Scottie," she said. "The party's on Saturday. Didn't I say that?"

"Wait, what?" Scottie barked. She'd been doing happy little hops in front of her locker, but Amanda's words made her stop so suddenly, she felt the reverberation in her knees.

"It's Saturday?" Scottie gaped. "It's not Friday? I was sure you said Friday."

"No," Amanda said. "I think I just said this weekend."

Scottie felt her face fall. She knew it *would* have been more sensitive to Amanda to mask her disappointment, just a little bit. If only her disappointment hadn't been so huge.

"But," Scottie squeaked, "Beck wants to go out on Saturday."

"So just see if he can switch it to Friday," Tay shrugged. "What's the diff?"

"Friday's only two days after our Wednesday date," Scottie breathed. She slumped so heavily against the locker next to hers that it clanked. "It's too soon."

"So Sunday then," Bella offered.

•• Chicks with Sticks

Amanda was silent—and back to twisting agitatedly at her notebook's wire. She might as well have been tying Scottie's insides into a similarly frayed coil.

So much for Saturday night being date night, she gloomed to herself. *I mean, for any of us except Amanda.*

Scottie buried her face in her locker to hide her huge sighs. Propping her bag on the edge of the locker, she carefully refolded Beck's note and tucked it into her wallet. As she listlessly stacked up her morning's books and binders, she imagined what her Saturday night date could have been. She saw Beck meeting her parents, then walking her out of the building, both of them giggling about the Shearers' dorkiness. A walk to a restaurant. Hand-holding across the table. Maybe going to Katarina's after dinner to hear some mus—

"Wait a minute!" Scottie blurted. She spun around so fast that one of her notebooks slid off her stack and slapped onto the floor. "Beck and I can still go out on Saturday. And Tay, so can you and John. We'll *all* go the party. It'll be a Triple Date!"

Scottie was mildly aware of the way "triple date" trilled out of her mouth. As if she were exclaiming, "hot fudge sundae" or "half-price Risdie yarn!" She couldn't help it. If she'd spent years dreaming about what it would be like to go on a real, live, actual date, she'd probably fantasized even more about double-dating. Doubling or tripling the couples made the whole thing seem more . . . datey, somehow.

"It'll give you a guys a chance to get to know Beck," Scottie added. "And we'll still all be there to support Amanda at the party!"

"Well, I already met Beck," Bella pouted. "And *I* don't have a date, remember? What, am I supposed do? Stay home?"

"Of course not!" Scottie said, tweaking one of Bella's dreads. "You're so coming. Bella, half the junior class is swooning for you. The only reason you don't have a date is because you don't want one."

"Well, I guess so," Bella grumbled. "This isn't really the same, though."

"No," Amanda said, thunking her locker closed quietly. "Not really."

"Not at *all*," Tay scowled. "You know, I don't think John's a Muppet kind of guy."

"It's just a name," Amanda offered lamely. "The band doesn't really have anything to do with Muppets."

"So John'll probably be into it then," Scottie said quickly. She knew she was pushing a bit too hard. She knew this wasn't the perfect solution to this quandary.

But it was the best one she had.

Now Scottie was envisioning a new date—a party in one of those rambling old houses in Hyde Park. She saw the Chicks dancing together while Toby thrashed. She saw herself and Beck taking a break to go outside, look at the moon, and kiss. John was coaxing Tay into a slow dance and melting away the brick wall she'd put up lately. Bella was meeting a college boy who wowed her with his maturity. Toby was sitting out a song so he could have some alone time with Amanda. . . .

They'll see, Scottie insisted to herself as she and her slightly stony-faced girlfriends fanned out to beat the first bell to class. *A party could be just the thing to ease all the tension going on here. I have a good feeling about this.*

And the good feeling lasted, oh, right up until the moment they all walked into the party.

That was the first time Scottie considered the fact that, this shindig? It was full of complete strangers. Complete strangers in *college*.

For a moment the six of them—Bella, Tay, John, Amanda, Scottie, and Beck—just stood in the doorway of the address Toby had given them and gawked.

"What *is* this?" Bella quavered.

They were in the formal foyer of a ramshackle mansion, the plaster on the walls so cracked and yellowed it was coming off in chunks. College kids slurping out of giant plastic cups were lounging on a spiral staircase covered in torn, beer-rank carpeting. The formal dining room to the left of the foyer was outfitted with two kegs propped crookedly in giant tubs of ice, each surrounded by a cluster of hungry-looking partiers. Blaring out of the giant living room to their right was the super-loud, shrill-with-feedback, screechy rock of Beaker's Revenge.

Amanda clutched her little Prada purse to her chest and curled her lip.

"Toby said it's kind of an anti-frat," she yelled over the music. "About thirty guys live here."

"No wonder it's so gross," Bella said, pinching her nose.

"Bella, this is nothing," John said, snaking his arm around Tay's waist and grinning at the scene. "Compared to the guys' locker room at Stark? This place is like a rose garden."

Beck grimaced at Scottie.

"He's right," he said.

Scottie stuck her tongue out and grinned as she headed toward the living room. She called to the crew, "Let's check out Toby's band."

But she'd only taken a few steps when two burly guys in U of C sweatshirts almost mowed her down! Clutching oversized science lab beakers filled with beer, they skidded across the cracked marble floor in a sock-slide race. One of the beers frothed over, spattering Scottie's carefully chosen A-line skirt and clingy, pale-blue top.

"Agh!" Scottie cried.

"Oh man!" Beck cried, trotting up to join her. He smiled sympathetically as Scottie flicked stinky foam off her soaked skirt. "Well, it only took you two minutes to blend in."

"Yeah right," Scottie grumbled. Glancing at the other girls milling around the party, she could see that she was completely overdressed. Most of them were slouching around in jeans and layered tanks or baggy T-shirts.

Amanda, in her silver, boot-leg pants; iridescent, cowl-neck tank; and strappy sandals looked even more out of place than Scottie did.

Scottie sidled over to her.

"So how did we not know that this was gonna be an . . . um, *kegger?*" she hissed.

"I don't know," Amanda said. Her face went dark, but for the shimmery makeup dusting her cheeks and eyes. "Toby told me to dress up!"

Amanda frowned at the living room. Scottie could see people churning around a makeshift dance floor, but the band was still out of sight. Amanda headed in. Shrugging, Scottie motioned to Beck, Tay, and John and they followed. She craned her neck, looking for Bella, but she'd disappeared.

Maybe she's already dancing, Scottie told herself. As Beck caught up with her, she gave him a rueful smile.

"I'm so getting in trouble when I get home," she yelled, "and I didn't even *drink* any of this beer."

"We'll come up with a solution," Beck yelled. "How about a dance? It'll dry you off!"

"Cool!" Scottie said. She grabbed Beck's hand and turned to her friends.

"Let's go!" she yelled, pointing at the dance floor. Amanda shook her head. She was staring up at the plywood platform serving as a stage. It didn't look like Toby had seen her yet. He was thrashing on his guitar, his scruffy dark hair covering his eyes, his face all sweaty and scrunched up as he wailed into the mic.

John and Tay settled into twin poses leaning against the wall, hands dug into their jean pockets, checking out the scene with bemused half-smiles.

Tay shook her head at Scottie, too.

"I don't dance," she said.

"I do!" John said. "Well, I pogo. I'm a badass pogoer."

"Oh, God," Tay muttered, but there was a laugh behind it. She motioned John onto the dance floor.

"So go pogo," she offered. "I'll watch. Maybe Bella and I will forage for chips. Hey, where is B?"

"Dunno," John said, using his height to do a crowd scan. "Not in here."

"I'll find her," Tay said. "See you in a bit."

"Eh, pogoing's no fun by yourself." John shrugged. "I'll go with you."

You could only see Tay's face harden if you were looking for it. And Scottie was. Tay's forehead furrowed and her lips tightened into a grim line. Hunching her shoulders up, she turned to mow through a cluster of girls who were swaying monotonously as they stared up at Beaker's Revenge. Without checking to see if John was following, she headed for a back room. John did follow, of course, reaching for Tay's hand as she plowed through the door.

Scottie tried to meet Amanda's eyes, but Amanda was still staring at Toby, an expression on her face that Scottie couldn't quite interpret.

Especially since Beck was taking her hand now, and pulling her onto the dance floor.

Which, of course, was when Toby thrashed out his final crunchy chord. The last line of his song sounded something like, "And she was so pretty it hurrrrrt!" But it was so deafening, Scottie couldn't be sure. In the hollow silence following the song, a screech of feedback rang out, making everybody in the room scream, cover their ears, then laugh, hoot, and throw plastic cups at the stage.

"We're taking a break," Toby told the audience. Scottie watched him finally spot Amanda in the crowd. Set apart from the grungy partiers in the back of the room, she almost glowed in her sparkly outfit. She also looked miserable.

"But first," Toby announced, "I've gotta admit something."

The kids on the dance floor elbowed each other and dimmed their chat for a second to listen up.

"That song I just sang," Toby said, looking intensely at Amanda now, "I wrote it for my girlfriend, Amanda. She's right over there. Hey, baby."

Amanda's skin went so pale she suddenly resembled a marble sculpture, planted awkwardly in the wreckage of this decrepit room. Her eyes shifted back and forth as everyone in the room swiveled to peer over at her.

A whistle rang out from somewhere near Scottie and Beck.

"Good one, Toecheese!" grunted the whistler. "Guess you're made for a poli sci major. Ugly politicians always get the best chicks."

"Thinking of transferring out of the math department, geek?" Toby ribbed back. His thin, sweaty face was flushed with the music, the lights blazing too close to the makeshift stage, and, it seemed, with smug victory.

"Amanda!" he called out. "Come on up here!"

Amanda glanced around, mortified, then shook her head hard.

"Aw, c'mon," Toby yelled, grinning and waving Amanda toward him.

Scottie looked anxiously at Amanda. She looked tragic—sad and bewildered, her eyes brimming. Ironically, this made her look prettier than ever.

For a moment, Scottie forgot all about Beck. She just wanted to get to Amanda. She began to push through the sweaty crowd. She'd almost reached the back of the room when a tall guy nearby peered over the top of the crowd and shook his head.

"That's what happens when you date high-school girls," he clucked.

Scottie bit her lip.

WHAT'S *what happens?* she wondered.

Only when she broke out of the clump of bodies could she see what the guy was talking about. Amanda was bolting for a door in the back of the room. And from the way her hands were covering her face, Scottie was certain she was crying.

"Amanda!" she yelled. She started after her, but hesitated at the doorway—which led to a glassed-in room that had probably been an elegant conservatory once, and was now the house's smoking lounge. She glanced back at Beck.

He appeared at the edge of the crowd.

"Why don't you go find her," he said. He jerked his thumb toward the foyer. "I'll go hang with the others."

Scottie swooned.

He's the best boyfriend ever, she thought.

She smiled at Beck, waved good-bye, and dove into the room, coughing and waving her hand in front of her face as she peered through a giant cloud of cigarette smoke. She couldn't see Amanda anywhere, but a short way off, Bella's spray of dreadlocks was unmistakable. Scottie fought her way through the murk to Bella's side—just in time to see her crunchy, peace-and-love BFF begin shaking her finger at a dumpy guy.

"Bella?!" Scottie called out.

Bella didn't hear her over the roar of voices in the crowded room. Scottie glanced at the guy Bella was berating.

He was the sock-slider who'd crashed into Scottie! His beer beaker had apparently been refilled. He was smirking at Bella, and winking at his pal who was lounging in a folding chair nearby. When Bella paused for breath, the sock slider's lip curled higher and he said something Scottie couldn't hear.

But Bella heard it, all right. She gasped and gave the boy the most withering glare Scottie had ever witnessed on her bud's beautiful face. Then Bella grabbed the beer out of the guy's chubby hand, and dumped it over his head!

13 ✤ (Frog down to dropped stitch)

"Bella!" Scottie cried.

The boy Bella had just doused was sputtering and spitting mad. Bella, on the other hand, was grinning for the first time that evening. When Scottie reached her side, she threw her head back and laughed.

"Maybe the band should be named Bella's Revenge!" she cackled.

"Oh, my God," Scottie muttered. She wrapped her arm around Bella's waist and dragged her out of the room as quickly as she could. Only when they'd arrived in the kitchen and ducked behind a tall cabinet did Scottie dare to look behind her. But the coast was clear. Nothing was coming through the door of the smoking lounge except billows of smoke. It looked like Beaker boy had left well enough alone.

Which was more than Scottie could say for Bella!

"What happened?!" Scottie screeched. She sniffed the air around Bella's face. "Are you drunk? You smell kind of beery."

"Ew, no!" Bella said. "I think you're smelling *you*."

She pointed at Scottie's beer-stained outfit.

"Oh, yeah," Scottie sighed. "Uch, this party gets grosser by the minute."

"Yeah!" Bella said, pinching her nose.

"So, um, Bella?"

"Yeah?"

"What just *happened* in there?!?" Scottie asked, completely bewildered.

"I was only defending your honor." Bella shrugged.

"What?!"

"The guy thunked into you, totally ruining your cute outfit," Bella said, "and then he dashed off and didn't even apologize! Boys!"

Bella shuddered in disgust.

"That part I remember," Scottie said, looking at the ugly stain on her skirt. "So then what?"

"I went and found him," Bella explained simply. "And I told him that he was really rude and he should go apologize to you."

"Um, okay, thanks I think," Scottie squeaked. She was totally mortified, but she knew this wouldn't compute with Bella.

"The jerk only laughed at me," Bella went on. "So I tried to talk some sense into him. You know, about the major damage he was doing to his karma and how you were only on your second date with Beck and how could he humiliate you like that."

Okay, mortification squared! Scottie thought.

"Bella, you didn't have to—" she squeaked. "I mean, that was sweet and all but—"

"So *then* guess what he did!" Bella fumed. "He said, 'You know, you're cute when you're mad. What do you say me and you go on a *first* date?' As if!"

"So you dumped beer on his head?" Scottie sighed.

"Well, it worked so well at Camp Hippie," Bella said with a mischievous smile. "With Peter and the goat's milk."

"Bella," Scottie said. "Okay, yes, that guy was a total idiot. But you can't keep dumping cold beverages onto guys' heads!"

"I can if they keep disrespecting me," Bella insisted, pooching out her bottom lip. "Asking me out and stuff!"

"Okay, beer beaker guy?" Scottie said. "That was disrespect. Peter the cheater? Him, too. But Sergio and those other guys asking you out, that's just them . . . liking you. What's so wrong with that?"

(Knit two together)

"I can't expect you to understand." Bella sighed. She shook her head sorrowfully. "You're in love."

"Bel-la," Scottie protested, turning bright red.

"No, that's okay," Bella shrugged with a sad smile. She put a hand on Scottie's shoulder. "I understand what you're going through, sweetie. This is what happens when you get a boyfriend. You actually *like* the shackles. At least, that's what you *tell* yourself. . . ."

"Shackles?!" Scottie sputtered. "Wait a minute, it's so not like that—"

A horrible screeching noise cut Scottie off. Someone was coming in from the dining room through the swinging—well, scraping—door. The door was so loose on its hinges, it had no swing left. John poked his head into the kitchen, looking flustered.

"Oh, hi, guys," he said. "I was just looking for Tay. You seen her?"

Bella elbowed Scottie and whispered, "See?"

"No!" Scottie scowled, elbowing Bella back.

"Okay, okay," John said, throwing his hands up. "You don't have to get huffy about it. What's with all you tonight?"

"Oh, sorry!" Scottie said, taking a few halting steps toward him. "I wasn't saying no to *you*. Although, actually, uh, no I haven't seen Tay."

"Huh," John said. He leaned wearily against the refrigerator and exhaled. "Listen, can I ask you something?"

Scottie and Bella glanced at each other, their eyebrows raised.

"Um, sure." Bella shrugged.

"Lately, all I seem to do is annoy Tay." John sighed. "It's like, the harder I try to make her happy, the less happy she is."

Scottie froze. She didn't know what to say. Frankly, she was terrified of saying *anything*, because suddenly she couldn't remember what Tay had complained about in person, and what T. C. Boil had snarked about in *In a Sknit*.

Before she could decide what to do, Bella spoke up. Scottie didn't know whether to be relieved or freaked. After all, Bella had already shown herself to be deep into psychoanalytic mode tonight. And if

Scottie had learned anything from her psych teacher this semester, it was that the brain's underbelly was never pretty.

"Well, see, John," Bella said, "you said it right there! You're *trying* to make Tay happy. But we all know, Tay doesn't like anybody fussing over her."

"That's true," John said, "but—"

"Like at one of our S.S.O's," Bella went on, her theory gaining strength now. "I *forced* Tay to submit to a facial cleansing and deep sea mud mask?"

At this, John's mouth popped open. Scottie snorted as Bella pressed on. "And then I was supposed to rub her temples for ten minutes, while she did some deep breathing and meditation. Well, two minutes in, she couldn't take all the warm fuzzies anymore. She spent the rest of her mud mask playing with her Xbox!"

"We really wanted to take pictures," Scottie giggled to John. "But Tay said she'd break the camera if we did."

John laughed wanly.

"That's my Tay-Tay." He sighed.

"*Your* Tay-Tay?" Bella said with a troubled frown. "You know, John, maybe it's this patriarchal sense of *ownership* in your relationship that's the problem! I mean, I know you don't mean to be oppressive, but let's face it, you *are* a boy, and—"

"I think what Bella means," Scottie said loudly, giving Bella a wide-eyed stare, "is, well, maybe Tay just needs a little space? I mean, some-times she even screens *our* calls."

Scottie looked at Bella for affirmation. Bella nodded hard.

"Wait, are you saying she's screening my calls?" John said. His face blanched and his wide shoulders sagged.

"No!" Scottie cried. "I mean, I don't know."

Even, though, she sort of did.

BF called three times tonight. Which, okay, two of the times were valid. The last was to say good-night and the one before that was a knitting emergency. (No, BF, you CAN'T add new yarn at the end of the row. Welcome to my world, frogger!) But the first time he called? Just to share with me that he was so hungry after practice that he fully ate three Stouffers pizzas? That I could have lived without.

"All I meant was, Bella's right," Scottie squeaked. "Probably the best way to try with Tay is to not *try* so hard."

"I know, it seems sort of opposite of what you should do," Bella said.

"But this is Tay we're talking about here," Scottie said.

While John nodded sadly, the door scratched open again. What do you know—it was Tay. She frowned at the three of them.

"I've been looking for you guys!" she said.

John's face lit up for a moment, until Bella subtly shook her head at him.

John rolled his eyes and sighed. Then, with exaggerated effort, he twisted the grin off his face, went even slouchier against the fridge, and sounded bored as he said, "Oh?"

"Did you forget," Tay said to John, "we were looking for Bella? Where'd *you* go off to?"

"You were going so fast, I lost you in the crowd," John spat back. "Not that you noticed."

Tay raised her eyebrows and gave John a long, hard look, which clearly made him squirm.

"Anyway," he said through a weary exhale of breath, "here she is."

He waved his lanky arm in Bella and Scottie's direction—which reminded Scottie of her original mission.

"Oh, my God," she said, slapping her forehead. "*I* was looking for Amanda. Then Bella distracted me with her beer brawl."

"What?!" John and Tay screamed together.

"Well . . . " Bella started to explain, looking sheepish and delighted all at once.

"You can hear the whole sordid story later," Scottie said, heading for the rickety swinging door. "I really think we should find Amanda. She's way upset with Toby and she was crying."

"Crying?" Tay sighed, plodding after Scottie with Bella at her heels. "Oh man, that is so not my area."

"Mine neither," John said with a sullen shrug.

"Actually, I was talking to those dudes," Tay said dryly, pointing at her girlfriends. "And besides, that *is* your area, John. You're like, more nurturing than my mother!"

"Am not!" John retorted.

"Okay, okay!" Tay said. "Man, is all the estrogen in the room getting to you or something?"

"Good point," John said, thrusting out his scruffy chin. "I think I'll go find some *guys* to hang with. See ya later."

Whistling a little, John skulked toward the kitchen's side door—the one that led to the conservatory-turned-smoking lounge. Tay huffed and plunged back through the swinging door. As Scottie followed, she peeked over her shoulder at John. He was, of course, peeking over *his* shoulder at her. He shot her a questioning thumbs-up.

Scottie shrugged and tried to smile. Inside, she felt a little sick to her stomach.

Okay, what's happening to my world? Bella's accosting boys with beer beakers, John's acting like a jerk and—

As she, Tay, and Bella passed through the dining room to begin their Amanda hunt, Scottie spotted something that made her stop and gasp.

—and Beck's flirting with two girls?!

Up until now, this smelly party in this decrepit house had been merely disorienting. But now? Scottie wondered if the beer fumes wafting off her outfit were making her hallucinate! Because she was *pretty* sure she was looking at Beck as he leaned against the dining room wall, smiling and talking to the only other girls at the party besides Amanda, Scottie, and Bella who weren't shlumped out in jeans and T-shirts. One was wearing a miniskirt and tank top. The other was in skinny black pants and high heels.

Tay and Bella had almost reached the front door when they realized Scottie was no longer with them. Tay turned around and scowled.

"Scottie," she called out, "come on!"

Of course, at the mention of her name, Beck looked up.

"Hey!" he called. With one look at her face, he added, "What's wrong?"

"Nothing!" Scottie said automatically, though she noted in her head, *Actually, so many things are wrong right now, I can't even begin to list them.*

"Amanda's upset," she said bluntly.

"Which is why we have to go!" Bella said, just as bluntly. She trotted back to Scottie, clamped her fingers around her elbow, and started pulling.

"Geez, Bella," Scottie snapped. "Whatever happened to your whole peace and love thing?"

"Somebody dumped beer all over it, I guess," Bella said. But the comment was more wistful than biting.

Scottie suddenly flashed to herself about a year ago. Back then, she'd been just like Bella, wanting nothing more from her friends than inertia. She'd wanted to freeze them in the same happy, knitty place forever.

It was only in the past few months that Scottie had shifted into Go mode. Go for a bigger bra size. Go for a boyfriend. Go for triple dates and anti-frat parties and everything that represents forward motion. Go for broke.

Broken is more like it, Scottie thought. That was exactly how she felt as Bella pulled her into the foyer. Beck waved at her before returning cheerfully to his flirt-fest.

But— Scottie stuttered in her mind. *What is he— How can he just— Right in front of my eyes—*

Tay had opened the front door.

"Let's look for her outside," she said. "No way would Amanda want to stay in here."

Bella hopped onto the front porch gratefully and took a deep breath of non-smoky, non-beery air. But Scottie felt paralyzed.

"You guys," she stammered, "I can't. Don't you see? Don't you see Beck over there?"

Tay peered over Scottie's shoulder and shrugged.

"So he's made some friends," she said. "Score two points for Beck—he can fend for himself at a party, unlike someone *else* I could mention!"

She shot a scowly glance in the direction of the kitchen where John had gone looking for her.

"Now let's get outta here," Tay said.

"Those aren't 'friends!'" Scottie hissed. "Those are *girls!* And they're all over him."

Tay and Scottie peeked into the dining room again. Girl One in the mini was whispering something in Beck's ear and giggling. Girl Two was giving him an up-and-down look that could only be described as *hungry*.

"Well . . ."

Tay was hesitating now.

"See?!" Scottie said. Her lip was already starting to tremble.

"Okay," Tay admitted, "the *girls* are definitely flirting. *Definitely*. But as for Beck? I really can't tell. He might just be innocently chatting."

"Well, what do I do?" Scottie asked. "Y'know, to find out if it's innocent or *not* innocent?"

Tay heaved a sigh and rolled her eyes.

"How'm I supposed to know?" she said. "It's not like you own him, Scottie. He's gonna interact with people on the planet besides you, y'know."

"I know!" Scottie pouted. "But with girls who are obviously macking on him? I mean, Beck is my *boyfriend*. We've made out a total of seven times!"

"Okay, *that* I didn't need to know," Tay said with a curled lip. "Anyway, if you guys are really a couple, you've gotta trust him."

"Yeah, I guess," Scottie said. But clearly she was broadcasting major angst, because Tay threw her a bone.

"Or I guess you could march over there and drop the BF-bomb," Tay said. "Y'know, let them know they should keep their mitts off your man."

"You guys!" Bella had just poked her head back through the door. "What's going on? Are we going to look for Amanda?"

Scottie barely heard her. She was already staring at Beck and the flirty girls, trying to devise an opening line.

"Uh," Tay said, "I think Scottie's gonna join us in a minute."

"What?" Scottie said. She peeled her eyes off Beck for an instant to refocus on her buds. "Oh, oh yeah. I just want to, um, give Beck the update."

"Yeah, the update being that his girlfriend is one of those rabid, jealous types," Tay muttered.

"Am not!" Scottie shrieked. "Or . . . well, maybe I am. How'm I supposed to know what kind of girlfriend I am? I just had my first kiss five days ago."

"Scottie," Tay sighed with an indulgent smile. "Just go do what you gotta do and then come find us, 'kay?"

"'Kay," Scottie said wanly.

This time, Scottie looked both ways for sock sliders before she headed back across the foyer. With each step she felt shakier. But when she arrived at Beck's side, she gritted her teeth and forced a smile. She wanted to slip her arm through his, but that seemed way too much like something a catty movie character would do; not something Scottie would do.

"Hi!" Beck said. "Crisis over already?"

"Mmm," Scottie said vaguely. She gave Beck a searching look, then glanced at Girl One and Girl Two. Up close, she noticed a couple other details about them. For one, unlike Scottie, they both needed darts in their fitted tops to accommodate their sproutage. For another, they definitely didn't like the fact that Scottie was crashing their little party.

"Scottie?" Beck said. "Meet Jessie and . . ."

Beck paused on Girl Two.

"Kayla," the girl supplied in a teasing voice.

"Sorry," Beck said. "I'm terrible with names."

"Scottie?" Kayla muttered in response. "What kind of name is that?"

"What, you never heard of F. Scott Fitzgerald?" Beck said. "Scottie's a direct descendant!"

Beck turned to Scottie with a grin.

"Well, it *could* be true," he whispered.

Inside joke! Scottie thought, her spirits lifting a bit. *That's very boyfriendy. Maybe the girls will get a clue.*

She glanced back at them. Clearly, they *did* know something was up. They were now sizing Scottie up with the same snake eyes Scottie was giving *them.*

Okay, Scottie thought. *This is the part where I set them straight.*

"Hey," Scottie said to the girls, "thanks for keeping Beck company. I was dealing with some party drama and totally neglecting him. I'm *such* a terrible girlfriend."

"Girlfriend!" Jessie said, her face going dark. Immediately, her eyes drifted away from Beck and began scanning the party, presumably for a new prospect. "Beck, didn't tell us he had a *girlfriend.*"

Beck shoved his hands in his jeans pockets and shrugged uncomfortably.

"I . . . um . . ."

Beck was looking at Scottie with an expression she couldn't quite decipher. He was surprised, definitely. And a little . . . bewildered? Or maybe he was just squinting because of all the smoke in the air. That was probably the reason Scottie's lungs were feeling so choked up, too.

Scottie *did* slip her arm through Beck's now. And she couldn't help flashing Girls One and Two—she'd already forgotten their names—a tiny, smug smile.

"Want to get some fresh air?" Scottie asked Beck. "Tay and Bella are outside, looking for Amanda."

"Uh, sure," Beck murmured. He glanced at the disappointed girls. "Nice meeting you guys."

"Yeah, it was!" Scottie chirped. "See ya later."

"Bye," Girl One said bluntly. Immediately, she and Girl Two formed a huddle. They began whispering and shooting angry glances at Scottie as she led Beck to the door.

That's right, girls, Scottie thought, grinning at Beck. *Keep your mitts off. He's mine!*

As she and Beck stepped out onto the front porch, Scottie took a gulp of cool, night air.

"Oh man," she said. "It feels so much better out here, doesn't it?"

"Um, yeah," Beck said, shoving his hands back into his pockets. "Listen—"

"Scottie!"

Scottie jumped at the sound of Bella's voice. Bella and Tay had just rounded the left corner of the house and were walking briskly toward them. Without Amanda.

"You didn't find her?" Scottie said. She was getting a little worried.

"Maybe we should look upstairs?" Tay said, gazing apprehensively at the second story windows, each of which were hung with blackout curtains, twisted mini-blinds, or frayed sheets. "I mean, I hate to come in contact with the *living quarters,* but—"

"Why?!"

That was Amanda's voice! She sounded both sad and strident. The three Chicks all jumped and swiveled their heads in the same direction—the right side of the house.

Without exchanging a word, they rushed toward the voice. Beck trailed a few steps behind them. When they found Amanda—standing

• • Chicks with Sticks

in a little garden, complete with a dank-smelling fish pond—she wasn't alone. She was talking to Toby.

Or rather, fighting with him.

"Tell me why *I'm* dressed up like a Michigan Avenue princess," Amanda demanded, "when everybody else here, including *yourself*, is wearing the clothes they slept in last night?"

"Amanda—" Toby protested. He was sitting on a bench next to the fish pond, looking bewildered. "Come sit down. We'll talk about this."

"No!" Amanda said. "I'm *not* gonna be all quiet and unobtrusive. Isn't that what you want, Toby? For me to be a . . . a show?"

"What?" Toby squawked.

"You guys," Tay whispered to Scottie, Bella, and Beck. "Let's get out of here. Amanda will find us when she's rea—"

Amanda whipped around and saw them. Scottie felt so uncomfortable, her skin crawled. But Amanda didn't seem to mind the eavesdropping.

"No!" Amanda said again, this time to her friends. "I want you to hear this. Because this is about you, too."

She turned back to Toby and crossed her arms over her chest.

"It's not like you haven't done this before, Toby," she said bitterly. "You know, conveniently not had any time for me unless it was some group thing with your friends. You just want me around to complete your new image—a cool crowd, a badass band, a . . ."

Amanda glanced at Tay before she finished. ". . . a hot girlfriend."

"What?" Toby said. "I'm not allowed to be proud of you?"

Amanda ignored him and pressed on.

"But now you brought my *friends* into it," she almost-shouted. "*They* didn't need to be dragged here, overdressed and looking like geeky high schoolers. *They* shouldn't have been humiliated like that."

Amanda whipped around to shoot her fellow Chicks a look of fierce loyalty—and maybe gather a dose of strength as well. Because when she turned back to Toby, she announced, "And you know what? *I* shouldn't have been humiliated like that either."

"Amanda!" Toby cried, jumping up and running over to her. "I didn't mean to—"

"I know," Amanda interrupted. "I know, Toby. I know you don't mean to do it. I know you haven't meant to get all distant on me. I even know that you didn't mean to become this . . . cool guy that you've become. But you did all those things."

Toby suddenly looked down at his calloused hands.

"It's not that I'm not proud of you," Amanda went on. Her voice was even softer now, and choked with feeling. "I'm glad you're happy. But you're not . . . the same."

"People change," Toby protested. "Especially when they're in college. But that doesn't mean I don't love you, Amanda!"

"Do you?" Amanda said. She was crying now. "Or do you just love the idea of me? Be honest, Toby. For my sake. Especially after what you did to me tonight."

Toby dropped his head into his hands.

"I don't know," he groaned. "Amanda, we've been together for almost a year. You don't just throw that away!"

"That's not really a great reason to stay together, is it?" Amanda said.

Scottie stifled a gasp. Was Amanda actually breaking up with Toby?! Reflexively, she glanced back at Beck. He was looking more uncomfortable than ever.

Well, duh, Scottie thought. *He barely knows Amanda and now he's witnessing the biggest drama of her life!*

When Scottie turned back to Amanda and Toby, Toby's arms were clasped tightly around Amanda's waist, his face buried in her shoulder.

Scottie nudged Tay and motioned with her head toward the lawn. Tay, looking pained, nodded and grabbed Bella's hand. With Beck in the lead, the Chicks tiptoed away so Amanda and Toby could finish their conversation—their break-up—in private.

Nobody said a word. The girls were too shaken and too eaten up with sadness for Amanda to dish about what they'd just seen. The only break in their silence came from Tay, who flipped open her cell phone and called John.

"Hey," she said raspily. "It's me. Can you come out front? We're waiting for Amanda, but I have a feeling she's gonna want to get out of here really soon."

Maybe ten minutes later, Amanda did appear. She'd driven them all to the party in her mom's Mercedes, but with one look at her tear-streaked face, John offered to drive the car home.

"Thanks," Amanda said, handing him the keys and ducking her head down so that her long hair covered her splotched face. Their crew trudged miserably down the road to the car. Amanda fell into the back-seat and shut the door behind her. She leaned heavily against the win-dow and buried her head in the crook of her arm.

Scottie, Tay, and Bella squeezed into the backseat from the other side of the car, while Beck sat up front with John. Scottie picked up Amanda's hand and held it in hers. Her hand felt so small, so cold, that Scottie's heart broke a little bit. She snuggled up to her quietly crying friend and rested her head on her shoulder, wanting to comfort her with her presence, even if she couldn't with words.

The whole, silent drive home, Scottie stayed just like that—cuddled up to Amanda and staring at Beck's poochy-lipped profile illuminated by the passing headlights.

14 *(Do not block)

The next day at noon—an hour before the Chicks were due at Hannah's for their first lace-knitting session—they gathered somberly around Scottie's dining room table.

Amanda looked ghostly pale. Even more alarming, she was wearing sweats! And not even shimmery Juicy Couture–type sweats. These were navy blue and elasticized at the ankle. They rivaled Scottie's lavender stretch pants for frumpiness.

Bella sat next to Amanda and plopped her canvas bag onto the table.

"Here," she said, pulling foodstuffs from the tote. "I brought some chocolate covered graham crackers and sparkling lemonade—your favorite comfort foods."

"Thanks," Amanda said wanly. "I totally don't deserve this. Not after I dragged you all to that awful beer-fest."

"Watch it," Tay said as she plopped down at the head of the table. She glanced back at Scottie's mom's curtained-off studio. Her painting music—some sweet Dar Williams—was pumping out into the loft and the air smelled of strong coffee. "There are parents present."

"No worries," Scottie said as she laid out plates, tubs of salads, and French bread for their lunch. "Mom's in the zone. Has been for a while now. She's not coming out for nothing. I was totally able to sneak my beery clothes into the washing machine this morning without either of the 'rents finding out."

"You could have told your parents the truth," Bella said with a frown. "It's not like you actually drank any beer."

"Yeah, well." Scottie shrugged. "Let's not forget I was on my second date ever. I didn't want them to get a bad impression of Beck and y'know, pull some Capulet moves."

"So now you're Romeo and Juliet?" Tay said. "I thought you were Annie Hall and Alvy Singer. Which is it, Shearer?"

"Actually?" Bella said carefully. "I think we should talk about Amanda and Toby?"

"Oh yeah," Tay said with a cringe. "Sorry. So Amanda—spill. How'd it end last night?"

"Tay," Bella whispered through gritted teeth. "Don't you think you should ask her a little more sensitively?"

"What?" Tay defended herself. "Do you want me to get Mr. Adrian over here to work some of his therapeutic mojo on her? Amanda knows I care, right, Amanda?"

"Yeah," Amanda said, flashing a grateful smile. Then she cracked open the sparkling lemonade, took a small sip, and announced, "We're taking a break. I mean it's not like we're never gonna speak again. But we need . . . We're taking a break. It was my idea."

"Whoa," Tay muttered. "Did Toby freak?"

"No," Amanda said calmly. "He did cry a little bit though."

"He cried?!" Scottie almost yelled. "In front of you?"

"What's wrong with that?" Bella said. "Everybody cries."

"I guess so," Scottie muttered. "I just never thought of a *boy* crying. I mean, unless it was at a funeral or something."

Amanda gave her a long look before she went on.

"So then—this is kind of strange—but *I* was the one who got all calm," she said. "I stopped crying and things just became really clear. We love each other, but we also both want to be free."

"You do, too?" Scottie said. "Since when?"

"Since Toby changed." Amanda sighed. "You don't know how much it was dragging me down, always waiting for him to call me. And then when he *did* call me, everything was just . . . off. I mean, maybe it'll hit me later, how much I miss him, and how sad this is. But on the other hand, I think I've been sad for a while. I was *already* missing him, when you think about it.

"Now I'm just kinda relieved," she said. "Because, if it's over, maybe I don't have to be sad anymore. And if we're meant to be, we'll find our way back to each other."

Amanda took a shaky sip of lemonade.

"Does that sound totally crazy?" she asked. "I'm just in major denial, aren't I?"

"I don't think so," Bella cried with a grin. "Amanda, I think you're totally empowered!"

"Okay," Tay said, grabbing a tub of chicken salad from the middle of the table. "This is getting a little too group-therapy, you guys. Do we *have* to go with the crunchy-feely verbiage?"

"Sorry," Amanda said. Her smile got a little bigger as she added, "And don't hog all that chicken salad. Suddenly, I'm starving."

Tay responded by plopping a giant dollop of the mayonnaisey stuff onto Amanda's plate. Bella giggled as she started dishing up some curried tofu for herself. Scottie tried to join in on the laughter as she tore the heel off the French bread and spooned some tofu onto her own plate. But her stomach was too fluttery for jokes.

"So that's it?" she asked, gazing at Amanda. "You guys just stop calling and stop seeing each other?"

Amanda nodded thoughtfully as she chewed.

"For now," she said. "I know. I can't totally wrap my brain around it, either."

She took another giant bite of chicken salad. Tay and Bella dug

• Chicks with Sticks

into their lunches with the same gusto, but Scottie could barely nibble at her tofu.

She couldn't believe that Amanda and Toby could go from madly smitten to so distant that they were relieved to split up. Of course, Scottie knew this could happen in theory. People grew apart all the time. But in practice?

It was incredibly depressing.

It occurred to Scottie, suddenly, that this word she'd been savoring all week—*boyfriend*—was even more loaded than she'd realized. Up until now, it had only meant hand-holding and Saturday night dates; kissing and belonging to a kind of club. But Scottie hadn't really considered the flip side of that—that gaining a boyfriend meant she had one to lose as well.

The Chicks arrived at Hannah's loft, still nursing their half-finished bottles of lemonade, knitting bags hanging heavily off their elbows. An instant before Scottie knocked, the door swung open.

"Beck!" Scottie said.

Beck, who'd clearly been about to plunge out of the apartment, skidded to a halt. He looked from Scottie to her friends, and back to Scottie.

"Hi!" he said, a bit uncomfortably. "Long time, no see, you guys."

"Hi," Amanda, Bella, and Tay drawled en masse, while Scottie just stared.

"You're leaving," she blurted.

"Well, yeah," Beck said. "You guys have to work, right? I'd feel like a jerk sitting around watching TV while you're all getting yarn callouses."

"Yeah, the yarn callous," Tay said. "That's actually a myth. You know, to make us look butch."

"Yeah," Bella laughed. "See?!"

She thrust out her right hand and flipped it back and forth.

"Injury-free," she pronounced proudly.

"Heh-heh," Beck laughed a little awkwardly, before shooting Amanda a shy glance.

"So, is everything okay?" he asked. "After last night?"

"Oh yeah, fine," Amanda said softly. "Well, not *fine*. But I'm okay. Thanks for asking."

"Sure, sure," Beck said. He dug his hands into his pockets and hunched up his shoulders. "Okay! Well, I should go. . . ."

Scottie felt a pang.

Well, hello and good-bye, Beck!

While Tay, Amanda, and Bella stepped inside the loft, Scottie hung back.

"I'll see you in there in a minute," she said.

"Sure," Amanda said, glancing at Beck. "We can introduce ourselves to Hannah."

Her friends shut the door and Scottie turned to Beck. Suddenly, it was difficult to remember all the easy, melty vibes that had passed so effortlessly between them for the past week.

"This is kind of weird, huh?" Scottie said apologetically. "Me finally showing up to work for your mom?"

Beck shrugged.

"Nah," he said.

Then he shrugged again.

"Well, maybe a little," he admitted. "But I swear, I'm cool with this knitty gig of yours."

"Really?" Scottie said.

"Really. And besides, we just hung out last night. I wouldn't want you to get sick of me or anything."

"Ha, ha," Scottie barked. "Wouldn't want that."

Okay, she groaned inwardly, *what's happening here? Am I crazy, or did I just conjure a self-fulfilling prophecy with my lunchtime freak-out?*

•• *Chicks with Sticks*

"So, okay, I should go," Beck said. "I'm gonna hang with the Burrito Brothers. We might see a movie. There's a Jim Jarmusch at the Music Box. He's the height of cool."

"Well, *yeah*," Scottie said, nodding way too much. Because, of course, she didn't have a clue who Jim Jarmusch was. "Okay, then . . ."

Scottie took a hesitant step toward Beck and relaxed her lips into a pre-pucker.

Beck glanced nervously at his loft door. Then he gave Scottie's upper arm a squeeze.

"Okay," he said again. "Talk to ya later?"

With that, he was gone—loping down the hallway, his hands still deep in his pockets, flicking his shaggy hair out of his eyes with a little swerve of his head.

Scottie stared after him, even after he rounded the corner to the elevator.

Okay, she asked herself, biting her lip, *how many ways could that have gone better?*

She imagined Beck giving her one of the sweet, smiley kisses he'd been planting on her all week.

Even better, he could have given her *several* sweet, smiley kisses.

Or, he could have stayed home, hanging out on the couch so he could shoot Scottie secret looks. Maybe he would have even dropped a cute note into her lap when he passed her to go the kitchen, a note that said, *Meet me in the hallway in five minutes.* When she did, he'd be waiting there to give her yet more sweet, smiley kisses.

Not that Scottie had lain awake in her bed that morning imagining this very scenario or anything.

Sighing, Scottie pushed open the loft door. Her friends were sitting at the dining room table, half of which had been cleared of sketches, samples, and sewing paraphernalia to give them a workspace. Clearly, the introductions had been made and the lace-planning had already begun. Hannah—wearing carpenter's jeans and a voluminous top made of filmy, hot-pink fabric—was enthusiastically flipping through skein after skein of glimmery cord, thread, and yarn.

"So this gold is for the sleeves of the eggplant dress," she was saying, "but I'm torn about the knickers. I keep thinking fringe, then I say, 'No, lace it up, baby. If it ain't broke, don't fix it.' You know what I mean?"

"Um," Tay said, "not really, but . . ."

She shot Scottie a prickly glance as Scottie pressed the door quietly closed. *This woman*, her look clearly said, *is a total case and later, I'm going to have to kill you.*

Amanda, on the other hand, was practically glowing. Her eyes gleamed as she reached into Hannah's sizeable yarn stash and fished out some coral-pink thread.

"Hannah," she proposed, "what if the knickers had this running through the cuff? I mean, we could literally use running stitch, ending in a little poof of lace with a hidden button. The lace can be the part that cinches it all together."

Hannah's face screwed up into a mass of wrinkles that Scottie assumed meant she was thinking hard. She fussed with one of her pigtails and chomped savagely at a hangnail on her thumb. Then she looked up abruptly and announced, "It works. It better than works. You've got an eye, Amanda!"

Grinning, Amanda extended a length of the coral thread to size up its weight. Meanwhile, Hannah spun around. Scottie realized that she was still cringing by the door.

"Ah, Scottie!" Hannah cried. "You're finally here. Sit, sit."

Scottie scurried over to the table and Hannah continued to outline her plans. She wanted Scottie to knit up the gold lace she'd envisioned for the eggplant dress, and Amanda should get started on the lace for the knickers.

"Now, *you* girls," Hannah said, pointing a raggedy finger at Tay and Bella, "you and I have to get to concepting. Tell me what *this* says to you."

Hannah presented a sketch of a gauzy skirt with two layers of fabric and jaggedy hems that floated around the ankles.

"Oohhh!" Bella cried, clapping her hands with delight.

"To me, it says Bella," Tay yawned. While Bella immediately chose a gossamer yarn that would give the skirt a sweet, subtle trim, Hannah led Tay over to a dress form, on which was pinned a pair of bottle-green bell-bottoms with an asymmetrical button fly.

"Pretty bad-ass, huh?" Hannah crowed, tapping Tay on the arm.

"Actually," Tay said with a raised eyebrow. "Yeah."

Amanda spun in her seat and grinned at Scottie.

"This was such a great idea," she whispered. "I can't believe we really get to design a little bit of something that people will wear!"

"Uh-huh," Scottie said dully. She grabbed her gold cord and pulled a lace pattern book and some #3's out of her bag.

"Um, how was Beck?" Amanda asked.

Awkward? Scottie posed silently. *And kiss-impaired. And I think it's all because of this gig! He says he's cool with it, but is he really? Maybe that's boy-speak for, "Guess what, Scottie. Now that you knit for my* mother, *my attraction to you has curled up and died."*

Normally she would have unloaded all this angst out loud. But since Amanda was still looking a little shell-shocked after her own boy drama, Scottie just shrugged.

"Oh, fine," she whispered. "I think. But you know, this is all so new, I'm still learning to read his signals."

An expression flashed across Amanda's face—a knowing look of concern.

"What?" Scottie said. Okay, she might have snapped. "What's wrong?"

"Nothing," Amanda said quickly. "It's just, the thing about boys, Scottie, is they're always gonna be kind of mysterious. Just like we are to them."

"Weren't you just telling me the opposite?" Scottie demanded. "You said I should *stop* looking at boys as 'mysterious' aliens and start treating them like human beings. Friends, even."

"Well . . ." Amanda began casting her coral thread onto a skinny needle. "I stand behind that. Of course, I do! It's just, you need to know that, even in the best conditions, the boyfriend thing can be . . . challenging. Look at me and Toby."

Scottie felt a stab of hurt. She knew Amanda was in a bad state, but it was almost like she was *trying* to drag Scottie down with her. Scottie looked down at her own yarn. Absent-mindedly, she made a slip knot and pushed it onto her needle.

"You know," she whispered, "just because it didn't work out with you and Toby doesn't mean that Beck and I are doomed."

Tears sprang to Amanda's eyes. Her pink thread went limp in her hands.

"I wasn't saying it did," she rasped. "Geez, Scottie. I was just trying to be helpful."

"I know," Scottie said, feeling teary herself. "I know you were."

"I'm sure everything with you and Beck is just fine," Amanda said. Now she was the one sounding snappish. She went back to her casting on. A row of neat stitches began to build on her rosewood needle.

"You think?" Scottie wheedled.

"It'd be nice if you were as worried about *me*," Amanda said. "I *have* just been through this major trauma."

"I am!" Scottie whispered. "Of course, I am. But you seem so okay with everything."

"Yeah, well . . ." Amanda sighed and finished looping her yarn. "Scottie, just be careful not to have crazy-high expectations. I mean, I know how your imagination works. But you've only known Beck for a little while."

"Oh, thanks," Scottie cracked. "Make me sound like more of a case."

"Seriously," Amanda said. She gave Scottie a hard—and loving—look.

Scottie rolled her eyes. Amanda really *was* reading too much into their psych class.

"I've got it under control," Scottie insisted, even as her mind drifted back to that missed connection in the hallway.

Amanda cut her off in mid-brood.

"Glad to hear it," she said. Her smile had returned. "Now, can you do me a favor and count these stitches? I need twenty-six and I'm not in the mood to deal at the moment."

"Sure thing," Scottie said. She grabbed Amanda's needle and began flicking away at the stitches, counting under her breath.

But even she had count three times to get Amanda's CO to the right number. And when she handed the needle back, her smile was way wobbly.

Because the whole boyfriend/girlfriend thing? She'd lied. It suddenly felt completely *out* of control. And Scottie didn't have a clue what was around the next turn.

The Chicks left Hannah's loft about two hours after arriving, each with three lace assignments to finish before they met again in two weeks.

Hannah had wanted another meeting after one week, but Bella explained that they were spending the following weekend at YarnCon.

"And, of course," Amanda added, grabbing Bella's hand to give her a twirl, "we also have to keep Sunday night open. It's Bella's birthday, which requires an emergency weeknight S.S.O. at her apartment."

"S.S.O," Hannah said. "What's that?"

"Oh, nothing," Scottie blurted, going red. She was still feeling a little weird about getting too chummy with her BF's mother. She wanted to keep things strictly businesslike between them, no matter how much she liked Hannah.

"It's so not nothing!" Bella retorted. She fingered her new swatch of pale green lace as she explained to Hannah, "It stands for Sacred

Sleepover. We have them every couple weeks. With mandatory junk food and chick flicks."

"And knitting, of course," Amanda added with a grin.

"And occasionally," Tay said, "birthday cake. Vegan, if preferred."

While Scottie squirmed, Hannah clapped her hands together.

"I love it!" she declared. "You girls are adorable. And more importantly, talented. Amanda, let me get another look at your lace before you go. It's incredible."

Amanda's free-formed swatch was shaped like a fan, with little lines of purls and yarn-overs swooping gracefully outward.

"It really is," Scottie said. She took Amanda's swatch and stretched it out to take in its eyelet-filled beauty. Of course, she wasn't just admiring Amanda's work—she was also asking Amanda for forgiveness for their little spat earlier.

"Thanks," Amanda said, winking at Scottie and giving her a poke in the arm.

Which Scottie knew was Amanda's way of saying, *Forgiveness granted, dork.*

So that evening, Scottie was free to angst about nothing but Beck. And the fact that he hadn't called. Or IM'd. Or knocked on her door.

Since homework was impossible, she stomped out to the red couch with her lace and flopped into the smushy cushions to knit.

She peered at the pattern in her book, then glanced at the adjustments that she'd scribbled into the margins in green ink.

"Yarnover," she muttered to herself, "Knit two together. Purl three. Yarnover. Knit two together . . ."

Knit two together.

Is that what we're doing, me and Beck? Scottie wondered. *Or am I just fooling myself?*

Scottie eyed her cell phone, which she'd just happened to place expectantly on the coffee table. It was deafeningly silent.

Scottie shook her head at it and tried to refocus on her knitting.

"SSK," she whispered to herself, "purl three, yarnover, knit two together."

Knit two together! This pattern just *had* to be brimming with them.

With a huff of frustration, Scottie tossed the Lace in Progress onto the coffee table. She needed a break. Grabbing her cell, she stomped toward her bedroom. In the hallway, she ran into her mom, who was leaning into the laundry closet across the hall from Scottie's room. She pulled a couple items out of the dryer, namely the clothes Scottie had worn the night before. Scottie could detect the faded outline of last night's beer on the blue top.

It stained? Scottie groaned, but not out loud, of course. *Lovely. A souvenir of the anti-frat party.*

"You were quick to do your laundry this morning," Mom said, tossing Scottie her clothes and raising one eyebrow. "Anything I should know about last night's party?"

"What do you mean?" Scottie said quickly.

"Honey," her mom said. "You *never* do your own laundry. Let me guess. Your clothes were reeking of smoke."

"And beer," Scottie blurted, looking at the floor. Suddenly she was too weary to tap dance around this subject.

"Okay," Mom said, crossing her arms over her chest and looking grim. "Was any of this smoke or beer consumed by you? Or just your clothes?"

"Just the clothes, I swear!" Scottie cried. "It was a really gross party. This guy doing sock-slides spilled his beer beaker all over me and—"

"Okay," Mom said, holding up her hand. "Here I thought I was being all savvy and hip to your game, and now you're using vocabulary I've never heard. Tell me this. Amanda drove last night. She did *not* drive under the influence, did she?"

"No!" Scottie said.

"And you swear that you didn't drink or smoke?" her mom said.

"No!"

"Did your—" Scottie's mom swallowed hard. "Did your boyfriend?"

"No," Scottie said miserably. "I promise."

"Okay," her mom said, shaking her head with a deep sigh. "I'm going to believe you, Scottie. But can I just say that I can't believe you have a boyfriend? My little girl!"

Little girl?! Ugh.

Luckily, Scottie's mom couldn't see Scottie rolling her eyes, because she was wrapping her up in a quick, hard hug. Her mom's usual tangy scent of spiky hair gel and acrylic paint was overpowered by the odor of coffee.

Well, being called a little girl is better than being grounded, Scottie allowed to herself.

Into her mom's sharp shoulder, she sighed, "I can't believe I have a boyfriend, either."

Pulling away, Mom ducked back into the clothes dryer. Scottie tossed her wrinkly party outfit over her arm and headed into her room. Before she shut the door, her mom added, "By the way, Scottie?"

"Yeah?" Scottie said, still shaky after being busted.

Her mom pulled the last of the clothes out of the machine, dropped them into the orange mesh laundry basket at her feet, and stared Scottie down.

"That's the last college party you're going to for a good long while," she said. "Possibly 'til you're in college yourself."

"Mom!" Scottie whined. "This is the thanks I get for telling you the tru—"

Her mom held up a single finger to make Scottie zip it.

"Ooh," she said. "Just got a brainstorm."

Before Scottie could utter another word of protest, her mom dashed down the hall. A few seconds later, Gwen Stefani began pumping out of her studio.

Scottie sighed and shut her bedroom door. Flopping into her desk chair, she flipped open her laptop and dragged her finger aimlessly across the track pad.

She skimmed up to her bookmarks and scrolled down through the long list of sites, both knitty and gossipy.

Almost against her will, her cursor hovered over the one site that was both: *In a Sknit.*

Don't do it, Scottie told herself. *This is none of your business.*

But Scottie couldn't help it. If anyone could distract her from Beck's silence, it was T. C. Boil.

Well, haven't heard from BF all day! I'm proud of him. And just in time, too. The static cling was getting to me.

Have been able to focus on my current WIP all afternoon. The thing about the WIP though is . . . never mind, I don't know if I can bring myself to type this.

Ah, what the hell—it's lace. Yes lace. Like the kind your granny puts on the back of the couch. If you have that kind of granny, which I don't. Thank god.

I'm only doing it because it's a job. I'm getting paid for this. Seeing as this is probably the only time in my life I'll actually make some money out of this obsession of mine, why not?

Plus, turning the gig down would have resulted in friend-based drama. And I get enough of that without saying a word. No way am I dumb enough to generate any of my own!

10 p.m. And still no call from BF.

Maybe I should call him?

Nah. Don't want to scut the day's progress. Besides, I'll see him in a matter of hours at school.

What's that phrase? Be careful what you wish for?

Whoever came up with that one should be punished.

Scottie logged off, feeling numb. Maybe it should have made her feel better, that she wasn't the only one going through bedtime BF angst.

But it didn't.

(Knit two together)

In fact, it only made her feel more worried.

Clearly *none* of her friends had all the answers when it came to the art of having a boyfriend.

Which means, Scottie sighed as she began to get ready for bed, *I'm flying blind.*

A few days later, she still felt, if not exactly blind? Definitely visually impaired.

Because Beck was harder to read than ever.

When Scottie arrived in the foyer Monday morning, her guard fully up, Beck surprised her by swooping her into a hug so big, he lifted her off her feet.

"Good morning," he said, planting a quick smack on her lips.

"Hi!" Scottie said, her eyebrows raised. "Better now?"

"What do you mean?" Beck said, with a confused grin. "Was I sick or something and I didn't know it?"

"Oh, no, it was just . . ."

Okay, he went from melty to awkward to kind of fizzy! Amanda was right. The boy is definitely mysterious. Which I guess is . . . normal?

". . . nothing," Scottie said with a sunny smile. "I didn't mean anything."

Deciding to just relax and enjoy the moment, she puckered up for another kiss. She and Beck held hands the whole walk to the L.

But that afternoon at lunch?

Beck loped into the cafeteria, stopped by the Chicks' table to say a quick hello, and then took his Sloppy Joe over to sit with the burrito brothers!

"What!?" Scottie squeaked, twisting furtively in her chair to watch him go. "What's going on?"

"Um, lunch?" Amanda said absently. She wasn't actually eating lunch. She was too busy working a tricky turn in her second fan of lace for Hannah's knickers.

"Beck and I are boyfriend/girlfriend," Scottie rasped. "Doesn't that mean we're supposed to sit together at lunch?"

"Don't you want to sit with us?" Bella questioned, a forkful of tofu loaf trembling before her lips.

"Of course," Scottie said. "And I want *Beck* to sit with us!"

"Well what about *his* friends?" Bella said, nodding at the burrito boys. One of them had a laptop open on the table. Beck and the other guy were peering at the screen over the boy's shoulder, snickering at something he'd written. A couple other guys and one girl were heading over to join them. A patch on the girl's satchel read, ARE YOU STARKERS?

Scottie's mouth hung open. The guy positively had a posse! When had that happened?

"Oh, I get it," Bella said. "You want him all to yourself."

"No!" Scottie said. "But shouldn't he want to spend time with me when he has the chance?"

"You mean *besides* walking to and from school together daily?" Amanda said. "Not to mention dates and drop-bys. I mean, you guys practically live together."

"We do not," Scottie sulked.

"Scottie," Bella said. "You've got to give Beck a chance to have a life."

"Of course," Scottie said petulantly. "It's not like I want to spend all *my* time with him, either. I just thought, y'know, lunch together . . ."

"It's a very boyfriend-girlfriend type of thing to do," Amanda said wistfully.

"Yeah," Scottie said, grateful that Amanda got it.

"Well, I bet he'll want to sit with us tomorrow," Amanda offered.

"Sure . . ." Scottie sighed. She chomped unenthusiastically into her turkey sandwich, peeking over her shoulder at Beck as she chewed.

"So how's your lace?" Bella piped up. She was clearly itching to change the subject. "Wanna see mine? As I was knitting it, I was thinking, 'Snowflakes!'"

Bella pulled her WIP out of her tote. Scottie took another bite of sandwich and tried to pay attention. But as Bella began to point out the intricacies of her mitered square, Scottie found her eyes drifting over to Beck again.

He was reading something else on the laptop screen and laughing uproariously. Scottie couldn't help but smile. He was *so* cute. She wondered what was so funny—

Oop! He's looking right at me.

Scottie started to glance away, but then she remembered something.

Hello, she told herself. *This is your boyfriend? Not some crush. You're allowed to make eyes at him.*

Scottie waved. A tiny, tentative little wave.

Still laughing, Beck waved back—a big, sunny wave—before returning to his friends.

Okay, Scottie thought. *So that was good. He's over there with his friends, I'm with mine. Everyone's happy.*

Scottie glanced up at Bella. Her pale eyes were hooded and sulky.

Whoops, Scottie thought. *Except Bella.*

Bella had pulled her lace back toward her and was knitting and purling madly.

"Wait," Scottie said. "I missed that last part. So after the slip slip knit, you . . ."

"That's okay," Bella said forlornly. "I already showed Amanda."

"Oh." Scottie slumped. She took another bite of her sandwich, which she decided was way too dry. She slapped it back onto her lunch bag with a sigh.

"Oh, God," Amanda sighed. "Just get it over with."

"What?" Scottie said.

"Just go over and say hi to him," Amanda said, nodding at Beck. "You're clearly dying to. A lot more than you're interested in our lace gig."

•• *Chicks with Sticks*

"I *am* interested in it," Scottie protested. She meant it, too. She really was psyched to see her knitting paired with Hannah's designs. "I just . . . can't focus on it."

"Until you get a Beck fix." Bella sighed. She turned to Amanda. "This is worse than her caffeine addiction."

"Ob-ses-sing," Amanda singsonged through clenched teeth.

"Hey!" Scottie said. "I'm totally offended by that." But even as she said it, she found herself glancing again at Beck—who was typing something into the laptop himself now.

"Go, go," Amanda said. "We'll see you in a minute."

So Scottie went. The trip across the cafeteria wasn't nearly the gauntlet it had been the week before. This time, Scottie had an entitled spring in her step.

Just going to say hi to my boyfriend, she told herself breezily. *That's all.*

Except when she arrived? Beck sort of didn't notice. He was still typing into the computer, laughing and shaking his head every once in a while.

"Um . . ." Scottie peeped.

"Hey," one of the burrito brothers said. "Scottie, right?"

"Right," Scottie said.

"Cool," the guy said, taking a massive bite out of his sloppy joe. "Except, you can't be here."

Beck suddenly emerged from his computer haze and glanced up at Scottie with wide eyes. He slapped the laptop shut as he blurted, "Hey!"

"Uh, hi," Scottie said awkwardly. "I just came over to say, uh, hi."

"Hi," Beck said. He smiled before glancing shiftily at the other folks at his table. He got to his feet and shoved his hands in his pockets.

"We're sort of in a meeting," Beck murmured in her ear. "Y'know, about that thing I told you about?"

"Starkers?" Scottie hissed. Unfortunately, her whisper was a little on the loud side. The burrito brother who'd banished her from the table raised a single eyebrow at her.

(Knit two together)

"Stark raving crazy?" Beck blurted quickly, covering up for Scottie's gaffe. "Nah, just a little overcaffeinated. I'm addicted."

Scottie plopped her forehead into her hand.

"Sorry," she groaned. This time it was low enough that only Beck heard.

"No prob," he laughed softly. "But you can't blow my cover. See you later?"

"On one condition," Scottie whispered with a crooked smile. She glanced subtly at the burrito brother. "Tell me which one that is. Strindberg or Beckett?"

"You're the one that's crazy," Beck said with another laugh.

"Okay, I'm going," Scottie giggled back. Almost without thinking about it, she leaned toward Beck, lips at the ready.

Beck's eyes widened and did a quick survey of the very crowded cafeteria, finally landing on his hipster friends.

"Okay," he said, leaning backward just a bit. A kiss was *so* not happening. "See ya, Scottie."

Scottie bit her lip as she trudged back to Amanda and Bella, feeling a lot less entitled now.

Could I be any more of a spaz? she thought. *Going for PDA in the* cafeteria? *Even Kate and Edward don't do that. Well, not very often.*

Scottie sat back down at the Chicks' table, feeling bereft.

"What's wrong?" Amanda said. "Of course, we were totally spying on you from over here. That looked like it went well."

"He was very smiley," Bella noted.

"Yeah, but I messed up," Scottie said. "Turns out he didn't eat with us because he's in some kind of secret meeting over there! I almost blew it for him."

"And then you went for the PDA," Bella noted, shaking her head sorrowfully.

"Yeah, we might have seen that, too," Amanda apologized.

Scottie groaned.

"Despite that, it looks like we're fine," she confirmed. "Beck and I are just fine. I don't know why I need to keep trying to confirm it! It's like I want some kind of guarantee. But the more I look for it, the less easy it is to find."

"The trick is not to look," Amanda said.

"That's always the trick, isn't it," Scottie complained. She flicked aside her dry turkey sandwich and dug into a bag of potato chips. "Don't look for a boyfriend, and he'll come to you. Don't look for signals from said boyfriend. Don't look for a leg to stand on with said boyfriend. Just be—"

"—breezy," Amanda sighed. "Yeah, not so easy, is it?"

"Well, it oughta be!" Bella said. "You know how I feel about boys, but Beck? Beck seems great! He's sweet. He's smiley. He's clearly smitten. He's even a good smoocher! What are you so worried about?"

"She's right," Amanda said, whipping a few stitches into her lace so, Scottie imagined, she'd have an excuse to hide her sad expression. "Scottie, you have to stop reaching so hard. It's all good!"

But it was like resisting that daily ice cream. Scottie just *couldn't* stop reaching! Over the next few days, she found herself going out of her way to swing by Beck's locker between classes. (She did this almost as assiduously, she noticed, as John made an effort *not* to run into Tay during the school day.)

She analyzed every kiss. Every non-kiss. Every returned phone call and every IM or lack thereof. Study Hall became Study Beck.

For instance, when Beck didn't stop by Never Mind the Frogs at Joe on Tuesday, Scottie wondered if it was because he was still a little weirded out by the fact that she was working for his mom.

When that week's issue of *Starkers* hit the Web on Wednesday, Scottie scoured the film section, wondering which of the pseudonyms belonged to Beck and whether he'd made any veiled references to her in his article.

When he hadn't asked her out for that weekend by Thursday morning, she wondered if this was a good sign: things were so coupley between them, he was just assuming they'd hang out together. Or bad: he was blowing her off!

Finally, she decided to ask him out herself.

"So," she said on Thursday afternoon as they walked from an after-school joe at Joe to the L. "Guess what's playing at the Twentieth-Century tomorrow night?"

"Um, *The Sorrow and the Pity?*" Beck quipped. That was this downer movie Woody Allen always made Diane Keaton watch in *Annie Hall.*

"No, Alvy!" Scottie scoffed. "*Kissing Jessica Stein!* I adore that movie—it's so cute."

"Scottie, it's a chick flick," Beck said with an eye roll. "If the *Chicago Tribune* hires me someday to watch chick flicks, I will gladly watch them. I'll even eat air-popped popcorn and diet soda while I watch them. But on a Saturday night?"

"Oh, actually, I was thinking tomorrow," Scottie said. "I've got Yarn-Con Saturday night, remember?"

"Whoops, actually I forgot." Beck cringed. "And I made plans tomorrow night. I'm going with the you-know-whos—"

By that, he meant the *Starkers* crew.

"—to Piece for pizza and trivia," Beck said.

"Oh," Scottie said. A wave of heat washed over her face as the horrible truth sunk in—she was available one night only this weekend, and Beck had made plans for it.

"You want to come?" Beck asked quickly. "They're a cool group. When they're not speaking in code and writing covert webzines, they're totally inclusive."

"That's cool that you've made all those friends so fast," Scottie said a bit flatly. "But no. I'm hopeless at trivia. I'd just drag you down. I think there's a YarnCon kick-off I could go to with the girls. . . ."

"You would not drag me down," Beck scoffed. "But hey, I understand if you want to make it an all-yarn, all-the-time weekend."

Don't protest too much, Beck, Scottie thought miserably.

They'd arrived at the L stop so she ducked her head into her bag, under the guise of searching for her fare card. But really, she was trying to choke back tears.

Even as she felt the pinprick of a pre-cry behind her eyes, she berated herself.

You're being insecure, she thought. *You're always waiting for the other shoe to drop. You're overanalyzing. Like Amanda and Bella said, you're reaching too hard!*

But the other side of her brain had a quick retort.

Look at Amanda and Toby, it keened. *If you don't watch out, the other shoe will drop. I'm only trying to make sure that doesn't happen!*

And besides, it wasn't like Scottie could control herself anyway. The more she ordered herself to stop reaching out to Beck, the harder she found herself reaching.

And the harder she reached, the farther away he seemed to get.

15 ✻ (Use three-needle bind-off)

"I can't believe we're here," Bella exclaimed. "It's like the whole city's gone knitty!"

Bella was prone to poetic exaggeration, but today, Saturday, all the Chicks had to agree—YarnCon was like Oz, with poofs of yarn instead of poppies and good witches everywhere staging classes, demonstrations, or just impromptu stitching and bitching. The outdoor gathering was nested amongst the department stores, theaters, and ornate office towers of Chicago's downtown loop on a giant patch of cement usually reserved for artists' markets and produce stands.

To help with their Hannah B. gig, the Chicks had all signed up for an afternoon lace techniques class, but they'd left the morning open for meandering.

Scottie couldn't stop gasping in delight as they began strolling through the fray. In one tent, she spotted a table brimming with Risdie's newest line. Three Risdie reps in pink and brown baby T's stood behind the table, looking smug and slouchy as they watched knitters descend on their wares.

At the next tent were jars of adorable stitch markers snazzed up with glass beads, tiny rubber animals, and fuzzy pom-pom creatures—as cute as candy.

There were giant displays of knitting bags, books, needles, and themed T-shirts. People strode around, nibbling chicken satay skewered on knitting needles and giant cookies iced to look like yarn balls. There were gray-haired ladies wearing cardigans, middle-aged mom types, and other teenagers in knitted tanks, badass ribbed wristbands, and bits of yarn woven into their hair.

"I've never fit in this much in my life," Bella giggled. Her own dreads were interspersed with a rainbow of I-cords that she'd pinned on with little butterfly clips. "It's weird!"

The more Scottie explored the convention, the better she felt.

"YarnCon," she breathed. She'd just alighted at a table full of fluffy wool roving. A woman sat in the tent's corner, spinning some of it into a homey, chunky yarn. *"Here's the joy."*

"Finally," Amanda sighed, poking at a puff of the baby-soft wool. "I could use some."

She shot Scottie a crabby glance.

"Hey, what was *that* for?" Scottie said.

"Oh man," Tay said, adjusting her messenger bag of knitting supplies on her hip. "This is gonna be an estrogen-packed day, I can already tell."

"I just hope you're not gonna pout all day," Amanda said. She prodded at another puff of wool.

"Can I *help* you?" the spinning woman said pointedly. "You know, I just washed that wool."

"*Mo*-ving along," Tay said loudly. She hooked her arms through Amanda's and Scottie's and propelled them to the next booth—a display of knitting books. Bella traipsed along behind, pointing out this and that knitty wonder.

"What do you mean?" Scottie demanded of Amanda, picking up right where they left off. "I'm not pouty."

Tay suddenly erupted into a coughing fit. Tucked into her hacking, Scottie thought she heard a breathy, "Bull!"

"Okay," Scottie admitted, flipping open a crochet book and thumbing through its pages without really seeing them. "So I might have been a little sad at *Kissing Jessica Stein* last night."

"A little!" Amanda said. "You were all, 'Oh, this is soooo romantic. Oh, it's such a perfect date movie. Oh, I'd soooo much rather be sharing my Good & Plenty with Beck than with *you* guys.'"

Scottie was horrified.

"I was not like that!" Scottie cried. "Was I?"

"Um, yes, you were," Bella said, as sweetly frank as always.

"I thought you were excited about spending the YarnCon weekend with us," Amanda said. Her lip trembled a tiny bit.

"I was," Scottie scowled. "I mean, I am. But aren't I allowed to be a little bummed, too?"

"Because you didn't get to have a date last night with the boyfriend that you see every day?" Amanda snapped. "Actually, no!"

Scottie had to grind her teeth to hold back a nasty retort. Instead, she said quietly, "I know you're sad about Toby, but you don't have to take it out on me."

"I'm not," Amanda said. "I'm just getting a little tired of your diva thing."

As a lump leaped to her throat, Scottie looked wide-eyed at Tay and Bella.

"I'm just scared, that's all," she squeaked. "Is *that* being a . . . a diva?"

She was on the brink of a sob. Yes, right there in the middle of YarnCon. Scottie flipped the crochet book closed and leaned against the table, biting the heel of her hand to keep from crying. She let her heavy knitting bag fall to the ground.

"*Shhh,*" Bella said. She was at Scottie's side immediately, stroking her shoulder. "Fear is a natural emotion."

"But dude," Tay added, "you've gotta find some balance. You're like a piano wire that's gonna snap."

"Balance?" Scottie said. It came out muffled by her palm.

"Never been your strong suit." Amanda sighed, pointing at Scottie's

•• *Chicks with Sticks*

overstuffed bag. She shuffled forward and gave Scottie a quick hug. "Sorry to harsh on you. It's been a tough week for all of us, huh?"

Scottie just nodded. She didn't know how she felt right then. A little resentful, and a little, *They're totally right!*

She looked at her friends, framed by this rainbow of yarn and autumn sunshine and suddenly blinked hard.

Because she realized something.

What she was *really* feeling? Was relieved. Relieved to have the entire weekend with her friends and her knitting, where no boy-speak was required. Excited to be spending the weekend in this world where everything was knitty; where she truly belonged. Psyched to while away the afternoon in a lace class, losing herself in stitches and soft, beautiful yarn.

If she was still trying to figure out what being a girlfriend was all about, she knew exactly what it meant to be a Chick.

"I'm sorry about last night, you guys," Scottie said. She hung her head. "I don't know what's wrong with me."

"Hello?" Tay said. "I keep saying—it's the estrogen!"

"Combined with testosterone," Bella pointed out. "That's a crazy mix."

"Well . . ." Scottie looked around. The knitters she saw in the booth across the way, pawing hungrily through milk crates of laminated patterns? The people ambling through the aisles, their noses buried in class catalogs or digging into shopping bags to take another peek at their purchases? The vendors perched in folding chairs at various tent entrances, effortlessly clacking away on their WIPs while they greeted shoppers? They were almost *all* female.

". . . there's barely any testosterone here," Scottie said. "And I'm going to enjoy it!"

Even as she made the declaration though, she hesitated. *But what does that mean? I'm still crazy about Beck, aren't I?*

A quick conjure of his hazel eyes and beautiful cheekbones—and the zing in her belly that accompanied it—confirmed that yes, she still adored him.

Then why—

Scottie paused in mid-analysis, aware of her friends' eyes on her. She'd been totally zoning again.

You know what? she told herself. *I'm as bored with my angst as they are.*

"Listen, guys," she said seriously.

She saw Tay's jaw clench, and Amanda's back straighten, and Bella's eyes go wide. They were steeling themselves for more drama—until Scottie cracked a wide grin.

"I don't think we can truly call this a girly weekend," she said, "unless we've got some sugar in our systems. I say we grab some of those yarn ball cookies before our class starts. My treat."

After a wary look at each other, her friends visibly relaxed.

"Cool," Bella said, clapping her hands together. "Since it's my birthday weekend, I'm totally doing dairy and eggs."

"Ovo-lactos unite," Scottie said, pressing her knuckles to Bella's. "Let's go get our knit on."

As they wended their way through the Con, Scottie began to feel more and more like herself.

Tay did a Hannah imitation that was so spot-on, Scottie spewed cookie crumbs all over her.

Then the girls happened upon a tiny yarn tent stocked with the most wild homespun yarn they'd ever seen—fat worms of wool conjoined with scraps of fabric or paper or even tiny plastic bugs, all in colors that weren't of this world. Amanda was the only one with enough cash to buy a forty-dollar ball of mocha-colored stuff called "Twigs and Sticks Con Leche." As the girls continued through the aisles postpurchase, they kept pulling the ball out to admire it.

Finally they grabbed some satay on knitting needles and headed for the large, airy tent where their lace class would be held.

As they arranged themselves at a round table, a teacher circled the space. She had a round, ever-smiling face and a head full of salt-and-pepper curls. She wore a plain tank top, the better to show off an incredible green-and-gold lacy shawl slung around her shoulders with European flair.

"Doesn't she kind of remind you of Alice?" Scottie whispered to Tay with a happy shiver.

"She doesn't look like the type who knits doilies for the back of the couch," Tay said with respect in her voice. "That's for sure."

"Well, we both know *that's* your worst nightmare," Scottie joked—before she froze.

Tay stiffened up, too.

"How do we both know that?" she asked, in chilly voice.

For a brief instant, Scottie just wanted to admit everything to Tay; to tell her she knew all about T. C. Boil and *In a Sknit*. She wished she could tell Tay that she didn't have to confide to the Web, not when she had the Chicks.

"You can say anything to us," Scottie wanted to tell her.

Of course, that begged a question.

Then why didn't you tell Tay when you first discovered her blog?

Scottie drew in a shuddery breath and shook her head, deciding not to go there. If her friends could forgive her Beck-based neurosis, she had to respect Tay's need for privacy.

"C'mon, Tay," she said. "You and doilies? That's like me and roller derby. We're talking no-brainer, here."

Tay relaxed visibly.

"Well, duh!" she said. "Although, purely from a knitting POV? I gotta admit, the lace is fun. I like all the holes and zigs and zags and stuff."

"Zigs and zags and stuff? Sounds like my kinda class."

Tay and Scottie looked up to see Polly and Regan standing behind them.

"Hey!" Amanda cried, hopping out of her chair. She stood on her tiptoes to give voluptuous, redheaded Regan a hug. Then she bent *down* to hug Polly, who was a tiny, wiry thing.

"Nice streaks," Amanda said, tousling the bright pink slashes in Polly's shag-cut, black hair.

"You guys are taking lace-making?" Tay said with a raised eyebrow. "I thought you were all, 'Free-form or die.'"

"Stereotype much?" Regan said with a grin. "Hey, you can't freeform without technique."

"Yeah," Polly said, plopping into one of the free chairs at the Chicks' table. "First we learn lace, then we *un*-lace it. It'll be very punk. We can start tomorrow at the free-form clinic. You're signed up, aren't ya, Amanda?"

"Course!" Amanda said. "And I'm going to the lunchtime crochet-a-thon."

"Ooh, maybe I'll try that," Scottie said as she pulled her lace-in-progress out of her bag. "I left my roster open for tomorrow. I figured I'd decide what to take on the fly."

"Uh-oh," Bella said with a cringe. "I went on the YarnCon website yesterday and it said most of the workshops are booked up!"

"What?" Scottie cried. "Oh no!"

She clutched her WIP so hard that she squeezed several loops off her needle. She stomped her foot as she strung them back on.

"I couldn't figure out what to sign up for," she complained as she squinted at her lace. "I guess I was just too uninspired slash distracted."

"So I've heard," Regan drawled.

Scottie started. She gave Regan a hard look before glancing at Amanda, who was squirming ever-so-slightly.

"Wait a minute," Scottie began, "what—"

"You guys!" Bella interrupted them. She was peeking over her shoulder, her celery eyes wide and weirded out. "This is so bizarre. Look over there."

Scottie scowled, but bit back her suspicions for a moment to follow Bella's gaze.

At a table right behind them were four girls who looked almost exactly their age. One of the girls had waist-length brown hair and the flariest, patchiest bell-bottoms ever. She was makeup and accessory free, but for a leather thong around her neck strung with a chunky turquoise bead. In other words, she looked like she'd just gotten off the bus from Camp Hippie.

Another girl was decked out in Adidas pants and pigtails. Her fingers were covered with band-aids.

"Full-contact knitter," Tay noted, disdain in her voice.

Sitting elbow to elbow, the two other girls were giggling and gossiping. As the one in the pink, long-sleeved T pulled back the other girl's hair to whisper into her ear, Scottie saw the flash of a diamond earring.

All four of the girls were rifling through pink Stockinette bags, patting at their spanking new supplies with the reverence of recent converts.

"They're our doppelgangers," Bella whispered.

"Are you kidding?" Tay scoffed, pointing at the girls (until Scottie grabbed Tay's hand and placed it back on the table). "They're nothing like us. Or more to the point, we're nothing like *them*."

"Just because they're trendheads," Scottie whispered, "doesn't mean we should *completely* dis them."

Amanda shook her head slowly. "They're not trendheads," she said. "They *are* us. Us a year ago—when *we* were newbies."

"No way!" Tay insisted.

But Scottie bit her lip and looked at the girls again. One of them was pulling a tendril of yarn out of a new ball of Risdie, studying the filaments of color with fascination. Another one was flipping through a beginner's knitting book, boning up on some technique. The tomboy was working on a scarf while she waited for the class to begin. She was playing it cool, but you could tell from the upturned corners of her mouth that she was having a fabulous time.

(Knit two together)

That is *us*, Scottie thought. The lump returned to her throat as she thought back to her first days with the knit—and with the Chicks. But before real tears could start behind her eyes, the teacher held up a hand to quiet the group and begin the workshop.

And soon after that, just as she'd hoped, Scottie got swooped up into the knits, purls, yarnovers, and other delicate operations of lace-making. She fell, blissfully, back under knitting's spell—at least for the next two hours.

"Okay, guys," the teacher said. "We've got some pretty, pretty lace happening."

Scottie looked up blearily from the swatch she was weaving out of Baby Cashmerino. She had no idea how long it had been since the teacher had spoken up last. She'd been completely zoned.

"Let's take a break," the teacher pronounced. Many of the knitters were already getting up to stretch. "Afterward, I'll show you how to do some funky stuff with a cable needle."

"Cool," Scottie breathed as Polly and Regan high-fived each other.

But Tay's face had fallen, despite the fact that she'd just knitted up a kick-ass length of lace.

"*Not* cool," she said. "I left my cable needle at John's house last week and I keep forgetting to get it back from him."

"Actually, that was my cable needle, sweetie," Bella said, flopping over to do a hamstring stretch. "I had to borrow Scottie's last week. I guess we're both bumming."

"Oh yeah," Tay said with a cringe. "Sorry, B."

"Well, I have one extra," Amanda said, pulling a U-shaped needle out of her bag.

"Bella's got dibs on that," Tay said. She slumped back in her chair. "I can just improvise with a double-pointed needle or something. Let's go get a snack. Though this is such a girly festival, I bet they don't even have funnel cake. Too fattening."

• • Chicks with Sticks

"Plus, you'd get powdered sugar on the yarn," Bella said.

Together the girls wandered out of tent, which was clustered with a few other classroom tents. Most of the other classes seemed to be breaking, too. Including one that was filled with . . . guys!

"I guess it had to happen," Scottie said. "The boys have invaded. But on the bright side, Tay, maybe you can join up with them and issue a demand for fried dough."

Tay glanced without much interest at the crowd of men and boys tucking needles into their back pockets and slipping crochet hooks behind their ears. It was only when one guy separated from the crowd that she froze.

The boy was tall and skinny, with blond scruff on his chin and blue eyes made bluer by the sporty sunburn on his nose.

"John?" Tay barked.

John looked around for a moment before he spotted the Chicks. When his eyes landed on Tay, his face lit up—before he remembered to play it cool and wiped the sloppy grin from his face. He sauntered over.

"Hey," he said. "How's it going?"

"What are you doing here?" Tay asked rudely.

"Hello?" John said, looking around and smelling the air. "It's YarnCon?"

"Yeah, I know," Tay said. "So there was *nothing* you could find to do today besides *my* thing?"

Scottie held her breath.

And so did John. For a moment, his face went a darker shade of pink. Then he let out a long, weary exhale. He reached into his back pocket and pulled out a couple things. The first was a creased and crumpled YarnCon program.

"All of YarnCon is not *your* thing," John said, his voice shaking a bit. He jabbed a knuckly index finger at the program. "Maybe you didn't notice this workshop?"

Tay peered at the program and read out loud, "The Guys' Guide to Knitting: Working the Sticks in a Woman's World."

"That's so cool," Bella breathed. "I don't know why knitting is so *gendered.*"

"Listen to you, Miss Anti-Boy," Amanda teased.

"Just because I don't like boys," Bella retorted, "doesn't mean I think they should suffer from knitting discrimination!"

Meanwhile John was holding out the other thing he'd fished from his pocket. It was a cable needle.

"I noticed you left this at my apartment," John said. "You know, before you stopped hanging out at my apartment. Thought you might need it."

Tay gave the U-shaped needle a long, hard look. Then, reluctantly, she took it from John.

"Tay!"

It was a single word, but coming from John, it was pumped with frustration and hopelessness.

"What is so wrong with bringing you your cable needle?" he yelled. He glanced wildly at the knitty tent city around them. "It's YarnCon! I thought you might need it. I was *trying* to be nice."

Tay looked stunned.

"I know you were trying to be nice," she said.

It was Amanda and Toby all over again. Scottie knew that she and the others should drift away and let John and Tay have this fight—one that had been brewing for a while. But just as she felt powerless to stop clicking on *In a Sknit*, Scottie couldn't bring herself to move.

And for once, Tay didn't seem to care that her friends—not to mention countless YarnConners—were there.

"You don't value nice," John said. "You don't like that I want to spend time with you. Or that I try to make you happy."

"I need to make myself happy," Tay said.

"Oh, does Mr. A say that?" John challenged.

"No, *I* do," Tay said. "John, I love you, but I also need my independence."

"What," John said, folding his arms over his chest, "I haven't kept my distance enough this week?"

Tay squirmed.

"I don't know," she said. "Maybe it's more that I want *you* to have more independence. I want you to do your own stuff. Hang out with your own friends. I love spending time with you, but John, you need to . . ."

Tay stared into John's feverish eyes and trailed off.

"I need to get a life," he said flatly. "That's what you're thinking."

Tay looked at her feet, scuffing one of her boot toes across the cement.

"Well, I wouldn't put it that way, but yeah."

"Yes, you would," John said. "I get ya. But guess what, Tay? Maybe you're the one who's not getting me. I *have* a life. My life is school, and basketball, and my annoying little brother. And yeah, it's also knitting. But that's cuz I *like* knitting. I'd be at YarnCon today even if I didn't *know* you."

Tay flinched.

"And guess what, Tay-Tay," John went on. His voice was softer now. And sadder. "My life is also being with you. Hanging with you and knitting with you. And your friends."

Next to Scottie, Amanda emitted a shuddery sigh.

"It's digging the things you're into because I dig *you*," John said, "not because I'm some co-dependent freak with no life."

Tay was silent for a long moment. When Scottie looked at her eyes, she realized why.

Tay was crying!

Okay, she wasn't exactly sobbing. Truthfully, there wasn't even any spillage of tears. But there was definite moisture hovering in her lids. Her almost-black eyes were glassy and pink.

"I'm an idiot," she finally rasped.

"No, you're not," John responded automatically. "You have been acting kind a dumb though."

"I thought," Tay stuttered, "I thought I wanted a relationship that wasn't so, I don't know, hands-on. But the truth is . . . the truth is—"

And now Tay really did start crying. Her face crumpled as she struggled against it, but tears trailed down her pale cheeks anyway.

"The truth is you missed me this week," John provided with a sweet smile. "When I was being 'hands-off.'"

Tay nodded quickly as she swiped at her face with the backs of her hands.

Before Scottie knew it, John had wrapped Tay up in his albatross arms. Tay gripped John's bony rib cage so tightly, her knuckles went white.

"I sense some reconciliation PDA coming on," Amanda whispered to Scottie and Bella. "Let's get outta here."

Scottie, feeling happy and mushy inside, started to follow Amanda. But Bella stayed put, her eyes wide and awestruck. Scottie trotted back to Bella and whispered, "Uh, sweetie. It's not polite to stare at your friends when they're swapping spit."

Bella shook herself out of her stupor and glanced at Scottie. Then she peeked at Tay and John, who were indeed in a major clinch by now.

"Oh," she said dully. She followed Scottie down the aisle between tents. But she tripped along slowly, and kept stealing looks over her shoulder.

"Bel-la," Scottie muttered through gritted teeth. "Stop looking!"

"I'm not looking at Tay and John!" Bella said with a grossed-out shudder. "I'm looking at *him!*"

Bella was gazing at a boy loitering at the doorway to the Guys Guide to Knitting tent. He was showing an older man—probably the teacher—a swatch of box stitch, and chatting animatedly.

He was also gorgeous, with high cheekbones, chocolate brown eyes, eyelashes so fringy they could rival even Bella's, and . . . dreadlocks!

With his baggy jeans and T-shirt, he looked about sixteen, but one look at the beautiful angora swatch in his hands made it clear that he was not your average teenage boy.

He *was*, however, a boy.

"Bella," Amanda said. She'd doubled back to see what Scottie and Bella were whispering about. "You do realize that's a guy, don't you?"

Bella didn't answer. She simply stared. And when, a few minutes later, she, Amanda, and Scottie made their way back toward their tent to start up class again, she was still staring.

Meanwhile, Tay was doing a turnaround of her own. She was tugging on John's hand, her face giggly.

"C'mon," she said. "Come check out this lace class. You'd love it, I know!"

"I like my guys' thing," John protested, though his grin was enormous. "There's a rumor we're gonna end the class with a drum circle. Major male bonding."

"*Uch,*" Tay laughed.

John pulled out his program again.

"Let's go to the 'Stitch 'n Bitch at Dusk,'" he proposed. "Then we can get some pizza."

"You're on," Tay said easily.

After one more hug good-bye, she walked with her girlfriends back into their class. Polly and Regan caught up with them.

"Whoa!" Polly said to Tay. "That looked like major BF drama."

"Yeah, it kind of was," Tay said sheepishly. "It's all good now, though."

Scottie gazed at her glowy friend and immediately felt a pang. For the first time in hours, she thought of Beck. She wondered what he was doing right then.

She wondered if he missed her.

She wondered . . .

I wonder if we'll ever be as solid as John and Tay, Scottie admitted to herself.

Almost without thinking about it, she dug into her Suki for her cell phone. Flipping it open, she searched the screen for the voice mail symbol. It wasn't there.

She frowned as she turned up the phone's ring volume and slipped it back into her Suki. Then she sighed as she extracted her Lace in Progress and readied her cable needle for the next part of the class.

"You okay?" Amanda whispered. She eyed Scottie's Suki. Clearly, she'd seen her checking her cell.

"Oh, I guess so," Scottie sighed. "I just wish . . ."

"Aren't you happy for Tay?" Regan said loudly. She was sitting on the other side of Scottie and must have overheard what they were saying.

"Of course I am," Scottie snapped. "I just—oh, never mind. It's nothing."

"Personally, I think it's impressive when a girl can have a boyfriend," Regan said, propping her head on her hand, "and maintain a little perspective."

"What do you mean?" Scottie said stiffly.

"I mean," Regan said, "it's really unfortunate when someone so loses it over her BF that she disses her own friends."

"Um, Regan," Amanda jumped in, "actually—"

"Thanks for sharing, Amanda," Scottie accused. "I *said* I was sorry about losing it over Beck."

Amanda glanced shiftily at Tay and Bella, who were looking pretty edgy themselves.

"I know," Amanda said. "I, we, really appreciate that. But that just happened a few hours ago. And, like I said, it was a rough week, what with Toby and everything. I might have confided a bit in Re—"

"Scottie," Regan interrupted, toying with a knitting needle, "I know it's none of my business—"

"No, it's not!" Scottie blurted.

"Whoa!" Amanda said.

But Regan seemed unfazed by Scottie's bluntness.

• • *Chicks with Sticks*

"Listen, I'm nineteen," Regan pressed on. Scottie hated how breezy she was acting. "I've seen this happen a million times. A girl falls in love for the first time and loses it. She forgets about her friends. She becomes all about *him*. What *he's* interested in. What *he* wants to do. Where *he* wants to go and when *he* wants to go there. And when the inevitable break-up happens—because what else can such an intense relationship do but crash and burn?—the girl's left all alone. Take my advice, girlfriend. Don't let it happen to you."

"You're not my girlfriend," Scottie cried, jumping to her feet so fast that her folding chair flipped to the ground behind her. "They are." She pointed at Amanda, Bella, and Tay.

"Although, clearly, my *girlfriends* have been talking about me!" Scottie added with a catch in her throat.

"Not in a bad way!" Bella cried. "Amanda's right. We were just worried."

"Scottie," Tay said evenly. "It's the balance thing. We just want to help you get there."

"Well, guess what?" Scottie said. She was annoyed to find that she was getting choked up *again*. "Talking about me behind my back isn't the best way to do that."

"You're right!" Amanda cried. She shot Regan an exasperated look. "Scottie, I'm really sorry."

Regan didn't look sorry at all. She simply shrugged and returned to her swatch of lime-green lace.

"I just call it like I see it," she said.

Sitting next to her, Polly sighed. "Regan, you *might* want to think about calling it a *little* less often."

Scottie got some grim satisfaction out of that one as she slumped back into her chair, her arms crossed and her face tight with a pouty scowl.

Only after several long minutes had gone by did Scottie glance up. Tay, Bella, and most of all, Amanda were peering over at her, their faces furrowed with concern.

"Okay!"

Scottie jumped and looked away. The lace teacher had just alighted at the front of the class. She was rubbing her hands together, ready for some serious work.

"Break out your cable needles and let's get started on a technique I like to call, 'The Death Spiral.'"

While the rest of the class chuckled, Scottie scowled. Her friends, meanwhile, hadn't even glanced at the teacher. They were still gazing at her, apology and worry palpable on their faces.

As Scottie picked up her lace, worry gnawed at her own gut. She'd always been able to count on two things to smooth her feathers and unfray her emotions: knitting and the Chicks.

Now, just as one of those things was coming back to her, the other— her friends—seemed to be drifting away.

Scottie glanced at the four girls sitting behind them—the doppelgangers. They were alternating between struggling with their lace swatches and giggling with each other. Scottie felt like she was looking at a photograph from her past that had gone out of focus.

Everything in her life, in fact, suddenly felt unsteady. Only the yarn and needles in her hand were clearly solid.

So, just as Scottie had so many times before, she gave herself to the knit. She dove into it with singular focus, blocking out everything else. Part of her wished she could stay there, in the orderly comfort of her knits and purls, forever.

16 * (Using running stitch, sew seams)

The class ended all too soon and Scottie emerged from her lace reluctantly. Her sticks had worked their magic. The anger that had been flowing through her, so hot that she'd felt feverish, had melted away.

In its place, now, was sadness. No—weariness. Scottie was so tired, she couldn't have had a heart-to-heart with her buds even if she'd wanted to.

And frankly, she didn't.

They of course had other ideas. As soon as they'd all packed up their gear, Tay snatched up Scottie's Suki. Then Amanda grabbed one of Scottie's arms and Bella seized the other.

"You guys..." Scottie protested irritably, but they ignored her. They propelled her out of the classroom tent and led her to The Yarn Garden—a little courtyard in the center of YarnCon stocked with park benches and sunlight. Knitters were perched around the open space, stitching and bitching, snacking, or just gazing at the surrounding tents with stupefied smiles, soaking up all the yarny goodness.

"What are we doing here?" Scottie sighed as the girls planted her on a bench and clustered around her.

"We're talking," Amanda said, "about the fact that you're mad at us."

Scottie looked at her friends' faces. Amanda looked thin and pale, and it occurred to Scottie that those Toby-based lost-and-found five pounds? Had probably been lost again since the beginning of The Break.

Bella's spidery fingers were knotted beneath her chin and her eyes, big as saucers, were fixed on Scottie's.

Even Tay's face—whose expressions usually ranged from defiant to bored—had softened considerably.

Scottie felt a wave of love for her friends. She knew they cared about her. She knew Amanda had meant well when she'd talked to Regan.

Even so, Scottie felt a new distance wedged between them. This made her more weary than ever. She didn't know what to say or where to go from here.

She only wanted to go home.

To rest.

To be alone with her knitting and—for once—try not to think about her friends, her boyfriend, or much of *anything* for a while.

"You guys," Scottie said, lurching to her feet, "I'm sorry, but . . . I've just gotta go, okay?"

"But—" Bella said, looking totally confused.

"Scottie . . ." Amanda protested.

But Scottie just shook her head, grabbed her bag from Tay, and walked quickly out of the courtyard. She wove her way through the maze of YarnCon tents and hurried to the L. Before the train even arrived, she pulled out her sticks.

She barely stopped knitting for the rest of the day until, around nine o'clock, she fell fitfully to sleep.

Her eyes didn't open the next morning until ten. She slumped out of bed, sluggish from too much sleep and restless dreams that (of course) she couldn't quite remember.

She fished her cell phone out of her Suki.

No messages.

It took her a long minute to realize that the Chicks would already be in their YarnCon workshops by now. And Beck must have assumed that she was wrapped up in knitty activity, too.

So, why did she feel so abandoned?

Scottie shook her head as she plodded to the bathroom.

Don't think about it, don't think about it, she ordered herself. Then she pulled a brush through her hair, splashed some water on her face, and got out the door as quickly as possible.

I'll just give myself some YarnCon time, she reasoned as she walked to the L. *Then I'll be ready to talk to the Chicks.*

When she arrived, she checked out the schedule printed on a giant poster at the entrance. Next to every cool class, from "Turning a heel without turning into a heel," to "Spin control—making your own yarn" to "Celebrity Deathmatch: Knitting vs. Crochet" was a red stamp that read FULL!

Scottie scowled and cursed herself for not signing up for any of the workshops earlier. Impatiently, she decided to just scroll the list and go to the first NON-FULL event she saw.

"Mini-fashion show," Scottie murmured, spotting an event near the top of the list. "I guess that means it's short and sweet. And it starts in five minutes. Works for me."

Scottie made her way to the right tent and went inside. The canvas room was bisected by a low runway with chairs arranged on either side. She grabbed a seat next to a middle-aged woman in a sweater elaborately intarsia'd with autumn leaves. Almost the moment Scottie sat down, the woman leaned over and whispered conspiratorially, "So do you have a model in the show?"

Scottie was startled.

"Do I have—?" she stuttered. "Uh, no?"

"Oh," the woman said, her face going a little less shiny.

"Um . . . do you?" Scottie asked, even though she didn't quite know what she meant.

(Knit two together)

"Oh, yes," the woman said, puffing out her ample chest proudly. "My Bitsy. I knitted her outfit myself."

Scottie smiled politely, then pulled out her lace work, hoping it would discourage the woman from making any more Bitsy-chat.

Who names their daughter Bitsy?! she thought as she threw a few new stitches into her swatch. *Parents can be so weird.*

"Allllll right everyone!"

Scottie started as a bubbly, amplified voice reverberated through the tent. An emcee was stationed at a lectern, complete with microphone, near the runway. She was a carbon copy of Scottie's neighbor—right down to the poofy hair and fussy sweater.

"Welcome to the Mini Fashion Show," the woman burbled. "Have we got some adorable, tiny knitwear to show *you!*"

Oh no! Scottie thought, a chill running down her spine. *Don't tell me this is gonna be baby clothes. I have about as much use for that stuff as I do for an underwire bra. Besides, I'm in no mood for cute.*

Scottie looked around wildly. She was hemmed in by what seemed like dozens of eager-looking, middle-aged women! And now, two YarnCon volunteers were closing the tent flaps, bathing the tent in darkness. She was trapped.

A couple spotlights above the runway flared to life and some cheesy disco music began thrumming out of the speakers stationed around the tent.

"Oy vey," Scottie muttered, slapping a hand over her eyes. She grimaced as the emcee began narrating.

"Let's get right into things, shall we?" she cooed. "Our first *model* is Flora, wearing an *adorable* pink-and-purple jacket, embroidered, appropriately enough, with *flowers.* Her booties are made to match. C'mon folks! Let's give Flora a hand!"

Everyone except Scottie burst into applause.

"Whatever," Scottie mumbled. She took her hand away from her eyes to give baby Flora a few desultory claps.

But when Scottie glanced at the runway, she got confused.

"Where's the kid?!" she whispered.

She'd expected to see a baby, crawling down the runway or held aloft by her mom/handler for all to ogle.

Instead, she was looking at a poofy-haired woman holding a leash! Scottie looked down at the runway in horror.

Yup. Flora was a Lhasa Apso. Fluffed beyond belief with yarn bows in her hair, she was strapped into a *doggie* jacket and wearing rubber-soled *doggie* booties. If a Lhasa Apso *could* possibly possess any dignity, then Flora had lost hers.

And Scottie was right there with her! Mortified beyond belief, she crouched down in her seat and prayed that the pain would be brief.

Alas, fifteen minutes later, the emcee chortled, "We're *approaching* the halfway mark, folks. But don't worry! We've got some busy knitters in our audience and there are *plenty* more mini-fashions to see."

Kill me now, Scottie groaned. She'd already seen a dachshund in a fuzzy tube top and a weimeraner in leg warmers. A fleet of beagles had yelped their way through their show of goofy hats. And panic had erupted when a trembly, bald Chihuahua had not only leaped out of its tiny sweater, but out of its handler's arms altogether. It had scampered through the tent, nipping at the ankles of everyone it passed, including, of course, Scottie.

"Now," the emcee trilled, "get ready for a bit of drama. A capelet, knitted to resemble a fox stole, draped around the graceful shoulders of . . . Bitsy!"

Suddenly, Scottie felt long fingernails digging into her arm.

"That's her!" her neighbor cried. "That's my Bitsy!"

One of the poofy-haired dog-handlers stepped into the spotlight with a silver poodle whose fur had been shaved away but for a few frizzy polka dots at her ankles, ears, and hindquarters. As if this weren't bad enough, the dog was wearing a *knitted* fox stole. The fox's felted head was embroidered with little Xs where its eyes should have been. Its French knot teeth gnawed on its own bushy angora tail.

Scottie couldn't take it anymore.

"That's just sick!" she said, jumping to her feet. Thrusting her knitting back into her bag, she began to pick her way down the aisle, stepping on several feet—but hopefully not the Chihuahua—as she fought her way out.

When she emerged from the tent, she breathed a sigh of relief and rolled her eyes. She felt something brush her hand and jumped. Was it some escaped "model," licking at her palm?!

Scottie looked down and sighed.

It was just some of her pink practice lace, peeking out of her Suki, beckoning to her like an old friend.

Scottie glanced at her watch. It was 12:30. At that moment, the Chicks would just be finishing their lunch breaks and delving into their afternoon workshops.

Without her.

Suddenly, Scottie didn't want to be at YarnCon anymore.

She could only think of one place she *did* want to be, in fact. Tucking her WIP safely into her Suki, she headed back to the L.

She was so distracted when she got to the top of the ladder in the sixth floor supply closet, she didn't even notice that the hatch door was unlocked.

It was only after she'd flipped the door open and poked her head through that she saw him: Beck. He was sitting in her chair in the corner of the coal-black roof, looking out over the treetops.

Scottie hesitated, but Beck had heard her.

"Hi!" he called out, clearly surprised. He waved her over.

It was only when Scottie had almost reached him that she realized he wasn't sitting in *her* folding chair, the one she'd found in the alley and lugged proudly to the roof. Her chair was next to Beck, empty. He was sitting in a battered wooden chair with peeling yellow paint and half the spindles missing from its back.

"Where'd that come from?" Scottie blurted.

"The alley, of course," Beck said with a small smile. "I brought it up here a few days ago. I was wondering when you'd come up and find it. I thought we should both have a spot on this roof. I know it was yours first, but I think I love it up here as much as you do."

Scottie sank into her chair and gazed out at the view with Beck.

"Hey, wait a minute," Beck said. "Weren't you supposed to be at YarnCon all day?"

Scottie felt a defensive twinge. "I guess I ran into some YarnCon snags," she said. "Sorry to disappoint you."

Beck's smile disappeared. "Why do you say that?"

"Because you've been sending me mixed signals ever since that anti-frat party last week!" Scottie declared. "Sometimes you want to see me, sometimes you make other plans without even considering me. Sometimes you want to kiss me, and sometimes you don't. And then, you were all too happy to hear that I was spending my weekend at YarnCon—and not with you."

Beck gaped at Scottie for a moment, but then he went thoughtful. He returned his gaze to the treetops.

"Maybe I did want a break," he admitted.

Scottie felt her heart jump into her throat.

A break! Like Toby and Amanda's break?

"But not from you," Beck went on. "From your, well, to be honest? From your scrutiny."

Scottie bit her lip.

"What do you mean?" she quavered.

"Scottie, has anyone ever told you you're kinda transparent?" Beck said with a little laugh. "And not just when you attack me behind the school."

Scottie felt her face go hot. "Oh my God," she groaned.

"No! It's not a bad thing," Beck assured her. Crinkly eyes. Crooked smile. "I think it's kinda cute. But here's the thing. All week I've been getting this vibe from you. I feel like you're analyzing everything I say or do. It's like you're sizing me up as a boyfriend."

Scottie's mouth had gone completely dry. "Wow," she croaked. "For a boy, you're, um, pretty perceptive."

"Okay," Beck said, rolling his eyes. "I'll let that one slide. The thing I want to know is, why are you doing that, Scottie? What am I doing wrong?"

"Nothing, I guess," Scottie said. Her hands felt nervous and twitchy, like they were missing her sticks. "Or maybe you are. I don't know. I guess this boyfriend/girlfriend thing is hard to get the hang of. And, y'know, after seeing Toby and Amanda have that meltdown? I just wanted to do things right so that didn't happen to us. Beck, I *really* like you."

Beck started to lean forward in his chair. His eyes were intense and his lips were puckered.

He's about to kiss me, Scottie thought, feeling the zing return to her belly.

But then, Beck stopped himself and slumped backward. He looked at his hands.

"I really like you, too," he said. "But I don't think you're gonna like what I have to say. I've been trying to say it ever since that party, actually."

Scottie's zing went flat.

"Remember when you told those girls at the party that you were my girlfriend?" Beck said.

"Yeah," Scottie said apprehensively.

"Well," Beck said, angling his head to look at her warily. "How did you get to that? That we were boyfriend/girlfriend? Because I don't really remember it coming up."

Scottie blinked hard.

"Well . . ." she stuttered. "We . . . um, we kissed, you know, behind the school."

"Yeah, I remember," Beck said, with a little smile.

"And we've been kissing lots more," Scottie shrugged, "and holding hands and going on dates and stuff. And, well, that *makes* us boyfriend/girlfriend, doesn't it?"

Beck just looked confused.

"OhmiGod," Scottie blurted. "Did it really never come up? You mean, I've been assuming all this . . . OhmiGod! Tay *asked* me if we were on the same page and I just thought we were! Amanda was right. I am *such* a spaz!"

"Scottie," Beck said, grabbing her hand. "It's okay."

"No, it's not," Scottie said. She pulled her hand away and slapped it to her forehead. She stared into her lap, too embarrassed to meet Beck's eyes.

A realization was seeping into her mind: *He doesn't want to be my boyfriend. He never did!*

"Listen," Beck said. "I know the whole coupley thing is a big deal at Stark. But . . . I just got here. And I'm trying to make friends and find my way around this crazy, bad-bagel city and I'm *just* starting to feel slightly less pissed-off at my mother. . . . Suffice to say, I've got a lot going on."

"And you don't have time for a relationship," Scottie provided dully.

"Well, maybe not the attached-at-the-hip kind you want," Beck admitted. "Yeah."

Scottie looked back out over the rooftops so Beck couldn't see the tears pooling in her eyes. Inside, she cursed herself. Amanda had been right when she'd warned Scottie to start off as friends with Beck.

Tay had been right about the importance of the "balance thing."

Even Regan, much as Scottie hated to admit it, had been right about her.

But no, Scottie thought bitterly. *I had to have ice cream every day. I had to spaz.* She lurched to her feet.

"I get it," she said. "And this is all my fault. And . . . I'm sorry, Beck."

She started to turn and rush back to the hatch, but Beck's hand stopped her. He'd grabbed her by the wrist, his dry, soft hand sending tingles up to her elbow.

(Knit two together)

"Wait!" he cried.

Scottie decided she no longer cared if Beck saw her crying. It wasn't like she could sink much lower. She looked down at him. Gravity made her tears overflow and run in twin streams down her cheeks.

Beck stood up and used his thumb to wipe one of the streams away. When he spoke, his voice was gravelly, the way it had been that night at Mandrake's.

"Does it have to be all or nothing?" he said. "Do we have to be either a couple or broken up? What about, maybe, just . . . dating?"

Scottie blinked hard.

"D-dating?" she said through a residual sob.

"Yeah!" Beck said. "Going out together. Hanging out together. Eating lunch together. But also . . . not. Y'know, having a life outside of the Beck-and-Scottie lurvefest, too."

Scottie emitted a soggy laugh.

"Wouldn't it be kinda nice," Beck offered, thumbing away the rivulet on Scottie's other cheek, "not to always be wondering if we were adhering to Correct Boyfriend or Girlfriend behavior? I think it would take some pressure off."

"Yeah," Scottie blurted. "Yeah! It would. Maybe it'd be just the thing to break me of my ice cream habit."

"Um, huh?" Beck said, looking confused.

"Never mind," Scottie giggled.

Maybe it's okay that he doesn't get all my girlspeak, she realized giddily. *Maybe it doesn't even matter!*

"What I mean," she explained, "is yeah. I think we should give it a try."

Beck's eyes crinkled into a relieved smile. Scottie's did, too. And when she leaned slightly forward, her lips pouted into a pre-pucker, he met her halfway without a speck of ambivalence. His arms wound tightly around her waist and Scottie's hair blew around their faces in a sudden gust of sweet-smelling autumn air.

Scottie wasn't sure how long they stayed on the roof, talking, laugh-

• • Chicks with Sticks

ing over each other's stories about YarnCon and Starkers, and kissing some more. By the time they wandered over to the hatch and back to their respective lofts, the week's tensions had been peeled away.

Scottie arrived back in her bedroom, so drained she was rubbery. There was no music coming out of her mother's studio—only her parents' quiet murmuring. She grabbed her lace out of her Suki. In a move that she'd perfected over the past year, she bounced backward against the edge of her bed, slid down the side of the mattress, and landed on the white shag rug in perfect knitting position—her knees hunched, her feet planted and pigeon toed, her fingers already flying through her knits and purls.

After about an hour of work on the practice swatch from the lace workshop, Scottie pulled out her doctored pattern and the gold trim she'd begun for Hannah B. It sucked her in immediately; so fully that Scottie didn't stop until she'd bound off. After soaking her work in water and pinning it to a towel to block it, she saw that she had created a beautiful starburst of gold lace.

She placed the towel and lace on the rug, then crawled up to her bed and lay on her stomach so she could admire it from a different angle. She felt the same yarn fizz she'd experienced when she'd finished her very first knitting project—her full-of-mistakes, fabulous blue scarf. She realized that even if a hundred Stockinette trendheads knit up this same swatch of lace—even if *Jordan* did—hers would still be different. The knit would still be hers, the secret she'd discovered that long-ago night at KnitWit.

She smiled as CC poked her way through her bedroom door, hopped onto the bed, and nestled into her side. The she replayed her crazy day in her head, a small, incredulous smile playing around her lips. Finally, her eyes grew heavy. She sighed contentedly and let them fall closed.

When she woke up, it was dusk—and a dream was dancing in her head. Scottie kept her eyes closed, still savoring the images until she realized— she was actually remembering a dream!

(Knit two together)

She shot up in bed and grabbed her dream journal from her night-stand. She opened it up, flipped past the boring dreams she'd made up over the past few weeks, just so she wouldn't get zeroes on Fisheye's homework assignments, and started writing. She scribbled with no regard to grammar or grades. She only wanted to get the dream on paper.

I'm with the Chicks. We're doing the smudge circle that we did last year at KnitWit—a ceremony we conducted to sort of seal our friendship. It sounds corny now, but at the time, it wasn't. It still isn't, actually.

For this smudge circle, we're not at KnitWit. We're on a roof. It's not the bread factory roof (my roof, Beck's roof). We're on a tall building. I peek over the edge and see YarnCon—a sea of tents. Only, they're not white anymore, like they were in real-life. They're the exact same pink as those bags from Stockinette.

The Chicks come to the edge of the roof and join me. They link their arms through mine so we all feel safe, even when a gust of wind comes, blowing so hard that Bella's skirt fills up with air like a big bell and the tuft of smoky sage in Tay's hand blows out. It doesn't matter. We'd finished the ceremony already. Now we're just looking down at YarnCon and we're all feeling super-content.

Amanda points at four girls leaving the pink tent city and walking down State Street. They're arm in arm, just like us. It's me who realizes they're the girls from our lace-making class—our doppelgangers.

Our past.

Amanda, Bella, Tay, and I look at each other and smile. We all know what to do.

1–2–3, we jump! But we don't fall, of course. We fly! We hover over the street for a moment until we swoop down together and land on the sidewalk, right behind the four girls.

Only the girls aren't there anymore. It's just us, sauntering down the street arm and arm.

Maybe they are us.

Or we're them.

Newbies again, starting over.

When Scottie finally finished writing, the sky had gone from hazy gray to black. She glanced at her bedside clock. It was eight-thirty.

On the nightstand in front of the clock was a stripy ring of knitting, wadded up and forgotten.

Scottie gasped.

It was Bella's hat! The hat she'd been making for her birthday. Which was today! Tonight!

At this very moment, Scottie realized, her three best friends were gathered at Bella's house for a Sacred Sleep-Over. Without her. They hadn't even called her!

With a sick feeling in the pit of her stomach, Scottie realized they'd probably been waiting—all day—for *her* to call *them*.

Her first impulse was to collapse back onto her pillow and burst into tears. As right as things felt with Beck now, the wedge between her and the Chicks was still there.

Or was it?

Scottie's dream was still with her—as vivid and colorful as Bella's rainbow hat. She didn't want to let go of it. So, she grabbed the WIP off the nightstand and began to bind it off. She raced through the stitches. In about five minutes, she held a knitted ring—a hat without a top. Both brims curled over upon themselves until the hat was little more than a wide headband. Scottie snipped off the yarn and hurriedly wove in the ends. She tucked it into her Suki, and while she was at it, swiped her Hannah B. lace off the floor and stuffed it in, too. Then she flew out of her room.

"Mom!" she yelled as she headed for the door. "Mom? Dad?"

(Knit two together)

Her parents were in the gallery. They crashed through the double glass doors.

"What's wrong?" her dad cried. "You've been napping for hours. We were getting worried!"

"I forgot about Bella's birthday," Scottie said in a rush. "The S.S.O. at her house!"

"Oh, is that tonight?" Scottie's mom said. "Well, sweetie, it's almost nine. Are you sure you want to go over so late?"

"They'll be up 'til midnight, at least," Scottie scoffed.

"Oh great," her dad said dryly. "Just what we want to hear when we've allowed you to have a sleepover on a school night."

"Dad!" Scottie yelled in horror. "You're not gonna make me stay here, are you?"

Her parents glanced at each other.

"No," her dad said. "But I'm not letting you catch a cab at nine o'clock. I'll give you a ride over."

"Thanks," Scottie said, shifting anxiously from foot to foot. "But can we go *now?*"

"We can go in a minute," her dad said. "I want you to see something first."

"I'm really in a rush," Scottie wailed.

"It'll only take a minute," her dad said, motioning Scottie into the gallery.

"I hope you like it," her mom said quietly. Scottie glanced at her. Mom was tapping a coffee-stained finger against her tight lips. She was actually nervous!

Her interest piqued, Scottie followed her parents into the gallery. Propped against the wall were five paintings, all splashed with earthy colors—clay yellow and cobalt, grass-stain green, and most of all, a wash of clear, pale brown that Scottie immediately recognized as the coffee her mother had been brewing every day.

Scottie's eyes skimmed across the canvases. Each one was filled with

•• *Chicks with Sticks*

slashy, abstract, yet, somehow, fully-fleshed-out figures. The people, even the ones in repose, seemed to move. Scottie felt like she was gazing upon an angelic new species of earth turned human; coffee come to life.

It was when her eyes rested on the largest canvas, in the middle, that Scottie clapped a hand over her mouth.

These weren't anonymous coffee angels. They were four figures—girls—that Scottie recognized. One had a wild mane of hair, another a body that was all graceful right angles. The third seemed to emanate sparkly light, and the last one held her arms aloft, beckoning the three others into a circle. A starburst of wavy lines—yarn?—emanated from behind this girl, undulating around the quartet.

The painting was beautiful.

With tears in her eyes, Scottie threw herself at her mom, giving her a long, hard squeeze.

"I don't like it," she whispered. "I love it."

"You helped," her mom said with a wink.

"Back at ya," Scottie said, wiping at her eyes.

Within ten minutes, Scottie was at Bella's front door. Bella's mom ushered her in with a look of concern.

"I was worried you weren't coming," she said.

"Me, too," Scottie admitted. She looked around nervously.

"Are they here?" she whispered.

"In her bedroom," Bella's mom whispered back. "You know the way."

Scottie gave Mrs. Brearley a tremulous smile and headed back to Bella's room off the kitchen. She hovered her knuckles in front of the door, but after a moment of indecision, decided to just go in.

Amanda, Bella, and Tay were sitting on the floor, clustered around a half-demolished carrot cake. Even though there was a little pile of burnt candles on the cake tray, the vibe was anything but celebratory. The girls were shoveling in forkfuls of cake with looks of grim determination.

Bella was the first one to see Scottie. She screamed, dropped her fork, and sprang to her feet. She continued to scream as she threw her arms around Scottie's shoulders.

"You're here, you're here!" she cried.

"If you'll have me," Scottie said. She realized tears were streaming down her cheeks again. "Why didn't you guys call me?!"

"Why didn't you call us?" Tay said. "You were the one who dashed!"

But she didn't seem angry. In fact, she seemed just as thrilled to see Scottie as Bella was.

"We were so scared," Amanda said, stepping forward and swallowing hard, "that things had changed between us forever. Scottie, I'm so sorry I talked to Regan about you. That was totally breaking the Chicks' code of honor."

Scottie waved her off.

"Nah, it wasn't," she said. "I deserved it. I hate to say it, but Regan knows what she's talking about."

"Well, she's *nineteen* after all," Tay said, waggling her fingers and bugging her eyes in mock-awe. "Ooooh!"

"Hey," Amanda admonished Tay, though there was a laugh in her voice.

Suddenly Scottie remembered the circlet of wool in her Suki. Biting her lip, she pulled it out and handed it to Bella.

"Happy birthday," she said lamely. On Bella's bed, she noticed a gossamer mohair shawl and a cute pair of chunky, purple socks. Clearly, Amanda and Tay had put a lot more thought into their gifts than Scottie had.

Not that Bella thought so.

"It's perfect!" she cried, pulling the tube down on her head and tugging her long hair through it. "Finally, a hat that lets my hair be freeeee!"

Bella did a pirouette that set her dreads flying.

Scottie could have gotten away with this, but she didn't even hesitate.

"Bella," she said. "I have to admit something."

Scottie glanced at Amanda and Tay before she said, "I didn't set out to knit you some custom-made, lock-friendly hat. It was just going to be a normal hat. But I lost track of it this week. I . . . I lost track of everything, actually. So what your hat really is, is unfinished. I'm really sorry, sweetie."

Bella pulled the hat off and looked at its twin rolled brims. She peeked over at Amanda and Tay.

And then all three of them started howling.

"Bwa, ha, ha!" Bella laughed. Amanda unleashed her trademark snorty giggles and Tay, her silent belly laughs.

"Hey," Scottie said, completely confused. "What's so funny. Hello? I'm crying here."

This only made her friends laugh harder. Of course, it wasn't long before Scottie herself had joined in, giggling with relief as she wiped her cheeks dry.

When Amanda finally caught her breath, she gasped, "Well, it's nice to see that you've finally emerged from your little swamp of self-absorption."

"Yeah, what made you see the light, Shearer?" Tay asked.

"Oh, I guess I got a little perspective," Scottie shrugged proudly. "And I had a talk with Beck. Who, I might add, is no longer my boyfriend."

Immediately, her friends fell silent. They gaped at Scottie.

"Oh, my God," Amanda cried. "Are you devastated?"

"Oh," Scottie said with mock casualness, "I've still got the boy. Just not the boyfriend. Beck and I are going to just date."

"Date," Amanda said blankly.

"As in, date *casually?*" Tay blurted.

"With no guarantees?" Bella squeaked.

"No standing lunch plans?" Amanda said. "No getting jealous at parties? No obsessing? Scottie, can you do that?"

Okay, Scottie was feeling a little less breezy now. She sat on the floor, picked up a spare fork and took a big bite of carrot cake.

(Knit two together)

"I want to," she said after swallowing. "I really do. But, I might need a little help from you guys. You know, a gentle reminder from time to time? That I really don't want ice cream every day. No matter how much I think I do."

This time, no translation was needed. Amanda and Tay exchanged a giggly glance, then nodded vociferously. Bella dropped to her knees and gave Scottie a squeeze.

"We are totally there for you!" she declared. She pulled her hat back on, picked her fork up, and took her own giant bite of cake. "Dating! What a cool concept."

"Wait a minute," Scottie said. "That's a pretty pro-boy thing to say! What's happened to you?"

"What's happened to her is Jaden!" Amanda cried with another round of snorty giggles.

Scottie was bewildered for a moment, until she remember the boy with the cheekbones and the knitting needles.

"The guy from YarnCon?" she screamed.

"*Bella* got his number," Tay said while Bella slapped her hands over her eyes sheepishly. "She *called* him. And they have a *date* next weekend!"

"No. Way!" Scottie screamed. She took another bite of cake, kicked off her shoes, and crossed her legs. "Tell me everything!"

"Well . . ."

As Bella launched into her story, her dreadlocks poking kookily out of her half-hat, Scottie looked at her friends and got a little weepy once more. She couldn't believe that even for just twenty-four hours, there had been a rift between them; three against one.

The Chicks were—had to be—a quartet, arms intertwined, holding each other afloat. It wasn't *just* their knitting that wove them together. Not anymore. But it was still their fulcrum. That's why Scottie knew Bella would always keep that goofy hat Scottie had made her. The woolly circle was just like the Chicks' friendship—better than perfect.

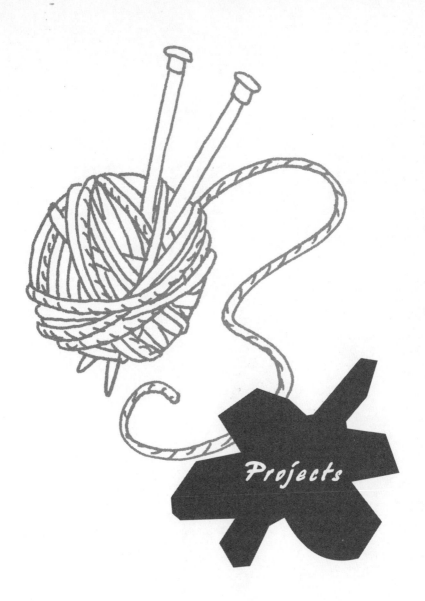

Projects

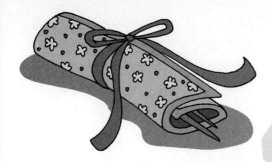

Needle Catcher
for the Hopelessly Disorganized

Well-behaved knitters keep their needles organized in their original sleeves. The rest of us invariably toss our sticks into the depths of our knitting bags, making them impossible to find, all mixed up, or even lost forever.

For us, there's the NCFTHD. It's so cute and crafty, you'll want to take that extra five seconds to slip your needles into it. This version is an especially good nest for the short needles in your stash—circulars and double-pointeds.

A sewing machine makes this project a snap, but it can be sewn freehand as well.

MATERIALS AND TOOLS:
- three (3) 12″ x 14″ pieces of fabric (cotton is best)
- 4 feet fabric craft ribbon
- sewing machine and thread
(For full-on fun, we suggest you choose ribbon and thread in a contrasting color that stands out against your fabric.)
- one (1) 9″ x 12″ sheet of felt or quilt batting
- straight pins or sewing needle for basting stitches
- scissors
- iron

Now what?

Take one 12″ x 14″ piece of fabric and fold approximately 3 inches behind one long side (so wrong side touches wrong side). Press flat and sew straight line along crease for a clean, finished fold.

Place this now 8″ x 14″ piece on top of one of the remaining 12″ x 14″ pieces, both right side up, so that the unfinished edges (bottom and sides) line up and the folded, finished edge is 3 inches from the top of the larger piece. Then cover both of these with the last 12″ x 14″ piece, WS up (RS facing in).

Sew along sides and bottom, about 1 inch from edges, stopping about 1 inch from the top on each side.

Snip excess fabric from bottom corners so they will turn out nicely.

Turn right side out and iron for nice, flat edges. Slide the felt sheet between the two larger pieces of fabric. This is for stiffness and padding.

Fold the unfinished top edges inward about 1 inch so that no WS fabric is visible. Press and use pins or basting stitch to hold in place.

Cut a 14″ length of accent craft ribbon and tuck ends into openings at top sides, with ribbon stretching across the top of the larger pieces. Sew across the top, both attaching the ribbon and sewing the top closed.

Pin remaining ribbon lengthwise across the center of the back of the now 10″ x 12″ unit. As you create the needle pockets, you'll be attaching the tie ribbon permanently, taking care to keep the loose ends of ribbon clear of the seams. Starting 4 inches from the left edge (pocket side facing up), sew a straight line from the top of the front pocket to the bottom. This pocket is great for circular needles or tucking away your current patterns. Sew more straight vertical lines as desired for additional pockets. Space them roughly every inch. Repeat larger 4-inch pocket on right if desired for more circulars or other larger knitting necessities.

Trim thread and fold rectangle closed in thirds, as you would a letter, and tie closed with attached ribbon.

With that, all your lost needles will be fashionably found.

Edge-Anything Lace

Antimacassar, shmantimacassar. This is not your grandma's dowdy lace. What's more, it's supremely versatile. You can use it to fringe up sweaters, socks, bags, hats, mittens—you name it!

SKILL LEVEL: Beginner

For extra funkiness, use thick-and-thin or variegated yarn.

SKILLS YOU'LL NEED: cast on (CO); knit two together (k2tog); yarn over (yo); knit through the back loop (k tbl); bind off (BO).

CO 7 stitches.
Row 1: K2, k2tog, yo, k2, yo twice (bring yarn to the front, then wrap it once around the right needle from front to back before you knit into the next stitch), k1—9 stitches on needle.
Row 2: K1, knit first part of wrap stitch as usual, knit second part of wrap stitch tbl, k2tog, yo, k4—9 stitches.
Row 3: K2, k2tog, yo, k5—9 stitches.
Row 4: BO 2 stitches, k2tog, yo, k4—7 stitches.

Repeat these four rows until edging measures desired length when slightly stretched. Sew onto knitted piece.

HELPFUL HINT: Remember, a yarn-over is only the act of bringing the yarn in front of the needle. Knitting into the next stitch is a separate action, and is written separately in the directions. In this pattern, the yarn-over always occurs just before you knit into the yarn-over from the last row.

Butterfly Socks

Socks seem scary, but trust us—once you've turned your first heel, you'll be hooked. This pattern is the perfect project for intermediate knitters getting restless with scarves and hats. The irregular ribbing sets off a sweet stripe of butterflies fluttering down your ankle. Very Scottie.

SKILLS YOU'LL NEED: cast on (CO); work in the round; knit two together (k2tog); slip slip knit (ssk); purl two together (p2tog); slip stitches with yarn held in front (sl wyif); follow instructions to work short rows; pick up stitches; graft or 3-needle bind off to finish.

MATERIALS:
- 2 skeins of fingering weight yarn, such as Koigu, at least 175 yards each, or 1 skein of at least 350 yards. A solid or gently variegated color will show off the pattern best.
- Set of 5 US #0 or #1 double-pointed needles

HELPFUL HINTS: Ribbed patterns are very stretchy, so one size will fit most. Use #0s if your feet and ankles are small, #1s if they are broader.

Always slip stitches purlwise, inserting the needle from right to left. When you slip the stitch, keep the resulting strand very loose.

* = repeat instructions within brackets to end of round.

DIRECTIONS: CO 64 stitches and divide 16 on each needle. Join to work in the round, being careful not to twist stitches.
Rounds 1–11: [P2, k2, p1, k2, p2, k1, p1, k3, p1, k1]*.
Round 12: [Continue rib pattern until 7 sts remain on needle 2, k7]*. These groups of 7 sts will form the butterflies, so we'll call them the butterfly sts.
Rounds 13, 15, 17, 19, 21: [Work in rib pattern. Butterfly sts: k1, sl 5 wyif, k1]*.
Rounds 14, 16, 18, 20: Work ribs as given, k butterfly sts.
Round 22: [Work ribs as given. Make butterfly: K3, on the next stitch (which is at the center of the slipped group), insert right needle down through the 5 loose strands, bring needle up and transfer the 5 strands to the left needle, purl the 5 strands and the next st together as one st; k3.]*
Rounds 23–27: Work ribs as given, k butterfly sts.

Repeat rounds 13–27 until you have made four butterflies down each side of the sock. This will yield a cuff of about five inches. If you want a taller sock, repeat as desired and as the yardage of your yarn allows.

Divide for heel:
Transfer last 3 sts from n4 to n1, k across needles 1 & 2 until 3 sts remain. Slip these last 3 sts to n3 without knitting them. Needles 3 & 4 will now hold the sts for the instep and won't be used until after you've worked the heel.

Work heel flap:

Slip all needle 2 sts to needle 1 (32 sts in all). Turn and p back across all heel sts.

Next row (RS): [Slip 1, k1]*

Next row (WS): Slip 1, p to last st, k last st.

Repeat these two rows 15 more times, ending with a WS row.

Shape heel:

RS: Slip1, k20, ssk, k1. Turn. (8 sts remain unworked on left needle)

WS: Slip1, p11, p2tog, p1. Turn. (8 sts remain unworked on left needle)

RS: Slip1, k12, ssk, k1. Turn.

WS: Slip1, p13, p2tog, p1. Turn.

RS: Slip1, k14, ssk, k1. Turn.

WS: Slip1, p15, p2tog, p1. Turn.

Continue as established until all heel sts have been incorporated, knitting or purling one more st on each row. 22 sts on heel needle.

Pick up sts for heel gusset:

K across heel sts. With needle 2, pick up 16 sts along the side of the heel flap. Pick up one more st to prevent a hole between gusset and instep. Place all 32 instep sts on needle 3 so that needle 4 is free.

K across instep in rib pattern, then, with needle 4, pick up 17 sts along other side of heel flap to complete round.

Work gusset:

Round 1: K across sole sts and up gusset to last 3 sts, k2tog, k1. Work in rib across 32 instep sts to gusset, k1, ssk, k to end of gusset.

Round 2: Work even.

Repeat rounds 1 & 2 until 64 sts remain. You can rearrange sts to work on 3 needles—1 for instep, 2 for sole.

Work foot: Continue to work ribbing on instep and knit all sts on sole until sock reaches the end of your little toe when you try it on. End by knitting across instep.

Work toe: Sole: K to last 3 sts, k2tog, k1.
Instep: K1, ssk, k to last 3 sts, k2tog, k1.
Sole: K1, ssk, k to end.
Work one round even, then repeat decreases on next and every other round. Continue until 24 sts remain. Place 12 sts on each of two needles. Finish by grafting (kitchener stitch), three needle bind off, or other method of your choice. Weave in ends.

Then wear them, Scottie-style, with your favorite pair of suede Pumas.

Buttered-Toast Tank

Don't worry if you're feeling indecisive. Buttered Toast—a breezy, seamless, tubular tank—is knit from the top down, so you can decide at the last minute whether you want to edge the hem in sweet scallops or make jagged little points like Scottie's.

Follow your mood for the straps as well. They can be pragmatic I-cord or prettied-up ribbon ties. Or, if you're feeling really *indecisive—both!*

SKILLS YOU'LL NEED: cast on (CO); work in the round; increase (M1); knit two together (k2tog); slip slip knit (ssk); yarn over (YO); make I-cord.

SIZES: Measure under your armpits, above your bust, where the top of the tank will fall. Inhale and make sure the measuring tape is still slightly loose. If you're between sizes, knit the smaller size if you like a tighter fit or the larger size if you're well endowed or just want more ease.

28" (XS); 32" (S); 36" (M); 40" (L); 44" (XL)

MATERIALS:

• 5 (6, 6, 7, 8) skeins (84 yards each) Mission Falls 1824 Cotton in color Maize

• 24" circular needle, US #7 (if you're knitting L or XL,

the needle can be 28" or 32")
- 2 stitch markers
- 2 yards satin ribbon for ties, if desired

Gauge: 18 stitches and 24 rows = 4" in stockinette stitch.

HELPFUL HINTS: When you need to change balls of yarn, do so near the stitch markers, which indicate where the side seams would be—if there were seams. The shaping will help hide the joins.

While you're working on Buttered Toast—beware of subway doors!

DIRECTIONS: CO 124 (144, 160, 180, 196) sts, making sure your stitches are not too tight and placing a marker when you have cast on half the total quantity. Place second marker and join to work in the round, being careful not to twist stitches.

Work ribbing: [P2, k2]* for twelve rounds, until ribbing measures 2".

Next round: XS, M, XL sizes: K1, M1, knit to marker, k1, M1, knit to end of round. 126 (162, 198) sts.
S, L sizes: K all sts.

Work body: Knit in the round until work measures 5" from CO edge.

Begin waist shaping decreases: Next round: K1, ssk, k to last 3 sts before marker, k2tog, k2 (one on each side of marker), ssk, k to last 3 sts, k2tog, k1.

Work 5 rounds even. Then repeat decrease round.

Rep from * to * twice more; four decrease rounds in all.

Work 2 rounds even, then work one more decrease round.

106 (124, 142, 160, 178) sts.

Work 12 rounds even.

Begin waist shaping increases: Next round: K1, M1, k to last 2 sts before marker, M1, k2 (one on each side of marker), M1, k to last 2 sts, M1, k1.

Knit 3 rounds even. Then repeat increase round.

Rep from * to * three times more; five increase rounds in all.

126 (144, 162, 180, 198) sts.

For scalloped hem, all sizes:

Work lace:

Round 1: Knit.

Round 2: Knit.

Round 3: *(K2tog) 3 times, (yo, k1) 6 times, (ssk) 3 times; repeat from *.

Round 4: Purl.

Repeat rounds 1–4 four times, or as desired for a longer or shorter hem.

End by knitting two rounds, then bind off loosely.

For pointed hem:

Sizes XS, M, XL: Next round: Increase a total of 6 stitches, spaced evenly through the round. 132 (168, 204) sts.

Sizes S, L: Begin lace instructions over 144 (180) sts.

Work lace:

Round 1: Knit.

Round 2: Purl.

Round 3: Knit.

Round 4: Purl.

Rounds 5, 7, 9, and 11: * (k2tog) twice, (yo, k1) 3 times, yo, (ssk) twice, k1; repeat from *.

Rounds 6, 8, 10, and 12: Knit.

Bind off loosely, or repeat rounds 1–12 for a longer hem and then bind off.

Finishing: Weave in all ends. If desired, crochet a single chain along the top and hem edges for a tidy finish. You can also use this technique to make the top fit more snugly, if necessary.

Straps: Make two lengths of I-cord, pin in place front and back to check positioning, then sew firmly to attach. OR: Cut satin ribbon into four equal lengths, pin in place front and back, sew firmly, and tie in a bow at each shoulder. Trim ends as desired.